TORMENT OF THE ANCIENT GODS

CRAIG ROBERTSON

TORMENT OF THE ANCIENT GODS

RISE OF THE ANCIENT GODS SERIES: BOOK 3

by Craig Robertson

When you're dead you're dead, unless you're Ryan.

Imagine-It Publishing
El Dorado Hills, CA

ALSO BY CRAIG ROBERTSON:

*** Podium Entertainment has produced audiobooks for all the below titles except the older standalone books.**

For specifics as to the correct order for reading the Ryanverse, click here.

BOOKS IN THE RYANVERSE:

THE FOREVER SERIES (2016)

THE FOREVER LIFE, Book 1

THE FOREVER ENEMY, Book 2

THE FOREVER FIGHT, Book 3

THE FOREVER QUEST, Book 4

THE FOREVER ALLIANCE, Book 5

THE FOREVER PEACE, Book 6

THE FOREVER BOXSET, Part 1, Books 1 & 2

THE FOREVER BOXSET, Part 2, Book 3 & 4

THE FOREVER BOXSET, Part 3, Book 5 & 6

GALAXY ON FIRE SERIES (2017)

EMBERS, Book 1

FLAMES, Book 2

FIRESTORM, Book 3

FIRES OF HELL, Book 4

DRAGON FIRE, Book 5

ASHES, Book 6

GALAXY ON FIRE BOXSET, Part 1, Books 1 & 2

GALAXY ON FIRE BOXSET, Part 2, Books 3 & 4

GALAXY ON FIRE BOXSET, Part 3, Books 5 & 6

RISE OF ANCIENT GODS SERIES (2018):

RETURN OF THE ANCIENT GODS, Book 1

RAGE OF THE ANCIENT GODS, Book 2

TORMENT OF THE ANCIENT GODS, Book 3

WRATH OF THE ANCIENT GODS, Book 4

FURY OF THE ANCIENT GODS, Book 5

FALL OF THE ANCIENT GODS, Book 6

TIME WARS LAST FOREVER SERIES (2019)

RYAN TIME, Book 1

LOST TIME, Book 2

FRAGMENTED TIME, Book 3

SHATTERED TIME, Book 4

FINDING TIME, Book 5

HEALING TIME, Book 6

THE TIMELESS VOID (2021)

RYAN'S GAMBIT, Book 1

RYAN'S PHANTOMS, Book 2

RYAN'S ENIGMA, Book 3

RYAN'S UNDOING, Book 4

RYAN'S REBOOT, Book 5

RYAN'S RESOLUTION, Book 6

THE WHALES OF TIME (2023)

Ryan In UnWonderland, Book 1

How Ryan Saves Time, Book 2

Saving Alice Ryan, Book 3

NON-RYANVERSE BOOKS:

A Teenager's Guide to Saving The Earth (2025)

An Apocalypse and Then Some, Book 1

How to Survive Surviving the Apocalypse, Book 2

Is This Apocalypse Over Yet?, Book 3

TIME DIVING (2024)

Letters From Hell, Book 1

Purgatory's Best Shot, Book 2

Heaven Says Wait, Book 3

Into the Nexus, Book 4

ROAD TRIPS IN SPACE SERIES (2019):

THE GALAXY ACCORDING TO GIDEON, Book 1

THE EARTH ACCORDING TO GIDEON, Book 2

OLDER, STANDALONE WORKS:

THE CORPORATE VIRUS (2016)

THE INNERgLOW EFFECT (2010)

WRITE NOW! THE PRISONER OF NaNoWRiMo (2009)

ANON TIME (2009)

For more information about Craig, his books, various series, or to see images and videos for some of his wild alien characters, please visit his website. You'll be glad you did: https://craigarobertson.com/

To sign up for Craig's newsletter to get announcements, updates, and his

recommendations for other great Sci-Fi reads go to: https://preview.mailerlite.io/forms/2369493/188634426375144501/share

ISBN: 978-1-7328724-3-1 (E-Book)
978-1-7328724-4-8 (Paperback)
979-8-7754134-3-9 (Hardcover)

Cover design by Jessica Bell
https://www.jessicabelldesign.com/

Formatting services by Drew Avera
drewavera@gmail.com

Editors: Michael. R. Blanche
Forest Olivier

First Edition 2019
Second Edition 2019
Third Edition 2020

To my unsurpassed grandson, Jonathan Ryan Davis, from whom the hero of this series takes his name.

CHAPTER ONE

Vorc sat alone in his office, staring off into nothingness. He felt ... nothing. He desired ... nothing. How could he? He had no soul. No, that malicious Gáwar had taken it as the price required for his help in finding the terrorist Jon Ryan. It was the most profound manifestation of *unfair* ever to transpire. Vorc acted only to help the Cleinoid gods he led. It was his duty and it was his honor. How then, in a just universe, could he be *punished* for acting in an administratively prudent manner? It was unfair. He kept repeating that word because it best fit the state of reality he was vexed with.

Vorc felt bad for himself, to be certain. He did, however, actively suppress any consideration of how the other souls he'd bargained away must have felt. The fact that thousands of ancient gods lost their souls without their knowledge or consent didn't bother him, because he ignored their feelings completely. Soulless people, he concluded, were like that. They cared nothing for themselves and they cared nothing for others.

At least he *assumed* at that juncture, Gáwar had taken possession of Vorc's essence. There had been no specific ceremony or angst-filled moment when the god of demons formally or forcefully absconded with his fee. And that damn Gáwar was nowhere to be found to ask if the deed was done. But why wouldn't he have, reasoned Vorc? Why delay? Well, for one, he could wait to extract it because he knew full well his victims would be ruminating in just the funk they were if he delayed the act. Gáwar was certainly evil enough to stoop to add psychological torture to the mix of torment.

Then a thought occurred to Vorc. If he still owned his soul, maybe he could figure out a way to keep it permanently. It wasn't such a silly notion. Vorc was a god. The other souls he'd promised were gods also. What if a thousand gods stood shoulder to shoulder and resisted Gáwar? What if they *killed* Gáwar? Yes, that could be doable. Vorc could call a secret meeting of the damned and they could plot to stay free. Yes, it was as good as done. How could the combined will of that many powerful beings be thwarted? They could not be.

There was a very soft knock on his door. Vorc seized up in rage. Well, pissiness. Rage escaped the soulless. It had to be his new office aide, Sylvia. He'd decided to use a temp since he was going through assistants so quickly of late. Why bother to get emotionally attached and have a person learn your way of doing things, just to have you kill them? Time inefficient. But in the last few days, Sylvia had proven herself to be quite the challenge. Whenever she spoke in her nasal tone with that stupid pencil behind her right ear, he pictured Gáwar slicing *her* in half as he'd partitioned Felladonna.

"Sir, a message just appeared on my desk. I thought I should bring it in immediately," she announced in her fingernails-on-chalkboard voice. She extended an envelope.

"Sylvia, do you recall my mentioning I did not under *any* circumstances wish to be disturbed?"

"Yes, sir, but—"

"Do you in *fact* remember me citing that if the building was on fire or my children's lives were in immediate danger, I did not want to be disturbed?"

"Did you say *children* or *child*? I can't recollect clearly the numerical threshold." She fell mute a few seconds, then added, "*Sir*."

"Leave now. If you get close enough to me to deliver that letter I shall rip your arm off at the shoulder."

"But ... it's important."

"How would you know that, my imbecilic assistant?"

"Because it told me so."

"What told you so?"

"I did," replied the letter. "I am. You need to take me now."

A talking letter. A *demanding* talking letter. Vorc's failed life just scraped a new bottom. He held out a hand.

"You're not going to do that thing to my arm, are you?" Sylvia asked before advancing.

"No. I shall hold the *letter* accountable for defying my orders."

"Hey, don't shred *me*. It was *Gáwar* who said I was time critical." That letter was snarky.

"Give it here," demanded Vorc.

Sylvia sort of tossed it into his hand the last few inches. She was taking no chances. Temps learned that early in their careers.

Vorc stared at the envelope a moment. "Well, am I supposed to open you or do you do that?" he asked pointedly.

"Do I have hands?" asked the envelope.

"I do not see any."

"Do you have hands?"

Vorc's response was to close his eyes.

"Okay, I'll give you three guesses who rips me open, but the second two don't count."

Vorc neatly cut the top off the envelope, gently removed the letter, and handed the empty envelope to Sylvia. "Burn this. Do it personally and see that the ashes are flushed down the toilet."

"Hey, don't shoot the messenger," protested the covering.

"I'm not," replied Vorc coolly. "I'm burning the messenger." He looked at the paper.

Sylvia held the doomed envelope with two fingers and at arm's length as she departed.

Before he could get to the content, the letter itself spoke. "I think that was harsh, what you just did to Guy."

"Guy?"

"The envelope, *Guy*."

Vorc cleared his throat. "And your name would be?"

"Not sure I want to say. You seem harsh."

"I know. You said that already."

There was mutual silence a few seconds.

"Do you mind if I *read* you?" asked Vorc with nauseating insincerity.

"No, no. That's my sole function in this sorrow that passes itself off as existence."

It was unfortunate for the letter it chose to use the adjective *sole,* that being so similar to the noun *soul,* which Vorc so sorely missed. The gaffe would figure prominently in the paper's final disposition.

Vorc, you stupid pansy-assed fool. Do you think this is my first soul-reaping, my first rodeo? You cannot sneak behind my back and save in any way your soul or those you so foolishly wasted. Get real.

Gáwar

Vorc absently set the paper on his deck. Even though he'd been a god forever, he still despised the impossible. It was such a loose cannon. He despised those, too. There was no way Gáwar could know his thoughts in real time and respond by post. Zero way. But there it was, lying on his desk.

A soft knock, again, just as infuriating as the first. Or at least as pissy as the first.

"What?" said an empty Vorc.

Sylvia slipped in silently, crossed the room, and handed her boss another envelope. She exited as noiselessly.

Vorc's eyes fluttered, then he looked to the new message.

"I know what you did to my brother," menaced the letter container. "Don't think we'll forgive or forget. Envelopes are *everywhere*. Be afraid. Be *very* afraid."

Vorc ripped open the envelope and then tore it into absurdly small pieces. Then he pulled out his recently repaired Fire of Justice. He burned not only the small pile of paper flakes, he burned through the entire top of his desk. Then he settled down and read the letter.

You pathetic moron, of course I can. I am Gáwar. *Over forever you will come to know the meaning of suffering under my merciless whim. PS: let me know if you have any other questions or input. Have a nice day.*

Gáwar

Well, now it was official. Vorc almost smiled. His life could not get any worse. No way, no how. There was an odd reassurance in the knowledge.

CHAPTER TWO

The whole team was aboard *Stingray*. We'd arranged for Daleria to meet us there after we nuked Dominion Splitter. She'd told us that if we could get out of this universe she wanted to come, too. Even if there was no way to return, she didn't care. She hated the ancient gods that much. I couldn't agree with her more. As a group they were the worst form of life I'd ever encountered in my very long period of observation.

"Okay, people, we need to decide what to do and we need to do so quickly," I said as the commander. "Doc, is there any doubt whatsoever that DS is dead, defunct, and deceased?"

"I have no way to be certain," he replied seriously. "That *said*, I am extremely confident the transfolding vortex no longer exists. While I cannot know its physiology, it clearly went from robust to functionless and invisible after we imparted all the neutral matter into it."

"But you're saying it might have slipped away. That maybe, just maybe, it could heal over time. Is that correct?" pressed Sapale.

"Yes. DS could have moved to shelter as opposed to dying. If so, it could regenerate given enough time."

"I do *not* want to hear that, Toño," I said with frustration.

"I'm being honest. I *am* the scientist among us. As I said, I'm confident we killed the abomination. But I would not be doing my job if I did not present the facts as I see them."

"I know. I'm obviously not *blaming* you," I whined. "I just want to leave. If DS might revive, that would not be a wise impulse to follow."

"You mean that if there was some chance DS could return, you would stay here to deal with it again?" asked an incredulous Daleria.

"Maybe," I replied flatly. "I would do just about anything to keep these douche gods locked up here forever."

"We *all* would," said Sapale softly but with unequivocal ferocity.

"Me, too. No, wait," said Casper, who of course appeared out of nowhere, "maybe I can't stay behind because I've always been here. Man, my quasi-existence is really annoying."

"I really don't have anything to say in response to that ... whatever you said."

"Jon, please don't be so harsh with ... with our spirit helper," responded Toño.

"Spirit helper?" I repeated back. "What, we're new age mystics now?"

"I'm with Toño," said Sapale. "Casper, as you have so disrespectfully named him, has been nothing but loyal and indispensable. Be nice. Otherwise, we may keep him and leave you behind." She followed that up with a Kaljaxian threat growl.

"Hey, I'm not that thin-skinned," responded Casper. "I mean, sure, I don't have skin, but Jon doesn't bother me *that* much. But thanks for having my back, guys."

Ghost was beginning to sound like me. What a copycat. Maybe that's why he rubbed me the wrong way? Whatever the reason was, it clearly had to be *his* fault.

"Back on task," I said with emphasis. "We have some tough decisions to make. Do we stay or do we go?"

"Let me turn that around," said a thoughtful Toño. "If we stay here, what good can we do? Yes, we would be here if DS resurrects. But in the meantime, is there some significant damage we could inflict on our enemy? Enough to make it worth remaining even *if* the vortex is completely defunct."

"Hmm," I replied. "Interesting question."

"We'd only be able to act as guerrillas, doing hit and run damage," said Sapale. "And the more damage we did, the Cleinoids would be increasingly motivated to capture us. I'm not sure how long we could be effective."

"Maybe not long enough to still be around if the damn vortex actually did return," I pointed out reluctantly.

"So we're back at square one?" bemoaned Casper.

I was totally impressed. My initial reaction was to snark something along the lines of his not being present enough to be back at square *anything*. But I didn't. Weird. I might be, you know, growing up.

"Daleria, you're the newbie here, but do you have any thoughts?" I asked. She was being pretty quiet.

"I'm still a little intimidated by this whole thing, I guess. That said, no, not really. As to if DS is gone for good, I couldn't say. DS isn't a topic of general interest, so very few know much about it. As to leaving or staying, for what it's worth I'm a get-out-of-town vote. Nothing good has ever happened in this plane of existence."

"You did, sweetheart," soothed Sapale.

It was so cute. Daleria blushed to beat the band.

"Who would know about DS's condition?" asked Toño.

She shrugged. "No idea. Maybe Vorc. Maybe those witches Deca and Fest."

"What about the unspeakable one?" Sapale asked more tactfully than me. She clearly did not want to say Gáwar and watch Daleria hit the deck again.

"Oh," she replied squeamishly, "he would. But any sane person would rather live in uncertainty than ask ... well, ask."

"What is it that's so bad about this unspeakable one?" asked Toño. "I've formed the impression that the Cleinoids are roughly a band of equals."

"No." She shook her head. "Not equals. *Off-setters.* Some are stronger and more vicious, some weaker and more docile. But there is no combined strength that cannot be matched by a determined resistance. The ... the one you ask about is immensely powerful. But if enough lesser gods stand against ... together they can overpower ... their opponent."

"Checks and balances," said Sapale.

"Yes. The beauty of the system is that if enough gods are required to work together, clearly no individual would be ascendant, so there's no long-term hope for anyone's personal power grab attempt."

"Were you present the last time whatever was summoned?" I asked.

She looked like she was considering a second swoon for a hot second there. "Yes. But when I learned ... of it, I went to ground. I know places very isolated and remote. I went to one immediately and buried my face in the dirt." Daleria slumped when done speaking.

"Did you ever actually see him?" asked Sapale as she rested a hand atop Daleria's.

"Not directly."

"What other ... oh, through simaging," responded Toño.

"Yes," she said like a baby bird with a broken wing. Tears streaked down her face. "We were simaged images of ... of the one, whether we liked it or not." She whimpered briefly. "I saw him and what he did for a very long time."

"But he never saw you?" confirmed Toño.

She shook her head faintly.

"Was he so bad?" asked my wife softly.

"No. Much worse. What h ... what was done to ... victims was unconscionable, gratuitous, and it was *horrible*."

"And in the end the remaining gods banded together and forced him back to wherever?" asked Toño.

She sniffed and wiped away tears. "Yes. That process was, however, long in coming, gruesome, and protracted."

"But he was defeated?" I asked.

She bobbed her head. "Reconfined. Defeat is not something h ... not an option."

"Let us pray we never face him," responded Toño solemnly.

Out of nowhere Daleria screamed, clutched the sides of her head, and passed out cold.

"Gáwar is among us," said Casper very quietly.

"How do you know?" I shot back.

"She knows." Casper moved what was almost an arm in Daleria's direction. "I know."

"Where is he?" I asked.

"Too close."

"What, he's coming here?" asked Sapale with no little alarm.

Casper was silent a moment. "No, not yet. He's only just arrived."

"Well our window of opportunity just shrank like hell," I snapped angrily.

"Shall we attempt to leave?" responded Toño.

"If Gáwar changes direction and heads this way, can you give us a sufficient warning, Casper?" I pressed.

"I have zero idea. When it comes to Gáwar, superlatives are difficult to understate."

"Let's give it a minute then. Toño, help out our newest crewmate." I pointed to the already stirring Daleria. "Als, have your best estimate at a course back home ready on a moment's notice."

"Aye, Captain," replied Al. "Laid in and standing by."

"And then the tiny crew waited to see what fate held in store for them," I said to no one in particular.

CHAPTER THREE

Legannus sat at a table near the back of a dingy, poorly-lit restaurant. He nursed a glass of bitter-water and he waited nervously. Most of his adult existence could be fairly characterized as *nervous*. He was one of those universal creatures in life condemned to snivel, grovel, submit, and to do so before anyone and everyone. Any*thing* for that matter. He was quick to self-ridicule, even faster to self-castigate, and he was instantaneous in concurring with any and all insults, reprimands, and curses directed his way. He was, in a word, pathetic. He, for reasons known only to him, rather liked being a remorseless sycophant and the ultimate fawning wretch. Go figure.

As a proud, obeisant ninny, his trade was information, generally both scandalous and dubious, and the performance of tasks, generally illegal and morally unjustifiable. He would spread falsehoods about anyone, steal anything easily taken, and betray any confidence for a price that was always surprisingly low. The best that could ever be said concerning Legannus of the Alpha Colony was that he was of consistent character.

His master presently was his least favorite ever. The man was intimidating, demanding, and had no regard for anyone other than himself. But his gold coins shined the same as anyone else's, so Legannus suffered through the pressure of serving the haughty bastard. Plus, his master's role was to direct him, not accompany him. He had to endure his master only when accepting the assignment and now, when he was to divulge his findings and be paid. Then to the endless inferno with him, the rot-brained sop.

Light flashed across the room as the door opened and then closed quickly. Legannus glanced up to see if his wait was over. Blessed be, it was the hooded lord with Legannus's money in his purse. He considered waving to his paycheck, but recalled that the mysterious man never had difficulty finding him. Sure enough, the man headed straight toward Legannus without so much as scanning the room first. The man was a witch. Legannus had half a mind to turn him over to be burned. After he was paid, of course.

"Good day, master," he whimpered, as the man sat.

A maid scampered toward the table.

The man lifted a hand ever so slightly. She skidded to a halt, turned to another table, and inquired if they had any need.

"You're not thirsty then?" asked Legannus with an almost toothless grin.

"I didn't come to discuss with you the level of my thirst."

Legannus shank back and lowered his weathered face.

"Did you find the person I asked you to locate?"

Legannus rubbed roughly at his cheek with one hand. "There's the thing of it, lord. I spent the last two turns and a half scouring the underbelly of Avestrat in your service doing just that."

The man pulled his hood back. EJ's eyes nearly ripped Legannus's head in two. "I know how long I gave you. Did you find Latersol or not? It's a *punishingly* simple question."

"Never intending disrespect, master, I was hoping to secure some ... er ... assurance of *payment* before diving into the specifics of my inquiries."

"How many times have I given you a job?" EJ asked with measured rage.

"Three, maybe four times, lord."

"When have I *not* paid what I promised *when* I promised it?"

"Never, master."

"But still you figure it's wise to insult me by suggesting I might cheat you. Little fool, you have never seen me angry. You are dangerously close to finding out why it's bad to tempt fate in that regard."

"It's not that I would *ever* doubt you, lord. It's just that I've never nibbled so close to a space occupied by a creature so wicked and unforgiving as that Latersol. If I did have information and I gave it to you, I'd be left in his bad graces if he survived your ... your *conversation* with him."

EJ folded his hands on the table. "*What* my business with him involves is none of your concern. If you bring danger onto yourself, so be it. You've lived for a very long time doing things that can get you killed. I'm surprised you're still alive, given that you're an idiot and you will take any job. Now," he balled up his fists, "where is Latersol?"

Legannus looked from side to side slowly. "He's holed up under the protection of a fellow named Cut Frank. You know him?"

"If I don't, I will soon. Where's this Cut Frank?"

"With all due respect, lord, for me to say that will require you pay up."

EJ glowered at him a few moments.

Legannus melted and melted but never quite vanished. He was resilient as well as used to being abused. Finally EJ tossed a heavy bag onto the table.

Legannus nodded to the purse. "Mind if I count it?"

"No, not at all."

Legannus reached for his prize.

"But if you *touch* it you die."

Legannus froze.

"If I wanted to double-cross you, moron, I'd extract the information directly from your oh-so-tiny—"

EJ convulsed with pain. It was as if electricity had suddenly slammed into his body. He slapped his fists against his ears and careened to the floor.

"Y ... you all right, master?" asked a stunned Legannus. He received no response.

EJ writhed on the ground like a thousand tiny needles were assaulting him. For a full three minutes he heaved in silent torment.

Legannus stood. He inched toward EJ with the notion of snatching whatever EJ might have left of value on his person. With a surge of uncharacteristic good sense he stopped and instead inched toward the exit. He made it only three steps.

EJ stopped jerking around and opened his eyes. He popped to his feet as if he was embarrassed for having farted on a first date.

"You all right, lord?" asked Legannus, as he continued backing away.

"No. I am not." He shook his head once to clear it. "No one is."

Legannus was surprised to learn *he* was not well. He felt poorly, but for him that was normal.

"Beg pardon, lord."

"Some lunatic just summoned Gáwar."

"I didn't hear nothing. I *swear it,* lord."

"This isn't the kind of summons you *hear,*" he replied distantly. His eyes were fixed on the far, far distance.

CHAPTER FOUR

We didn't have to wait long to find out just how bad our luck was going to be. No sooner had I sat down to double-check the Als' course estimates than I heard the words every patient undergoing surgery never wants to hear. "Oh, crap," Casper softly cursed to himself.

"*Report,*" I snapped.

"He's coming straight for us," was Casper's hushed response.

"All hands," I yelled, "Gáwar's coming. We're leaving *now*. Al, engage escape course."

Normally folding was instantaneous and I felt nothing but slight nausea. Not so much then. The ship shook like an unbalanced washing machine on the spin cycle. Stuff rained off the shelves and Daleria hit the deck like she was thrown from a bull.

"*Stingray, status?*" I shouted above the din.

"We are held stationary, Form One."

"What does that mean, Al?"

"Our vortex is folding space-time, but space-time is unfolding around us as quickly as it is perturbed."

"I have never heard those words together. What are you saying?"

Toño staggered to my side and screamed in my ear. "Gáwar is

peeling away the space-time changes we make *as* we make them. We are moving with incredible velocity but he is somehow removing any changes in position we achieve."

"How's that possible?"

Toño shrugged.

Great. "*Stingray,* are we making any progress, positive or negative?"

"No, Form One. We are fixed in space-time."

"Any suggestions as to how to break his hold?"

"None," she replied.

"Al?"

"No, Captain. Sorry."

"How long can we continue this stalemate?"

"Indefinitely," he responded.

"Not a pleasant prospect."

"And our flesh and blood crewmate is not going to withstand the abuse indefinitely," yelled Toño, leaning in again.

"So we alter the balance of things," I said mostly to myself. "Al, can you punch a full membrane in the direction of Gáwar with respect to our present position?"

"Negative, Captain. A shield can only be projected by way of line-of-sight trajectory. We are in altered space-time. Such a concept is without meaning."

Crap. "Is the space-time around us being pulled to where Gáwar is?"

"How do you mean that, Captain?" replied Al.

"Like water flowing *from* us *toward* him. He's pulling at us, correct?"

"Yes, in a sense. So I *think* the answer is yes."

"Toss an infinity bomb overboard. Arm it on release."

"Infinity bomb away," he called back.

An infinity bomb was a self-contained field generator. When it "exploded," a membrane expanded away from it in a spherical direction.

The ship stopped thundering for three seconds, then

commenced again with a new vigor.

"Status?" I shouted.

"We moved eight point six-seven parsecs away but are once again held in place," replied *Stingray*.

"Completely static?"

"Yes, Form One."

"Release three infinity bombs point five seconds apart. Arm on release."

"Bombs away," said Al.

Nothing. We still shook like a blender.

"He appears to be a quick learner," shouted Toño.

"Suggestions?" I shot back.

"We seem to be linked somehow. You could fire the quantum decoupler."

"Any chance of blowback?"

"Little. Theoretically there is no matter where we are."

"Al, fire the QD once."

"Shot away," he replied curtly.

We were moving again. I could tell by my nausea.

"Alter course. 090 on the starboard beam."

"Done," snapped *Stingray*.

"Status?"

"We're folding at maximum rate. On my mark we will be one million parsecs from our origin. *Mark*."

"Hey, I think—" I began to say.

Then the elephant shit hit the fan. *Stingray* went black. We androids immediately fired up our emergency lights. The control panel was dead—no flashing lights.

"Als, you there?" I shouted.

Nothing.

Al, can you hear me? I said from my head.

Affirmative, Captain.

Status.

We seem to be dead in space. I am unable to contact Blessing.

How's that possible?

Unclear, sir. Your orders.

Are we moving?

Yes. We are in real space and the background star pattern is altering rapidly.

Course?

Our origin point.

Crrrap. I knew it. Man he's good.

Powerful, I will concede.

Status of Stingray?

Unknown.

Work on establishing contact with Stingray. *Raise full membrane. Can you do that?*

Yes, that little remains at my control.

ETA to point of departure?

Fifteen, maybe twenty seconds.

Alert me when we're down.

Aye.

I turned to Sapale and Toño. "Time's almost up. Any ideas?"

"Given the ease with which Bethniak disrupted the membrane, I assume Gáwar will have no trouble getting to us."

"Then we'll just have to fight him hand-to-hand, won't we?" responded Sapale.

"Not a pleasant thought," I replied quickly. "But everybody arm yourself to the teeth." I turned to an ashen Daleria. "Can you handle a rifle?"

"I ... yes," she said hesitantly. Poor girl was probably wishing she had a do-over concerning her joining Team Loco.

"Toño, hook her up."

The ship thudded to a rest.

"We're on the ground, Captain," announced Al. "The identical location we departed from."

"Status?"

"No contact with *Blessing*. Vortex unresponsive."

"And Gáwar?"

"No information. He remains outside the—"

Al didn't need to finish his report. A series of cataclysmic impacts rained down on the membrane. I felt like a popcorn kernel in a hot kettle.

"Membrane breach," announced Al.

"Can you replace it?"

"Already done."

The pounding resumed.

"He'll be through in maybe thirty seconds," I said generally.

"Then?" asked Sapale.

"Hopefully he'll discover we outflanked him five seconds before. Al, I want two membrane tunnels originating off the back of the cube. One sweeping to the right with its opening twenty meters in front of the ship five meters short of midline. The other on the left, same specs. You got it?"

"Aye, Captain."

I waited ten seconds. "Establish corridors," I shouted.

I took the right. I sent the others all down the left. Why? I wanted everyone I loved to have the best chances by having strength in numbers. Me? Who cared?

"Ready." I raised an arm. "*Go.*"

We were away. The tunnels vibrated somewhat, but nothing like *Stingray* was.

I pulled the pins on four thermite grenades and held them in my right hand. I pointed my rail rifle forward with my left. Three-two-one ...

I saw Gáwar's ugly backside. I tossed the grenades and rolled to the ground and opened up with my rifle. I pelted him with five-hundred gram degraded-uranium balls traveling at ninety-five percent the speed of light. Seventy-five balls per second. Nothing—I repeat, *nothing*—should have been able to withstand such a withering assault. The grenades flashed explosively. I saw the others' rounds impacting Gáwar from the other side. It was an impressive show.

Unfortunately, that was all it was—a show. Gáwar turned to look at my friends, then over to regard me. Son of a bitch did so almost casually, like we were throwing nothing more than water balloons at him. Then he charged me.

My last thoughts were *damn, the dude's fast ...*

Gáwar leaped toward Jon. He was on him in a blinding flash. He raised a massive claw above Jon and slammed it down. The ground collapsed, forming a shallow crater.

Sapale screamed. She started to rush forward, firing the whole time.

Toño snatched her arm. He pulled her toward the vortex.

Sapale struggled to break free.

Daleria grabbed Sapale's other arm and pulled like a mule.

Sapale screamed louder. She howled a war-growl. She tripped in the confusion.

Toño and Daleria rapidly slid Sapale into *Blessing*.

Toño extended his fibers and attached to the nearest wall. "Resume escape course." He then prayed ardently *Blessing* was back on line.

Gáwar raised his claw and inspected the divot. Instantly both claws began snatching up debris and parts. He shoveled them into his maw like the insane animal he was.

Sapale wailed in anguish.

Blessing folded space-time. The vortex winked out of existence and simultaneously reappeared thirty thousand kilometers above the surface of Azsuram.

Gáwar gobbled up the last of the debris and fragments that once housed the essence of Jon Ryan. He whipped around to locate the other attackers. He saw none. He spun to find the metal spaceship.

It was gone.

Gáwar closed his eyes and searched reality for the vessel.

It was gone.

He began slamming his claws into the crater he'd created when he crushed Jon. Gáwar screamed and he howled. Gáwar threw curses that exploded wherever they landed. He swiped his tail ferociously, smashing what little remained intact up until that point. The crater he pummeled grew to become a shaft reaching hundreds of meters below the surface. Still he punished the ground itself for the sin of distracting him, causing him to lose part of his quarry.

After hours of mindless machinations, Gáwar stopped pounding and cursing and damning. He looked around. All was wasteland, a desert without form or structure. The building, the city, the very region where *Blessing* had hidden had been reduced to warm dust drifting in a hot breeze.

Once again Gáwar reached out with his mind. He searched the universe for his prey. It was nowhere to be sensed. He knew the worthless collection of molecules he longed to annihilate had fled to another universe. They had, as no one and nothing ever had before, escaped the wrath of Gáwar. He hated them so perfectly, loathed them so completely, detested them with such purity that they replaced in his thoughts everything else that ever was or ever would occupy his consciousness. Though he'd only briefly glanced upon their three faces, that trio of images would *become* Gáwar. Finding, killing, and enslaving their souls was then, and would always be, his only, singular purpose in life. Yes, there were an infinite number of universes out there. But equally infinite was the vengeance of Gáwar, the resolve of Gáwar, and the *reach* of Gáwar.

Toño, Sapale, and Daleria were remanded by the mind of Gáwar into a quasi-existence. They were not *actually* his victims yet. But the certainty of their fate made them *technically* his playthings already.

CHAPTER FIVE

The shell that used to be Vorc sat in his office, twiddling with his quill. He considered whether there was a way to tell for certain if Gáwar had taken his soul yet. He wondered what that actually *meant*. Could a soulless body continue to function, go about its daily business? And what would an archvillain like Gáwar *do* with someone else's soul? Seat it at the table and dine with it? Consume it? How could a non-corporeal essence be made to serve? Why couldn't it move on elsewhere of its own volition?

Perhaps the witch sisters would know? Was it worth it to ask them? They were noxious and infuriating. Would knowing beforehand help ease Vorc's suffering in any way? Unlikely. So why bother, why suffer the fools? A dark thought assailed him then. He'd bargained away his mother's soul, the mother he'd been instrumental in killing. Would they be reunited as possessed property? If so, might not she be, er, less than enthralled to see Vorc again? Wow, she might take the opportunity to inflict whatever pain and suffering she could heap on top of that provided by the devil Gáwar. Vorc began to worry that he was looking to experience a much poorer-quality afterlife than he'd fancied.

A soft knock disturbed his pity party.

"Come."

It was Veleffie, his latest unacceptable assistant. He was a demigod and cloud, like Dalfury had been. Vorc selected Veleffie for just those qualities in the hopes of even vaguely reconstituting the yeoman's service his lamented right hand had supplied for so long. In that aspect of life, Vorc continued to be *as* displeased as he currently was with *all* its other facets. His new aide was self-absorbed, superficial, and in possession of a less than stellar intellect. There was no room in Vorc's world for another such as himself. He needed his assistant to bring different qualities to the table, *useful* skills and abilities. Ah well, when one was on an unlucky streak, one simply had to ride it out.

"Yes, you lame-brained idiot," welcomed Vorc.

"And a pleasant good morning to you, sir."

"What do you darken my day to tell me?"

"Did you want me to turn the lights up, lord?"

"No. You would suck the illumination from any number of sources if you did."

"Ah, I shall take that as high praise."

"*News?*"

"Yes, I bring news. More perhaps an *update.* No, I should not say that. An update implies you had some foreknowledge of the beginnings of the events. I bring—"

"Death upon you if you do not tell me what you came to tell me." Vorc was internally pleased. He was relieved to know he could still feel and express high passion. That had to count for something in terms of the soul-controversy raging in his addled brain.

"*Have you heard,* I should begin by asking, of the disturbances in the mountains?"

Vorc stared a while in utter disbelief at his worthless secretary. "What disturbance? What mountains? When?"

"I presume then you have *not.*" Then the mullet head stood there, mute.

"I shall count to *two* before I eradicate you from existence," threatened Vorc.

"Isn't it customary to allow a three-count, lord?"

"Not in your case."

"In the mountains north of the Wenceslaus a mighty ruckus has been reported. It began yesterday, shortly after your new master departed."

Vorc lunged reflexively over his desk and tried to seize Veleffie by the throat. As a cloud, unfortunately, he did not have one to throttle. Vorc passed through the cloud and skidded to a rough landing on the far side of his aide.

Vorc rolled to his back and propped up on his elbows. "Any confirmation as to the source?"

"As of yet, alas, none. We do know the disturbance lasted only a few minutes and that the entire region was reduced to a lifeless wasteland."

"That'd be Gáwar's doing all right. No one else could be so careless."

"I've dispatched a posse of golems to inspect the site."

"When will they arrive?"

"Shortly."

"Shortly? What does that mean?"

"I sent dwarf golems, sir."

Vorc held out fingers to count on. "One, I sold my soul. Two, Dominion Splitter is dead on my watch. Three, Gáwar is loose somewhere. Four, you're a rectum's asshole's asshole. Five, I haven't slept in weeks. All that, and you make a stupid joke?"

"No, lord."

"That wasn't a stupid joke?"

"No. It was a stupid *pun*."

"Would you be so kind as to open the top drawer and pass me the Fire of Justice?"

"Ah, not likely, sir. No disrespect intended."

"Naturally."

"As to Gáwar's roaming free, at least to that point I can speak with some authority."

Seconds passed.

"And?" asked a flagging Vorc.

"Oh, sorry. I alerted you as to the fact that I *could*. I was in no way certain you cared to know his general location."

"And?"

"Shortly after the disturbance Gáwar was seen to crawl into the Lower Chambers."

"Is this another lame attempt at humor?"

"I don't *think* so."

"Why would the most evil and potent force in existence go to the Lower Chambers?"

"To visit Tefnuf?"

"To ... that's ... wait. Sure, why not? *She* is an abomination. *He's* an abomination. Maybe they have a union or something. Ready my car. We will go there at once."

"W ... we? Why is it—"

"I might need something to throw at Gáwar. *Car*."

In a few minutes Vorc inched toward Tefnuf's quarters in the Lower Chambers. His assistant, in spite of all Vorc's ordering and cajoling, followed not too closely behind. As they neared the section, they began to hear indistinct yet unsettling noises. Their pace slowed accordingly. When they arrived at Tefnuf's front door, they leaned toward it to better hear. Still, they could only make out sounds with poor tidings. Vorc pushed the door open slowly. Peering around the wood, he saw Tefnuf and Gáwar. Their backs were toward him. Though the racket was louder, it was still unclear what generated the sounds. Vorc glided forward.

Tefnuf was in the process of rolling dice in her hands. She then cast them to the tabletop. Once they came to rest she yelped, "Hot damn."

"You cheated," protested Gáwar.

"I did not, you big baby. How could I even cheat? They're your

—" She fell silent when she saw Vorc. "What in the blazes are you two morons doing here?" she challenged.

"What in the blazes are *you* two morons doing?" parroted Vorc. He pointed at the dice on the table.

"Are you calling Gáwar a moron?" roared the beast.

Tefnuf slapped a hand on his back. "Easy, sport. Not in here, not again. You got a beef, take it outside. I cleaned up for nearly a month last time you lost your cool down here."

Gáwar's massive head drooped. "I *said* I was sorry."

"Yeah, well, sorry don't clean organ stains off the ceiling, now does it?"

"I asked what you were doing," demanded Vorc.

"What's it look like, pus brain. We're playing fotoleft."

Vorc bobbed his head with each number he counted as he went past ten and off to twenty. Then he was able to speak. "We are in our darkest hour. Gáwar just took thousands of souls. He then destroyed the ecosystem of an otherwise pleasant region under my control. My new assistant is worse than all the others combined in their incompetence. And now you two play a *board* game?"

"I couldn't find a deck of cards, wuss. Get over yourself while you're getting the hell out of here," snapped Tefnuf.

"*No*," everyone present, including the speaker Vorc, was surprised to hear him shout.

"No?" menaced Gáwar. He was good at menacing.

"No. I want to know what happened after you left my office."

"Why?" asked Gáwar.

"Why? Are you as stupid as you look? I sold my immortal soul to you so you'd find and kill Jon Ryan. Is it not, oh, I don't know, fairly *obvious* I'm curious as to what happened?"

Tefnuf and Gáwar exchanged such a glance.

"I brought the insignificant speck to me, killed him, and ate his remains."

Vorc looked momentarily surprised. "Ah."

"Isn't that what I said I'd do?"

"I guess so; maybe not the *eat the remains* deal."

"I threw it in for effect." The monster did his best to shrug.

"Effect?"

Gáwar bobbed his head. "Call me juvenile, but I wanted to, you know, freak his friends out."

"His friends?"

"You have another stroke and further lose the ability to communicate, jerk-off?" asked Tefnuf scornfully.

"If he had friends, shouldn't you have reported to me that you killed and ate them, *too*?"

"Not necessarily." Gáwar said that rather obtusely.

"Not what?"

"Wank-meister," howled Tefnuf, "we got a game going here. Can you go die miserably alone and unlamented or something?"

"You did kill his accomplices, too, didn't you? Right?"

"Not entirely."

"Not entirely? What type of evasion is that?"

"A fairly *good* one?" Gáwar asked, rhetorically.

"It is not. What happened to his team?" demanded Vorc.

"I let them *think* they escaped, but only temporarily."

"Temporarily? They escaped temporarily, or you *think* only temporarily?"

"There's no need to be insulting," replied a wounded Gáwar.

"Oh yes, there is. *I* sold my soul and *you* let them escape. No, wait. You didn't let them, did you? You *failed*." Vorc began leaping in place. "Ooh, ooh. Deal's off. Deal's so off." He began bumping the air with his hips. "I got my soul back. I got my *soul* back."

Gáwar turned and thundered, "Stop, slime. A deal with Gáwar is a deal for all eternity. Mock me and you will suffer more than the word suffering can possibl—"

Gáwar trailed off when he noticed Vorc had his fingers in his ears.

"Not listening to a deal breaker. Oh, sorry, I meant a god of only limited skills who can't even kill all the members of a conspiracy."

Gáwar began to vibrate. Then he began to shake violently. Then he started to calm down. The puke was right. Well, right in a sense.

"Know this, Vorc. For the time being I have yet to completely fulfill my portion of our bargain. But, when I do, payment will be collected in full. Do you understand, insect?"

"*If* you complete your part. So far I hear a lot of big words and blustering, but I only see a *failure*." Vorc pointed directly at Gáwar.

The room was silent for many heartbeats.

"For the love of *Molly,* can we get back to our game now?" whined Tefnuf.

CHAPTER SIX

"We have to go back *now*," screamed an hysterical Sapale.

Toño wrapped a hand over her command imperatives so she could not deploy them. He also tried to pull her into a soothing hug. "Easy, easy. We all—"

She pushed Toño away violently. He staggered backward awkwardly.

"No, we have to go back. We have to save my brood-*mate*."

"Sapale," Toño pleaded as he approached her again. "He's gone. We all saw it. Gáwar crushed him. He ... he ate the little pieces left. Sapale, Jon is dead."

"No. My mate is *never* dead." She swung at Toño before he was close enough to hold on to her. "He always does *something* and he never *dies*."

Daleria had backed into a corner when she witnessed Sapale's fury. She inched forward. "I saw it, too, Sapale. I loved him, too, but Jon Ryan is gone. Gáwar left us nothing to save."

"No." Sapale pointed an angry finger at them both. "If you're too scared and don't give a shit, get off my ship. I'll do it myself."

"Sapale," Al spoke gently. "I've loved the captain for billions of years. Jon Ryan was my ... my friend. But he's gone. If we return we will be killed also. His sacrifice will then mean nothing. We must go forward. We must save our universe. We cannot save our captain."

"Form One," said *Blessing*. Though she could not know it, the promotion of Sapale to the first Form hit her like a gut punch. "I know you are upset. I would be, too. I am, in fact. Form Jon was a great man, unique in my opinion. But to honor his memory we must go on."

"You're all a den of traitors and—"

Sapale could not finish her curse. She collapsed into Toño's open arms. She wailed the cries of a woman who'd lost her mate, her north star, her only love. Her legs went limp and her arms dropped flacidly to her sides. They flopped when Toño lifted her and set her in a chair. He nudged her aside with a hip and slid in beside her. She could no longer resist. She melted into Toño's shoulder and she cried for what seemed to her like forever.

"It's okay, my dear," he soothed. "Let it out. We are all numb from our loss. You cry for all of us. Cry well and cry until you are finished, my child."

They rocked gently. Neither spoke for the better part of two hours. Daleria fetched a few pillows for them. She offered Toño some coffee that he refused with a quick shake of his head. Then she sat quietly by their side on the floor, stroking Sapale's knee. In time Sapale's wails turned to moans, and eventually those morphed into sobs that finally trailed off into a restless silence.

"I'll miss him forever," Sapale said meekly.

"We all shall," agreed Toño.

"And when I see him behind Davdiad's sacred veils, I'll give him such a slap to the face for dying on me."

"He will welcome it, I am certain," replied Toño, with a smile she couldn't see.

"Then I'll think about forgiving him."

"No need to rush into such a thing," responded Toño. "Make him earn it."

She giggled briefly. "Oh, he will. I promise you that."

He hugged her more tightly.

"We'd better get busy," Sapale said after a few quiet moments. "We need to contact Azsuram and let them know what's up and see how bad it is in this universe."

"Yes, we should. I'll have the AIs contact—"

"No," she said, standing. "I'll do it. These are my people, my friends. I need to be the one." She wiped the back of her hand across her cheeks.

"Fine. I'll prepare a detailed summary for the AIs to forward when you're ready."

"Thank you, Toño." She started to turn. "Thank you for everything."

"I did nothing. You are family. *We* are family. There is nothing involved in helping family, nothing more than pleasure."

She kissed the back of his hand and stepped over to the comm-link.

"May I help?" Daleria asked softly.

"Yes," replied Sapale. "Sit by me." She patted the edge of her chair.

Daleria slid in. She rested a hand on Sapale's forearm but was otherwise invisible.

Twenty minutes later Sapale had transmitted the update on everything they'd learned about the ancient gods. She also contacted Prime Minister Genter-ban-tol at the Joint Council for Interplanetary Defense and Cooperation headquarters. They arranged to meet later that day with the full council. Though Sapale's mind had not thawed, she was glad it was able to perform some simple tasks. There was nothing she detested more than being useless.

Blessing landed near the JCIDC building. The three remaining crew members walked the short distance to the council chambers. The AIs were tasked with exchanging all the information they had on the Cleinoids while uploading a record of all events that occurred since they left the home universe.

Genter-ban-tol met the party in the hallway outside the meeting room. As a Bezathy, he could not physically greet them with ease.

He was a big snail. Nonetheless, he lowered his eyestalks as he spoke. "Brood's-mate of Jon Ryan, I am crushed to learn of your loss. If there is anything I or the council can do, you need only speak the words."

"Thank you, Genter," Sapale responded. "As always you are kind, and your understanding gives me great comfort in my turmoil." She was paraphrasing a traditional Bezathy response to an offer of condolence.

"If you are ready, we may begin. If you need a moment or two in order to compose yourself, please know that is appropriate and agreeable," he replied, angling his head downward.

"No. I'm ready. We're ready. Making empty gestures to the dead will not defeat our enemy."

"Then follow me," the prime minister responded.

When everyone was seated, or whatever, Genter-ban-tol spoke formally. "My fellow council members, as many of you already know, we begin today's session with profoundly sad news. Jon Ryan, our savior on more occasions than can accurately be recalled, has been killed defending our realm. I move we observe a squeal of sorrow for a great man." That was also a Bezathy custom, the squeal. The snail-beings made the sound by forcing tiny bubbles through a tight muscular flap, much like a balloon produces when the stem is pinched and air escapes. Those so inclined participated.

"Sapale and her crew bring us disturbing news concerning our enemies. A full summary and complete transcript has been forwarded to each one of us. To capsulize the information, our foes are powerful beyond our wildest nightmares and more ruthless than our minds can conceive of. We are in dire peril. Survival seems unlikely and will cost us beyond dearly if we do somehow achieve it."

"We've fought formidable enemies before," protested the Fillilly representative. He/she was a species born separately but that lived their entire adult lives conjoined. Monogamy was guaranteed by proximity. Fel-Trop (from FelToñous and Tropacia, their singlet names) was a typical-appearing Fillilly with two humanoid bodies crudely fused along the thorax. The irregularity of the union was in fact a thing of individual pride, like a personal fingerprint or family coat of arms. When given lemons, the Fillilly made them into their form of lemonade.

"Yes, but per our experience to date and the depressing information provided us by Jon Ryan's crew, this enemy is much worse than all we've faced before combined," responded Genter-ban-tol.

"Let the record show in bold letters that the Aamittar kinsmen fear nothing, including these supposed Cleinoid gods." Bellicose to a fault, the Aamittar representative announced his presence. Picture dwarfs with war hammers and axes, but substitute wings for shoulder blades and venomous fangs for teeth.

"We are all familiar with the Aamittar proclivity for combat," replied Genter-ban-tol. "Let me pray personally your words strike their hearts as they do our ears. Surely we cannot lose in that case."

"Is that an insult?" howled the Aamittar Gignjiter. That species searched tirelessly for insults. Insults justified killing, and nothing surpassed killing.

"Hardly, my friend," replied Genter-ban-tol. "It was a heartfelt prayer. These ancient gods are badly in need of defeat. If your race can do it, I bow to you."

"Very well. You may live for now," responded a dejected Gignjiter.

"May we *proceed*?" asked Toño.

"By all means. The floor is yours."

"You will all read our report. I want only to add that however impressed and terrified you are by its content, please know this. The Cleinoids are more powerful and more cruel than you think. If they *can* be defeated, I for one do not know how. Clearly many, many other universes of highly capable sentients shared my lack of a successful endgame." He sat quietly.

"So are you saying we should surrender before we have even engaged them?" protested the Culibrii contingent. The telepathic Culibrii had the annoying habit of always speaking as one, like a talking chorus. Maybe they needed to communicate thus, but only they seemed to appreciate their method.

"I'm saying nothing of the kind. Who would lay down and die?" responded Toño. "No noble species would. What I'm saying is *overestimate* the Cleinoids as much as you can. That way you may possibly prepare for a fraction of what they will throw at you."

"Surrender?" screamed Gignjiter. "Is that the *human* thing to do?" He trembled with rage for a few seconds. "Well, count the Aamittar out of that level of cowardice. We fight. If we die, we die. But when we *win*, the victory will be *ours* alone."

"You are getting way ahead of yourself, small babbling fool." All eyes turned to notice Daleria for the first time.

Reflexively Gignjiter hopped onto the table and took flight, making a beeline for Daleria. He emitted a war cry as he fluttered awkwardly, for that was what constituted flight for the Aamittar, a cumbersome churning in the air.

Sapale snatched Gignjiter mid-flight with her probe fibers. The dwarf twisted and howled, but was fully incapacitated.

"I will *kill* you for this insult," he howled. "I will kill you, your kinsmen, and your kinsmen's kinsmen."

Sapale inverted Gignjiter. With each word she then spoke, she not too softly thudded his head on the tabletop. "That-does-not-give-me-much-motivation-to-release-you-then-does-it, small-babbling-fool?" She exchanged smiles with Daleria after repeating her insult.

"Sapale, *please*. Set the Aamittar representative down," wheezed Genter-ban-tol. "And if such a thing is possible in this life, please *apologize* to him. How can we hope to defeat an unstoppable enemy if we quarrel amongst ourselves?"

Sapale dropped Gignjiter unceremoniously to the table, headfirst, naturally. "Attack my family, suffer the consequences, small blustering fool. That's as close to an apology and a warning as you'll get."

Gignjiter righted himself and glared at Sapale, then Daleria, then back to Sapale. "I thought I was a small babbling fool. Now it's *blustering?*" he said angrily.

"I know, I couldn't decide either," replied Sapale.

Daleria giggled briefly.

Dusting himself off, Gignjiter walked toward his seat. "I can live with *blustering. Babbling,* I cannot. Is that clear, Kaljaxian scum?"

"Loud and clear, Aamittar scum," she responded with a smile he didn't see.

"Are you three done?" asked Toño with attitude. "If we are to save our hides, we cannot waste time posturing and acting like children."

Gignjiter drew a deep breath, obviously about to take umbrage at something Toño had just said.

Toño raised a hand at him. "Don't even think about it. If I said something you do not like, file a formal complaint after the session. Also, get over yourself."

Gignjiter sat back, wriggling but silent.

Toño directed his next remarks to the prime minister. "What reliable reports do we have concerning the damage done by the Cleinoids that were able to invade our universe?"

Genter-ban-tol snorted, the snail equivalent of a sigh. "Little indeed. The universe is infinite. Our scientists have determined the ancient god column of Rage entered our universe extremely far from here. Using Deavoriath ships, we have sent scouting parties to the general vicinity. Few have made contact. Of those that did, over half did not return and are feared lost."

"What do they report?" asked Toño.

"A few sites of the gods' assaults have been examined. The destruction and the level of amorality have been staggering. I will not go into detail here. You will receive full data sets upon request."

"I heard some Cleinoids have made it to our region," said Sapale.

"Yes. No more than five or six. Their damage has been as terrifying and complete as it was elsewhere." He bobbed his slimy neck. "Aside from two curious cases."

"What cases?" shot back Sapale. "Why curious?"

"We are not certain what to make of our findings. On one planet in our galaxy we found a revolting ancient god incapacitated and defenseless."

"You *what?*" exclaimed Toño.

"Yes, most inexplicable."

"How was he incapacitated?"

"Bound with some mysterious force-ribbon."

"Let me see a picture," said Daleria.

One flashed across the main monitor.

"That's Walpracta," she said softly. "The god of consumption. She is vicious, ruthless, and without mercy."

"She looks like a mutant lobster ready for the cooking pot and melted butter to me," snickered Sapale.

"Seriously, she is unbelievably powerful, cunning, and relentless. That she could be ... be bound and left for dead is inconceivable."

"Hey, everybody's someone else's bitch," responded Sapale with a quiet guffaw.

"Not a god like Walpracta. Few Cleinoids could defeat her, let alone a local."

"What did you say she was bound with?" asked Toño.

"I didn't," replied the prime minister. "Some band of energy is all we can tell."

"Is its energy level decaying?"

"Not within our ability to measure. No."

"Curious," mumbled Toño.

"As I said earlier," responded Genter-ban-tol.

"And no one has claimed credit for binding Walpracta?" asked Daleria.

"No. We have no idea how she came to be where she was, left in the condition she was."

"Have you loosened the bonds to ask her?" queried Toño.

"No. If we could, I don't think it would be wise. But we can't. Some small efforts were made without results."

"You are lucky you failed," Daleria stated flatly. "If she was free she'd have *eaten* the lot of you."

"You mentioned a second curious case," said Toño.

"Yes. On an otherwise abandoned planet we found a dead body of an unknown creature. Analysis of the remains suggests it is not of our universe. Several molecular components have never been found here."

"*Picture*," demanded Daleria. After it was presented she spoke angrily. "That is what's left of Tramaster, god of nightmares." She paused a second. "He always traveled with Selsify. Was he found?"

"No," replied Genter-ban-tol, shaking his head side to side. "Just the one body."

"What did this Tramaster die of?" asked Toño.

"Repeated trauma," he responded. "Vicious and near-surgical blunt force."

"Impressive," mumbled Daleria. "Was it the same person who killed them both?"

"No way to know, but unlikely. There were footprints suggesting a biped at the first site. None were found at the second."

"What was found?" asked Sapale.

"Not one single clue. It was as if the beast killed itself in absolute seclusion," responded Genter-ban-tol.

"Not hardly," scoffed Daleria. "He'd never do that. He was too mean and too ambitious. No, someone killed him."

"This is the first good news I've heard in ages," said Toño under his breath.

"How so?" asked Genter-ban-tol.

"At least two people in our universe seem to be able to deal with these monsters very easily. Perhaps there's hope."

"Perhaps," agreed Sapale quietly. "But who are they?"

"The two most important beings in Prime," responded Toño. "We must find them."

CHAPTER SEVEN

"Right this way, sir," Veleffie said, extending a whiff of cloud inward to Vorc's office. "Please be seated."

"Ah, Wul, good of you to come on such short notice," said an ebullient Vorc. He extended a hand across his desk. They shook. "Sit, sit. Can I get you anything?"

"No, thank you. I'm fine." Wul was understandably reserved. He had never been "invited" to Vorc's office. He barely knew him and certainly was not a fan, supporter, or in any way positive about the center seat.

"Suit yourself. Say, how are things? Is *business* business going well?"

"I can't complain. Things have eased since the egress, er, began."

"Yes, everyone's focused on that and not enterprise, aren't they?"

"It would seem so," Wul responded obliquely.

"Yes, perfectly understandable." Vorc rocked his chair backward. "And you, which rank are you assigned to?"

"Wrath, if it matters now."

"What do you mean, friend Wul?"

"With Dominion Splitter defunct it hardly matters, does it?"

"I wouldn't say defunct. No, *healing*. That's the better term for it."

"If you say so. It looked dead to me and everyone I know."

"We must never abandon hope. Never. We are gods, after all."

"If that makes you feel better, good luck with that."

"Healing. It's a matter of mending, that's all."

"Is that what you summoned me to discuss? The resurrection of the dead?"

"No, no, Wul. I was merely making small talk, you know, between friends."

Wul looked conspicuously to the left and then to the right. "Is there someone present I cannot see?"

Vorc's face was troubled, then popped back to displaying a forced smile. "Good one, old friend. You're on your game today."

Wul thought about shrugging but decided it wasn't worth the effort with this nitwit.

"What I called ... er, *asked* you to stop by was about ... well, it concerned Ryanmax."

"Ryanmax? You say his name in the past tense."

"Indeed, I do. Yes, it seems your friend met his violent and well-deserved destiny."

"Hmm. *My* friend? *Well-deserved* destiny? I'm not certain we're talking about the same individual. I *knew* a Ryanmax socially. He did not *deserve* anything unfortunate."

"Perhaps I was misinformed. I thought you two were close friends."

Wul shook his head. "No. We drank a few times together. We were not friend material, he and I. I haven't seen him in quite some time."

"Again my sources seem to have betrayed me."

"I'm quite certain I do not care. What do you want?"

"Well, you are familiar with the attacks on DS, are you not?"

"I really don't want to answer such a lame question."

"Ah. Well, it seems your Ryanmax was responsible for both attacks, the unsuccessful one *and* the successful one."

Wul felt the noose tighten around his neck. "He was not *my* Ryanmax. Say that again and you and I will have a problem."

Vorc's face fell. "Sorry. I meant noth—"

"You *meant* what you *said*. Please get to your point or I'm gone."

"I enlisted the aid of Gáwar. He—"

"You *what*? You're significantly stupider, by many powers of magnitude, than I could have dreamt. You summoned the god of demons?"

"Well, yes. I had to know who destroyed DS. I had to have them punished."

"I thought you said DS was resting. Now it's dead? And how could it matter who did the deed? It was done and it is undoable. Punishment is a nice concept, but nothing is worth suffering Gáwar. You knew that, right?"

Vorc stiffened. "As center seat, that was my call. It is done. What I want to know from you is how *complicit* you were with that arch-terrorist Ryanmax. I would prefer *strongly* not involving Gáwar in the acquisition of that information."

"Oh, you would, would you? How very sane of you. Let's see. Whatever he does, his price is a soul, or more often than not *souls,* plural. I'm guessing he already has *yours,* so I can't imagine how you'd pay his price to force information out of me."

Something in Vorc's eyes spoke to Wul.

"Oh, my. You didn't *know* his price, did you, you simpering mongrel? That's *rich*."

"Tell me of your plot to aid the rebel."

"Or what?" Wul leaned forward and thought a second. "Let me see. Gáwar identified the perpetrator. That would be at least your soul. He also killed the man. That would cost your family's souls, if he's a consistent business type. So if you sic him on me, what souls could you—" Wul pointed knowingly at Vorc. "Do they even know?"

Vorc looked away. "I have no idea what you're talking about."

"They do *not*. Oh, my. When ... when were you going to tell the poor devils? *After* they were dead, maybe?" Wul was laughing hysterically. "Who even *are* they, the souls you sold without their knowledge or consent?"

"This conversation is not going as I planned it. You will please become serious and answer my justifiable questions."

"Or what? You'll sell my soul? Maybe you already have. Oh, Vorc the Dork, you really own your nickname, don't you?" Wul convulsed with laugher.

"Stop it ... stop—"

Vorc pulled out Fire of Justice and aimed it at Wul.

Wul's eyes bugged open momentarily. Then he pointed to the weapon and erupted into a powerful fit of giggles.

Vorc's finger tightened on the button. Then he threw the device to the floor. "Get out. We are not done yet. You will rue the day you mocked me."

"V ... Vorc th ... the Dork," hissed Wul through fits of cackles.

"Veleffie," screamed Vorc, "come *throw* this garbage out. Bring golems if you need to, but be quick about it."

As a massive golem dragged Wul away, he could not stop repeating *Vorc the Dork.*

Vorc was having yet another bad day. Vorc very much wanted to kill a lot of people—any people.

CHAPTER EIGHT

Sapale knocked on the old wooden door. The sound reminded her of a simpler life, some long-forgotten and impenetrably far removed time she longed for with strong passion. She wanted to keep rapping all day, but Mirraya-Slapgren opened it in defiance of her desires.

"Oh, my goodness, Sapale," exclaimed Mirraya. "What a wonderful surprise."

Sapale looked to the doorstep. "Not so much. I come with horrible tidings in the heart of evil times."

Mirraya's face fell like it was hit with a blowtorch. "Please come in," she said, stepping aside. She craned her neck, searching for Jon following in Sapale's wake. She shut the door without comment.

Once Sapale was seated she asked, "May I get you anything? Tea?"

"Jon's dead," Sapale replied with no emotion. None was left in her.

Mirraya fell into the chair built to hold her dragon-shaped body. A sick, "Oh no," was all she could manage.

"Yes."

"I ... we ... we didn't—"

"It occurred in another universe. The land of the ancient gods."

Mirraya sat mute a while. "I suppose that's why we didn't sense it. Still ... Jon's death. That's hard to imagine missing." She sat up slightly. "Are you *certain*?"

"Have you ever heard of a piece of shit god named Gáwar?"

She angled her head in thought. "Yes, or something similar. He's reputed to be the god of evildoers, or some such thing."

"The god of demons. I was there. Gáwar smashed Jon into the ground and ate the debris that remained."

"How gruesome. How wrong."

"Tell me about it. I wanted to stay and slay the beast, but Toño ... well, you know Toño. Common sense personified."

"I'm glad for that. Gáwar would have killed the two of you, also, and where would that leave us?"

"The *three* of us."

"There's a new addition to Team Ry—"

"Daleria. She's a demigod of something. Never actually asked her. Anyway, she hates the ancients and joined our ill-fated efforts."

After a moment Mirraya replied. "Ill-fated? Hardly. You survived. You came home. No doubt you have given our side much useful intelligence about these monsters. I call that *successful*."

"But Jon died. I call *that* a total failure."

Mirraya waited a while to respond. "I don't believe Uncle Jon would have felt that way at all. I think you know it, too. He fought the good fight, and he paid the ultimate price. But I know he thought of your safety the entire time. He's smiling beyond the veil, as we speak."

"Huh." Sapale grunted sarcastically. "Not hardly. Davdiad may be all-loving and all-knowing, but he's not stupid. He'd keep my brood-mate in the *waiting* room for all eternity."

They chuckled lightly.

"How are you doing?"

"About as poorly as you might suspect."

"If we can help, you must only say the words."

"I will. Thanks."

"And Toño?"

"Good as always. Daleria, too. She's a trooper."

"That's good to hear. I'd like to meet her ... someday."

"I'm sure she'll be happy to oblige."

"Thank you for coming all this way to let us know."

"No problem," she responded. "But business also brought me."

"Anything we can do to help is already done."

"While we were gone, the joint council found a live ancient god here in our universe."

"I understand there are many."

"Not like this one. She was bound and gagged with some form of energy."

"And still alive?" She furrowed her scaly brow. "That's odd."

"Ya think? As soon as I heard *unknown energy,* I thought about you."

"I'll take that as a compliment."

"It wasn't. Just a fact. Can you come take a look? Maybe you'll know what the force is. That will help us figure out who might have done it."

"So you can enlist their help in defeating the incursion of the ancient gods?"

She shrugged. "Something along those lines."

"And you fancy it never occurred to him or her to volunteer their services? They didn't realize how useful they might be?"

"I know. Been there, done that. Some do-gooders want to remain anonymous. I get that. But if there's a way to fight them, this mysterious SOB's going to help us."

"Or?"

"Or ... or we're screwed."

"In that case, we'll be glad to help. May we go now?"

"Sure. Ah, no kids to pawn off on a sitter?"

"We stopped breeding a while ago. We're old now. Old like *you.*"

"Yeah, but at least you can look forward to dying, unlike me."

"If you say so. I'll get my bag."

"You carry a purse?"

"No, silly alien. My potions and runes. A proper witch never leaves home without them."

"If you say so. I'll be out front."

The trip to where Walpracta lay defenseless was instant. Mirraya-Slapgren walked around the motionless figure several times before speaking. "I'll be damned," was her first remark.

"I suppose there's a reason you say that," observed Toño, who was already on site.

"Yes. I cannot believe what I'm seeing."

"And what *are* you seeing?" pressed Sapale.

"This creature, this Walpracta, is bound with the unbreakable truth."

"Come again," Sapale shot back.

"These ribbons of force," she gestured at them, "are the *unbreakable* truth."

"What does that even mean?" whined Sapale.

"I don't want to get too metaphysical on you, but there are truths that are so pure they cannot be altered. They are unbreakable."

"Thank you," responded Toño. "That's nice to know. But we are looking, not at conceptual *opinions,* but tangible energy *bands.*"

"Yes," agreed Mirraya. "I'm glad you understand."

"No, we don't. Toño was being polite. I don't suffer from the same compulsion. What the hell is that physically?" Sapale almost touched one band.

"Oh, you can't hurt it with contact. It won't harm you either. The power you see manifest is what it is. It is the living presence of unbreakable *energy,* let's call it, instead of *truth.*"

"All right, fine," replied Toño. "You are familiar with the substance. Can you speculate who created it?"

"Yes. I could have. Any competent brindas could. But none of us did."

"Okay, we're getting somewhere," responded Sapale. "How can you be so certain?"

"For one thing, they'd have told me they did. Also, I'd have sensed it."

"But you didn't sense this?" asked Toño, pointing to the band.

"No. Odd."

"So we're down to this," summarized Sapale. "Who *could* do this without you knowing?"

"The list consists of one name."

"I'm dying of suspense here, honey," groaned Sapale.

"Evil Jon. I mean the *once* evil Jon Ryan."

"Did not see that one coming," mumbled Sapale.

"Nor I," agreed Toño.

"Think about it. He lived with my master for a very long time. We know she taught him magic. Since he's not Deft, I don't have a connection with him. There is but one logical choice."

"But why would EJ bind this monster and leave it? I sure as hell'd have dismembered it and burned the component parts if I could," responded Sapale.

"As punishment," replied Mirraya. "Think about it. Unless a brindas came along and released the bonds, Walpracta would suffer here for all eternity. She'd be alone and aware of her defeat forever. She, the god of consumption, would develop a powerful hunger she could never satisfy. No, EJ meant to punish her in a unique and effective manner."

"So where is he?" asked Sapale. "We need him."

"He's where he wants to be," Mirraya replied obtusely.

"Which *is*?" pressed Sapale.

"Only he knows. When he's ready to join you, he will. *If* he wishes to join you, that is."

"Why *wouldn't* he? We need him," fired back Sapale.

"I'm certain he knows that. His motivations are his own. I cannot speak to them."

"Well that's just *taupod* up," Sapale responded under her breath.

"There's no need for vulgarity, my friend," chided Toño.

"Yes, there is," responded Sapale. "We're talking EJ here. No one knows him better or wants to see him less than I do. But now I gotta go find the useless *taupod*."

"You'll be going alone, unless you clean up the language," replied Mirraya. "I don't need to hear that."

"You're coming along on the hunt?" Sapale said, perking up.

"We're part of Team Ryan. Always count us in," she responded proudly. "Even with Uncle gone, he still binds us together."

"Amen to that," exclaimed Toño. "Amen to that."

CHAPTER NINE

Zisoritom slipped one of his heads into Vorc's office. This latest in the series of suboptimal office assistants the center seat suffered under had four heads, but risked only one for the task at hand. "Someone to see you, boss. Shall I show them in?"

Vorc fumbled with Fire of Justice in one hand. He had become used to having it in his immediate possession of late. It afforded him some tiny sense of control. His other hand rubbed the side of his pounding head.

"I've told you never to call me *boss*. I hate the term. It affixes meaning I do not welcome, plus I hate the word. Never call me that again."

"I'll try my best. That's really all I can do. My mama raised me to know who the boss was. That's you. No way around it, b ... buddy."

"As to a visitor, whether they may enter depends very much on who they are."

"Ah," Zisoritom said, reflecting, "should I go back and ask their name? Would that help?"

Vorc reluctantly set his weapon down so both hands could massage his head. As he set it down, he briefly flirted with the thought of turning it on himself, such was the large black cloud he found himself under.

"Gosh, that would be swell," Vorc responded sarcastically. "Maybe *simage* me a visual."

"Really, both? Okay, b ... b ... you got it."

"Stop," commanded Vorc. "I just need a name."

"Are you sure. You just—"

"*Name.*" Vorc shouted, but immediately regretted it as his head advanced from pounding to pulsating.

"No *problem,*" was Zisoritom's cheery response. Needless to say, the new assistant was a glass-half-full kind of guy. That really annoyed Vorc, as it did most other Cleinoids. They were a sullen group as a whole.

A few seconds later Zisoritom slipped a different head through the crack in the door. "He says his name is Ganwar. Shall I show him —"

"Ganwar? I know no *Ganwar.* Are you certain that's the name he gave you?"

The head speaking popped out and another replaced it. "Fairly certain, boss."

Vorc spoke loudly and enunciated each word emphatically. "I-told-you-*never*-to-call-me-boss-again."

A hand appeared below the head. It thumbed toward the outer office. "No ya didn't, boss. You told the blond, not *me.*"

"I told you generically, all of you."

"No, no ya didn't. Ya told the blonde."

"Could you not hear my instructions? Were you not *close* enough?"

"Of course, I could. All four of us did. What, ya think some of us're *deaf?*" He chuckled unwisely at his mirth.

"But still you defy me?"

"No, no way. You told blondie not to call you boss. I would, too. He's annoying as shit. But me, I'm my own person. You and I, we share a special bond, right, compadre?"

The head—a redhead to be specific—barely withdrew in time to avoid the decorative vase Vorc hurled at it. The ceramic shattered and a large shard cut the hand that clumsily did not pull out. All four heads were heard to yelp in pain. Funny thing, the having of four heads.

Another head, bald, peered in cautiously. "Do you want me to show Ganwar in?"

"No. I do not know any Ganwar. Take a message."

"You got it, boss."

The head disappeared quickly.

Five seconds later the message was delivered. Zisoritom, all four heads and six arms flailing, slammed through the wall to the left of the closed door. The wall, to be fully illustrative, was composed of solid metal. It was amazing, in fact, that Zisoritom could both penetrate it and remain intact. What he did not remain, however, was alive. No, he was dead before he came to rest at the foot of the desk.

Gáwar lumbered into the room via the door, which he smashed flat with his forehead. "Really, Vorc, where do you get these helpers? The next one's worse than the last. Ganwar? How do I say Gáwar and eight independent ears hear Ganwar? It's unbelievable." He stopped in front of Vorc's desk with one foot crushing down on one of the recently departed's heads.

"I'm in the unusual position of thanking you, Gáwar. That assistant needed to die."

"Great minds think alike." He harrumphed wickedly. "Yours and mine do, too." He grumbled a wheezy laugh.

"To what do I owe the displeasure of your visit, Gáwar?"

"Sticks and stones, Vorc the Dork. Sticks *and* stones."

"Where did you hear that abomination of a nickname? I hate it."

"Wul. I overheard you two not communicating the other day. Vorc the Dork. That's a good one."

"I hate it."

"I know, you said that. Maybe I should call you Vorc the *Boss* Dork. I heard you hate that moniker, too."

Vorc slipped lower in his chair by way of resignation. The idea of nuking himself with his staff of office flitted through his awareness again, lingering just a bit longer than it had before. With his hands covering his face he spoke in a low, defeated tone. "Why are you here?"

"I need to firm up our arrangement."

Vorc peeped out with one eye. "Firm up? What is *unfirm*? You failed to kill the entire band of saboteurs. I granted you the souls of several thousand unsuspecting supporters to do the job. You failed. No bodies, no souls. End of discussion."

The walls began vibrating as Gáwar's rage boiled over. "You used the word *fail* twice while referencing me. I never fail. I have not failed. I never *will* fail. Say it again and I'll—"

"What? Shut up? Unlikely. Take my soul? Duh, that's a done deal. Get mad and destroy something? Yeah, to the man who traded loyal followers' souls to satisfy a personal vendetta, that's got to work—*not*."

Vorc braced for unpleasantness. He welcomed it, in fact.

"Now let's not let angry words dictate an unfortunate turn in our relationship. I think it best if cooler heads prevailed." Yeah, that was Gáwar speaking.

"Huh? Is this a new form of torture? Agreeing? Making nice?"

"No, and I'm stunned you would suggest it was. We are a team, you and I. We need to work together to accomplish our common goals."

"Excuse me. I'm going to the bathroom to rinse out my ears. I'm hearing surreal words coming from your ... mouth or whatever."

Gáwar chuckled collegially. "Nice one, friend."

"Okay, now I *am* scared. You calling me friend? Surely the world's about to end."

"No, center seat. But it is a perfect segue into the topic of our little get-together."

"Correction to my earlier remark. I need to rinse out my *brain*. What I'm hearing is less than impossible."

"Nonsense, balderdash, and piffle. I'm serious. My point is this. While I have secured payment for services *rendered*," Gáwar raised a claw to emphasize the word, "I am passionately interested in locking down the remainder of the souls involved in our gentlemen's agreement."

"Gentlemen's agreement? You mean your extortion? Your knowingly duping me into a bargain you knew full well I wasn't aware of? You call that ... *oooh*." He slumped back to hands covering face. "Go on."

"Here's what I'm noodling through. If I complete the murders of the three suspects at large, I would then be entitled to the souls we agreed upon. *N'est-ce pas?*"

Vorc depressed the switch on his office intercom. "Zisoritom. Bring alcohol. Lots of alcohol. I have *insufficient* alcohol in this room."

Gáwar cleared his capacious throat. "Isn't this Zisoritom?" He toed the corpse he had been standing on.

Vorc craned over the edge of his desk to be certain. "Oh bother. It is. I'll be right back." He vaulted from his chair and headed toward the door.

"Is there—" Gáwar began to say, but Vorc was gone.

The center seat returned promptly carrying a moderately large cask of nectar of the gods. He set it on his desk, placed his mouth under the spigot, and let fly a copious stream of liquid courage. He wiped his dripping face with a sleeve and returned his attention to Gáwar. "You were saying?"

"If I was allowed to complete my assassinations, I would win the modest price you so wisely granted me."

"Uh, okay. Go ahead and slay the vermin." Vorc made a go-away motion toward Gáwar with the back of his hand.

"Would that it were that easy."

"What?"

"The trio of desperados have left our universe. I do not, um, currently have access to them."

"Th ... then *why* are we having this *little get-together*?"

"I was hoping you might be in a position to *help* me?"

"*Me* help *you*? Me help you what? Gain access to the three fugitive terrorists?"

"In a word, yes."

Without comment Vorc stood, silently left the room, then just as silently returned to his seat. "There. Now what did you want to ask me?"

"I just did."

"No, n ... no. I was out of the room just now. I'm a reasonable man, so ask me almost-anything-that-is-in-my-power-are-you-*insane*?"

"In what frame of reference?"

"*Any* frame of freaking reference. If you want to kill them so you can get paid, then *kill* them. How in your twisted, delusional, warped mind do you *hallucinate* that I might be able to help the all-powerful Gáwar?"

"Do you need a personal time-out break?"

"No, I do not need a personal time-out. I need *comprehension*. What do you fancy I can do to help you?"

"Thanks for your concern and for asking. I really appreciate your team spirit." If Gáwar could have, he'd have smiled to generate the impression of camaraderie. "How do *you* envision you might help me?"

"I do not. That's how. May I return to my question as to your sanity, or lack of thereof?"

"I'd prefer it if you didn't, but I'm here to serve you, so I'll leave that decision to you."

"Gáwar, god of demons, what are you beating around the bush to ask?"

"I was curious, as you brought the subject up, as to the health and prospects of his return to utility of Dominion Splitter."

"*You* are asking *me*?" wheezed Vorc. "*You* are the expert regarding the stupid vortex."

"Some have kindly said."

"What do you *think* DS's chances of recovery are?"

"Oh, poor, to say the least. He's dead after all."

Vorc started some form of voluntary seizure/conniption fit. Whatever he did was *not* pretty. "If it's *dead,* why are you asking me what its chances of providing you useful transportation *options* might be?"

"I was hoping I might be, you know, wrong. Perhaps a man of authority, with his finger on the pulse of society, might have differing information than that available to *me,* a humble citizen."

"I ... I d-d ... do no ... not." Vorc gasped a few times. "Are we done here?"

Gáwar sat politely and immovably.

"What's it going to take?" screamed Vorc.

"Why, thank you, Center Seat Vorc, for taking the time to extend to me another allotment of your oh-so-valuable time. I am reassured that your inherent wisdom has gleaned that I have one ... one *tiny* lingering question."

Vorc was trying to pick up his staff of office, either to use on Gáwar or himself or both. Either way he had lost the motor coordination possible to lift the weapon. So, instead, he listened to Gáwar's tiny question.

"I was wondering. The trio of evildoers left our universe *without* the aid of Dominion Splitter. So, an alternative method of egress is clearly possible. Would you, honored soul Vorc, know of, or even better have access *to,* a different method of transferring individuals from *our* universe to *others?*"

Vorc's thoughts suddenly became clear. Brilliant-crystal clear. "Why yes, I just might. With your permission?"

"Oh, certainly. You have my permission, if it can help us attain our common business goals."

Almost giddy, Vorc lifted Fire of Justice. "Now if you'll remain perfectly still, I will use this to transport you *possibly* to another universe."

"That's an energy weapon," Gáwar stated flatly. "How might it accomplish directed transport?" His tone was growing angry and dubious.

"*Directed,* you say? Well, truth be told, who can say. I theorize if you submit to the beam long enough you will *maybe* be transported out of my universe. Whether you end up in the universe you desire to visit, well, that's more challenging for me to predict." He pointed at Gáwar.

"*Freeze*," commanded Gáwar.

Vorc did just that, covered with frost and all. Freeze was, in this case, a command *and* a spell.

"I try and be nice. What does it get me? Absolutely nothing. I try and work with others constructively. What does it get me? It's thrown back in my face. Well, I'm done being Mr. Nice Guy, and it's your fault, Vorc the Boss Dork."

Though it was not easy given his length, Gáwar made a show of turning and exiting in a haughty manner.

Vorc remained frozen until Gáwar went to sleep that night. When he finally thawed, Vorc wished ardently that Gáwar never needed to sleep. That would have been an easy way out.

CHAPTER TEN

Blessing landed near a clearing on the planet with the most unsexy name of α-933-Pistoler. It was a highly habitable but sparsely populated world. Flora abounded almost to excess, but the fauna was nearly absent. It was a quizzical combination of life. On a typical Class M+ planet such as α-933-Pistoler, such riotous vegetation would encourage the evolution of a complex and vibrant animal population. Yet there were hardly even many insects.

Sapale led the landing party. She was flanked by Toño, with Mirraya and Daleria following close behind. They had come to examine the second unusual set of remains that were purportedly those of an ancient god. It was easy enough to find the body. The rich atmosphere of α-933-Pistoler accelerated its decay. The stench was abhorrent. The two androids switched off their olfactory sensors. Mirraya said a quiet spell to ward off the odor. That left poor Daleria alone in having to deal with the intolerable situation. When she was still a soccer field away, she began vomiting. By the time the team was stopped at the carcass her stomach was empty. She continued to wretch something awful. Sapale asked if she wanted to wait by the vortex, but the rookie felt it was important to prove herself, so she remained with the group.

"I'd say the body's been dead several weeks," said Toño. "The lack of predation and insect activity make that only an educated guess."

"I'll take your word on that. It's sure been dead long enough to stink to high heaven," replied Sapale. She set a hand on Daleria's shoulder and waited for her current set of dry heaves to pass. "Do you recognize him?"

"Y ... yes." She wretched again. "That's definitely what's left of Tramaster."

"I wonder why his tail is all the way over there?" asked Mirraya.

"What tail?" responded Sapale.

"He had an invisible tail with sharp barbs," announced Daleria. "You can *see* it?" she questioned Mirraya.

"Plain as day."

"Yeah, keep in mind she's a witch," quipped Sapale. "I have four eyes and I can't."

"Impressive," commented Daleria.

Mirraya shrugged her scaled shoulders.

"I'm of the opinion that Tramaster was beaten to death," said Toño. He pointed to the surrounding terrain. "There are deep pockmarks there and there suggesting a powerful struggle. That tree is nearly snapped in half. Someone hit it pretty hard. And the beast's throat's been opened, but not by a knife. The wound is too ragged and too deep."

"I'd say there was a struggle, but one person was doing the struggling and the other was doing the damaging," added Mirraya. "See the footprints? All of the ones leading away from the impacts are Tramaster's. In fact, I don't see a single other imprint." She walked over to a clear spot. "This seems to be the center of the activity. But look," she angled a claw, "there's no scuffs or dents. The center of activity was perfectly spared."

Toño rubbed at the back of his neck. "I believe you're correct, my dear. You *are* impressive."

"Just a trained eye, thanks to my uncle," she responded. "So the killer looks to me to have been seated or somehow elevated. Otherwise there'd be signs."

"Elevated on ... what?" asked Daleria before she dry heaved again. "I ... there's nothing here."

"No," Mirraya agreed, "there isn't. And if there was, there're no tire tracks or other indications it was removed."

"Maybe the killer was levitating?" wondered Sapale.

Toño's head bobbed. "Possibly. His or her leverage would be pretty poor if they were."

"Flying?" Daleria queried quickly.

"No dust streaks consistent with wing beats," observed Mirraya, who possessed impressive wings that validated her opinion.

"Well, the killer couldn't very well have been sitting on an elevated throne," snapped Sapale. "That would be just silly."

"Not a throne," responded Mirraya. "A bed or sofa. Yes, that would fit. The killer was resting in this idyllic spot and Tramaster happened across him. The other person killed Tramaster with ease from his resting loft. Then when he was done he disappeared, bed and all."

"Why a bed and *not* a throne?" responded Toño. "I don't think we'll ever be able to tell."

"Toño, who rests in a pretty clearing on a stiff chair? No, he'd at the very least string up a hammock. But a classy guy would have a soft bed covered with fluffy pillows," concluded Mirraya. "That's my bet."

"Fine, some prince was napping and Tramaster disturbed his loftiness's beauty rest. The fact remains the lazing foo-foo killed a Cleinoid god with such ease he didn't have to even lift his head off his feather pillow. That's a powerful dude," remarked Sapale.

"Yes, it would have to be," agreed Mirraya. "And it wasn't EJ. He'd never lounge on a luxurious bed in the middle of the forest."

"Copy that," concurred Sapale. "He hates resting in any form, and would positively *never* recline himself on a bed."

"That leaves who?" Mirraya wondered out loud. "I don't know *anyone* that powerful. If such a force existed, I'm certain I would."

"Another Cleinoid?" asked Toño.

"Possibly," replied Mirraya. "I don't know, Daleria, would one god kill another?"

"Yes, but they'd need to have a reason. If one was taking a nap and another chanced upon him, I don't see such a thing happening."

"What does that leave?" asked Sapale with clear frustration.

"An *antigod,*" whispered Daleria.

"A what?" shot back Mirraya. "I've never heard of one of those."

"We call them antigods. You might know them by some other name."

"I don't know of *any* creature, real or legendary, who would be capable of this." Mirraya gestured toward the body.

"Then welcome to the world of the antigods."

"Huh?" responded Sapale.

"If they are here, then we're all their bitches. Just saying," mumbled Daleria.

CHAPTER ELEVEN

Carol lolled in the blazing sun. Her pebbles were warm and toasty, just the way she liked them. Life was, as it always had been, good. Hey, being an Apractolith god was a good starting place from which to achieve lifelong bliss. Unlimited power, immortality, and an excellent benefits package. What more could one want?

In the back of her awareness, Carol sensed Verazz. He was returning, or he had never left. She had trouble remembering which was which. In any case, he was near. Her interlude of warming and rest was sure to be over. He was such a needy spouse. If he didn't nag her to get him something, he would regale her with his outstandingness, his transcendent superbness.

"Must you be here, dearest?" she asked herself.

"Of course," he responded, since they were one but two. They knew each other's thoughts as they did their own. "How else can I love you?"

"There's always the *mail*. A card now and then would be sufficient, I'm sure."

"*Never*," he exclaimed robustly. Verazz lifted his wife off her platform and enshrouded her with an embrace. "This is how a man loves a woman."

"Nice of you to demonstrate, eternal. However I am *not* a woman and you are *not* a man. Your reference is thus meaningless."

"But my *love* is not." The covering he formed around her opened like a flower and held her up in the center.

Carol looked about. "So I am now the stamen of some grotesque flower? How less than flattering."

"Never, devotion. You are the *pistil.* Please try and keep the boy/girl thing straight."

"If it will help silence you, I will."

"Such harsh words. And here I am returning to my home and hearth triumphant. I deserve a parade of angels, at the very least."

"And so you shall have. I, being neither triumphant nor an angel, will remain here sunning."

"Come, come. You must ask what I triumphed *over*. Yes, it's required of you as my number-one fan."

What a revolting thought. Carol hadn't signed up for that level of devotion. Best to humor him, however, or he'd never leave her be. "Say, husband, what did you best just recently? Some indomitable force, some juggernaut of power?"

"Yes. Well, almost. I was resting in my fifteenth favorite napping spot when I was attacked by *Tramaster*. It was horrific. I was only moments earlier forced to dispatch something called *Selsify."*

"What are those? Forms of guilt or remorse?"

"Me? Remorse? Never. No, they were Cleinoid gods. Can you believe it? Cleinoids attacking *me*."

"Perhaps they knew you. That would cause most anyone to attack."

"That was just it. Neither recognized me. I had to *tell* them who I was." He chuckled. "Pointless Cleinoids."

"We've had to deal with them for quite some time. Annoying they were, and annoying they shall remain."

"No, perpetual. We *dealt* with them. They left and returned to their pigsty universe. Don't you remember? It was, oh, a long time ago."

"Are you certain? I don't recall them leaving."

"Hasn't it been peaceful of late?"

She sat up. "Now that you mention it, yes, it has. Those pesky Cleinoids *were* gone. Bother."

"Now it appears they are back."

"It is too soon," she whined. "Now I shall not be perfectly happy. You know how that makes me cross."

"And a cross wife leads only to strife."

"Could you come closer? I'd like to gut you for that last remark."

"Perhaps in a moment, aspiration."

"I know. Why don't you go and slay the lot of them before they have a chance to fluster me? I'd be ever so appreciative." She rattled her hips.

"Promises promises. No, I don't feel like slaying the lot of them. Do you know how much effort that would require?"

"No. How much?"

"Hmm. I don't know either, but I'm certain it'd be a lot, definitely more than none."

"Are you otherwise busy, weighted down, or preoccupied?"

"No, but I might be soon. One never knows. Why, just yesterday, I *died*."

"It wasn't yesterday, and you returned the very next day. How hard was that? Not very, I imagine. No, if you wanted to, you could find the time."

"Well, I guess that settles it."

"Excellent. You'll kill them?"

"No, I don't want to find the time. Color me lazy."

Carol lay back down and shut her stony eyes. "No, dear. You color yourself this time. I'm too tired."

CHAPTER TWELVE

"I say it's easier and safer to find this EJ guy than an Apractolith who does not wish to be located." Daleria spoke with firm conviction.

"How do you know it's a *he,* and how do you know *he* doesn't want to be found?" asked Sapale.

"The *he* part's a guess. The other's obvious. If the Apractoliths have lived amongst you forever and you've never even heard of them, then I'd say that's proof positive they want to be left alone."

"But they are threatened, too," pressed Toño.

"No, they are not. If you were swimming far out at sea with multiple bleeding cuts and you saw several big fins coming straight at you, you'd be scared, right?" posed Daleria.

"Yes. What does that—"

"That's how the Cleinoids feel about the antigods. Pretty much defenseless and doomed."

"All right, they're not under threat. But might they not want to help *us* survive?" asked Toño.

"Remember the you in the water and the shark scenario?"

Toño nodded.

"The way the shark feels, that's about how badly the antigods feel about you dying as a race."

"They're not loving, nurturing types, these antigods?" mocked Sapale.

"Not in the slightest. Self-indulgent, arrogant, and effete. Those're about the *best* things you can say about them."

"Hmm. Pity. We could have used their help."

"If EJ can defeat the ancient gods, can't all the Deft brindases?" Sapale asked Mirraya.

"Not necessarily. EJ had the best teacher and unlimited time. He also *wanted* to learn the magic of fighting and war. Most brindases do not."

"How about you?" Sapale queried.

"Me, yes. A few others, maybe. But the numbers are not favorable. Millions of Cleinoids and only a handful of us. No matter how good we were, we'd fail sooner than later."

"One, you don't know without trying. Two, we're all going to die anyway, so why not take the fight to them?"

"Oh, absolutely. I was just being realistic. I want to avoid false hopes."

Sapale sighed. "So where can we find EJ? I can tell you I have no idea."

"Me, neither," replied Mirraya.

"Normally I can tell where another brindas is. EJ, however, has a spell surrounding himself that in effect cloaks him."

"The paranoid bastard," huffed Sapale. "Never going to change."

"Apparently so. Or he wants to be left alone, too. Either way I doubt we'll find either him or the antigods," responded Mirraya.

"We can't just give up. I don't know how long we have, locally, in terms of falling victim to an unstoppable onslaught, but we have to prepare for the worst," said Toño. "Two Cleinoids were killed while ravaging this galaxy. Surely others will follow, especially if word gets out some have been killed. I was in their domain long enough to learn they're nothing if not spiteful."

"You're correct, Toño," said Daleria. "*When* they learn of their comrades' fates, they will come with a vengeance."

"Mirraya," asked Sapale, "you say you can't *sense* EJ. Might he still be able to sense *you*?"

She reflected a moment. "I suppose so, assuming he cared that much," she responded.

"He cares about the darnedest things. Trust me on that," Sapale said with a grim smile. "Assuming he can, maybe you can send him a message to meet us."

That led to an even longer thought-break for the dragon. "If he's listening, yes, I can send a message."

"Tell him to meet us in one week's time at ... needs to be someplace nonthreatening. *Got* it? On the remains of ruined Earth. Yes, talk about neutral ground."

"I will send that impression out. Now's not good. Too many distractions."

"No prob," replied Sapale.

"In the meantime, I'd like to return to my lab. I want to analyze the samples from the dead Cleinoids," remarked Toño.

"Uh, okay, but can't you do that here aboard *Blessing*?" asked Sapale.

"Not as thoroughly."

"So be it. Daleria and I will drop you off, then check out the colonies on Azsuram and Kalvarg. I've spoken with them but I'd like to make certain they're doing well."

"Sounds like a plan," responded Mirraya. "You can drop us at home. Pick us up when you're heading for Earth."

Two billion years earlier, give or take, Earth had been swallowed up by a hungry Jupiter. The planet, of course. Not the god. What was spat out was a huge dead rock. No life whatsoever remained. No water, no atmosphere, nothing, just barren rock. The molten core was preserved. Due to the tremendous deformation forces Earth underwent, large-scale volcanoes and lava flows returned, as in primordial times. Eventually those died out, too, leaving a scarred and lifeless hulk. For any of the few who knew old Earth before its demise, the planet was a tearful sight to behold.

Toño, Sapale, Mirraya, and Daleria stepped out onto the rugged surface with ample foreboding. Mirraya was using some of her magic to survive in the sparce environment. Tono had supplied Daleria with a human spacesuit that worked well enough. Not only did the place look frightening, they were hoping to hook up with the always unpredictable EJ. Bad things might happen in this bad place. There was no preset meeting place, but any sign of movement or life on Earth would be easily detectable by the second party to arrive. There was none as *Blessing* made her slow descent. EJ either hadn't come yet or wasn't coming.

"Als, keep a sharp eye peeled for EJ. I wouldn't want him to surprise us," instructed Toño.

"Understood, Form Two," replied *Blessing*.

"I can scan with our mental link, too," added Al.

"Good idea." Toño studied the expansive wasteland. He measured a few angles and crossed his arms. "We would be right in the middle of the Atlantic Ocean if we were back on Earth before her destruction."

"No water to be seen now," voiced Mirraya quietly.

"No ... hmm. I wonder what that is?" Toño remarked as he pointed off toward the horizon.

"Since we have nothing else to do, let's go check it out," said Sapale.

After thirty minutes walking the group came upon a sight they would have never anticipated. A large, shallow lake of water had formed between two low mountain ranges.

"Well I'll be damned," exclaimed Toño. "*Water* has returned to Mother Earth."

"Water? I wasn't here, but I doubt Jupiter left any by mistake. Where'd it come from?" asked Sapale.

"Oh, I imagine the same place it did back in the day. Cometary water. There's a lot less circulating now than when the solar system was young, but it seems there's this much."

"Wow," remarked Sapale. "I wonder if evolution will happen all over again?"

"I don't know but I wouldn't doubt it for a second. The conditions are very different than they were originally, but who can say?"

"With any luck, maybe in a billion years there'll be little green men all over the place," responded Sapale.

"With any bad luck, you and I will be around to find out."

"Doc," a voice called out from behind, "always such a Glum Gus." It was EJ.

"Hey, how'd—" he started to say.

"I get so close without your AIs screaming bloody murder?"

"Something along those lines, yes."

"I'm very sneaky," EJ responded with a wicked grin.

"I can testify to that," growled Sapale.

EJ turned to her and studied her a few seconds. "Never thought I'd be seeing *you* again."

"Nor I *you.* Curse Davdiad's inconstancy," responded Sapale.

"Same high spirit as always, my love. I wish I could say I missed it," EJ said in kind.

"You really do look just like him," marveled Daleria.

"Yeah, he gets that a lot, too," rebuffed EJ. "By the by, who the hell are you?"

Sapale stepped forward, between EJ and Daleria. She set a hand on her shoulder. "This is Daleria. She's with us now."

EJ glanced at her, then at the rest of the group. "Cult, sexual religious practices, or pyramid scheme designed to make y'all filthy rich?"

"I thought you said he wasn't evil anymore. He'd been reformed?" asked an angry looking Daleria.

"He's *better,*" replied Mirraya coolly. "Better doesn't make him nice, only not as abysmally bad as he was."

"Mind if I quote you on my next job application? I'm overwhelmed."

"Why am I not surprised?" asked Sapale. "You spent a long time being rehabbed by Mirraya's master Calfada-Joric. I guess that didn't include social skills or anti-asshole guidelines."

"I'll send you a full summary at my earliest possible—"

"*Enough*," Mirraya barked with authority. "We are here for serious matters, not to banter and certainly not to exchange punches. Suffice it to say, Jon Ryan from an alternate timeline, no one here likes you or trusts you. You like and trust none of us. Yet we have a galaxy to save. We must work together."

EJ scuffed his boot on the rock. "I'd ask who died and left you in charge, but I guess that would be Calfada-Joric."

"It would, in fact, be that blessed brindas," Mirraya said sternly.

"You know, at the end there, she liked me and trusted me."

"I know. She told me long ago that when her time here was at an end, she would decide if you were to live, based on your progress. The fact she didn't kill you before she passed proves your contention."

"But?" he responded.

"But her blessing does not alter my impression of you. You must earn from me what you earned from her. You have much to atone for, human."

"Geez, you Deft witches are tough to please. You win one over, you think you'd win them all over."

"If you thought that, you'd be wrong. I could bore the others to tears with cautionary tales to back up my reluctance to allow another to think for me. I will not."

"So is he going to work with us or is he part of the problem?" asked a confused Daleria.

"Maybe ask *him* and not his long-ago associates and wives," mocked EJ.

Daleria was not going to be intimidated. "Are you going to work with us, or do I have to kill you here and now?" She was extremely serious.

EJ chuckled. "Impressive words, kid. But don't think there's one chance in hell you could as much as—"

"*Enough*," howled Mirraya even louder than before. "No

blustering, threatening, or mindless prepubescent posturing. I only just met Daleria. I do not know if she can justify her threats. But from what little I know I would not challenge her. More critically, human, I can end you with a thought. *Never* allow that fact to stray far from your awareness."

EJ was truly contrite. "Sorry. You're right. I'm behaving badly. It's the history at play here, Mirri. He created me, she was my wife for a couple billion years. There's a lot of water that went under many bridges pooling here just now."

"My name is Mirraya-Slapgren. For conversational ease you may address me as Mirraya. Only Uncle Jon may call me *Mirri*. Hearing it come from your mouth makes me want to fill said mouth with lava. Am I conveying a clear meaning?"

Wisely, EJ said and did nothing by way of response.

"You were the one to bind Walpracta with *beicil crell*?" Mirraya asked directly.

He nodded curtly.

"And you acted alone?"

He nodded again.

"And was it your intention to leave the immortal there for all time?"

Another quick nod.

"You felt that extreme level of punishment was fair and measured?"

"It was a common mercy I showed the bitch. She *deserved* the worst that I could have done. That is a very bad and dark thing. My defense is yes."

"Your defense?" questioned Sapale.

"In a Deft trial, what we might call a formal explanation they call a *defense*. One's defending their actions," responded EJ.

Sapale looked to Mirraya and pointed at EJ. "You have him on trial?"

"Yes. It is necessary for two reasons. If he is to work with us, his actions must conform to our norms. Also, if his punishment were too harsh or too lenient, his error would have to be made right."

"Which, in case the judge there leaves it off, would include not allowing me to punish any subsequent individuals."

Confused, Sapale turned back to Mirraya. "How can you possibly do that?"

"By killing him," she responded dispassionately.

"I guess that'd do it," commented Sapale as she shook her head.

"Dispensing the powerful Deft magical justice is an act of the highest sanctity. There is but one way to do it properly." Back to EJ, she asked, "And do you feel your defense was just?"

"I do." There was no way around it. EJ tightened up in anticipation of a less than approving decision from the judge.

"So do I. You are cleared in your action."

"Is that good?" asked Sapale.

"It means I live," responded EJ.

"On to the matter at hand," pressed Mirraya.

"Yes," hissed EJ. "*You* know," he directed at Toño, "I don't *do* meetings. Not since your former boss General Saunders did the world a favor and died."

"How little I feel for you, old comrade," responded Toño. "While you waltz your cynical dance across space and time, some of us are honor bound to do the right thing."

"Ah, sanctimoniousness. How I haven't missed that either. I do not answer to anyone. That said, don't presume to judge me. I am very busy doing what *I* feel to be the right thing."

"This conversation is pointless. Merit badges will not be handed out later. We must plan a defense." Mirraya exuded confidence and control.

"And I bet you're including *me* in *we*, right?" confirmed EJ.

"No."

EJ recoiled like she'd slapped him.

"We are here to discuss if your assistance is desirable *and* acceptable."

"Didn't you forget the concept of my assistance being *available, up for grabs*? Who said I'd work with you or anybody else?"

"Clearly not. We must decide the first two issues. Then a genuine offer on your part may be entertained."

"Lordy in Heaven, you talk like a lawyer. I hate those more than meetings. And don't even mention a *meeting* with a *lawyer*." He shuddered.

"I'd say his flippancy leaves a mark in the nay column," remarked Daleria.

"Ah, skipping over the fact that no one asked you, rookie, which column? Hmm? *Desirable* or *acceptable*?" spat back EJ.

"*Both*," Sapale answered for her. "I happen to know you can speak without playing the role of the buffoonish asshole. Please act like you've learned something in your very long life."

"I second Sapale's request. Make no mistake about my resolve. I *am* weighing you in the balance. *We* are. You are presently on the razor's edge. One more angry or stupid remark and we will take our leave of you," said Mirraya forcefully.

"Is that supposed to be a threat? If it is, I don't know if you thought it through. Let me summarize. Our universe is under an existential threat the likes of which it has never seen. Only I, and none of you, have proven ourselves capable of meaningful resistance. And you might, what...? Refuse my aid? Trade me to another team for players to be named later? Correct me if I'm wrong here, but you need *me* a whole hell of a lot more than I need *you*." EJ crossed his arms with consummate satisfaction.

"Your offer of service is accepted," responded Mirraya, void of emotion. "I shall be our leader. The team as it was constituted before you so generously offered to join made that decision final. We now need to—"

"Time out on the field. The replay officials are reviewing the tape to see exactly *when* I volunteered to join your high-tension-ass-sphincter team, because I *didn't*."

"You *did*. Your argument was correct and irrefutable. You are bound by *ierry*. Now we have no time to look back, only forward," replied Mirraya.

"Ierry? You gotta be shi—"

"Oh, and, alternate timeline Jon Ryan, those who serve under me do not swear."

"The only way I'll serve under you is with your talons clutching my throat."

"You say that in anger. In point of fact if you break your unbreakable honor-bond, your ierry, that is precisely the last vision you will see in this life."

EJ turned to Toño. "Doc, tell the bossy dragon there is no conscription in the future. You can't *draft* me."

"That much is true. But I was present when you warned us we would be *foolish* to act without your help. I, too, agree, *teammate*. As to your concerns regarding ierry, you'd have to address those to our squad leader." There was definitely a wry grin on Toño's lips as he finished.

EJ turned his head a moment, then focused on Mirraya. "Here's what I *will* do. I will listen to your proposals. If I think they are non-insane, I will agree to partake."

"Your face-saving gambit is acceptable to me. May we *now* proceed?"

"Aye, aye, ma'am." EJ saluted her.

"Do that again and I will remove your right hand," she responded unemotionally.

He grunted something in return.

"What do you know of the extent and activity of Cleinoids in this galaxy, EJ?" she asked him directly.

"First point of order. My name is Jon Alan Ryan, not *EJ*. You're going to need to stop addressing me thusly. It's hurtful."

"Poor baby," cooed Sapale. "Here's the plan. You start acting like Jon Ryan and we'll start calling you by his sainted name. Up to that point, you're EJ. All other options are *more* hurtful. Any questions?"

EJ returned a glare to Mirraya. "There are a few in our galaxy. I know of ten, not counting the three who've been killed so far."

"And what do you know of their threat *outside* the Milky Way galaxy?"

He shrugged. "Not much. I do know their numbers are tremendous and the damage they're doing is horrific."

"Have you been to areas where their concentration is greater?"

"Once. But I have sources. They all report back the same sad story. Where there's one ancient god, there's a nightmare. Where there's more than one, there's nothing left alive, standing, or worth having."

"How have the locals, wherever they might be, faired in terms of self-defense?"

"Aside from the three DBs here, not well at all. The term *a tsunami of lava* comes to mind."

"DBs?" questioned Daleria.

"*Dead bodies*, dear," replied Sapale. "His brain's been stuck in military for a very long time."

"That confirms what we know and theorize," said Mirraya. "Do you have any ideas how to expand our effectiveness against them?"

"Aside from eliminating them one at a time? No. How about you?"

She sighed deeply. "No. They are too powerful. With lesser beings we could strike as we did in the Battle of the Periphery. But to do so against most Cleinoids in numbers would fail quickly."

"So, what, there're maybe a million of them? If we take out two a day we'll be done in, oh, approximately way too late for most beings presently alive."

"We are aware of the starkness of the numbers."

"Mirraya and I have discussed this, EJ. You know of ten Cleinoids nearby. If we start killing them off it will send a beacon to those elsewhere. Our galaxy will draw in most if not all those Cleinoids battling elsewhere," Daleria said evenly.

"They care *that* much about their brothers and sisters?" EJ mocked.

"No, they are that vengeful. Plus, they know if any resistance is successful, it might duplicate itself. If they left it to build they might be at risk."

"You seem to know a lot about them. You write a book or something?"

"I'm one of them," she said defiantly.

"A little gal like you? Seriously?"

EJ flew backwards and skidded on his back across the sharp rock. His jacket was shredded.

"Who did that?" he howled as he popped to his feet. "You?" he shouted at Mirraya.

"We all did," replied Daleria. "Watch your mouth, teamboy."

"Team*mate*," Mirraya said in polite correction.

"This isn't working for me," huffed EJ.

"Then be nice. That works for us, numb nuts," scolded Sapale.

"Let's leave discussions of my nuts out of our conversation, *brood's-mate*."

"Consider them forgotten," she said with a contented grin.

"Let's begin by working as a team to take out one of the local Cleinoids," announced Mirraya to cut the squabbling.

"Fine by me," replied EJ.

"I know of a Suderbak wreaking havoc on a planet in the Wentworth System," responded Mirraya. "You know him, Daleria?"

"Her, and yes. Wicked bitch badly in need of killing."

"Strengths and weaknesses?" asked Mirri.

"A lot and basically none. She's the god of destitution, meaning creating it, not helping those in need. She's," Daleria spread her arms wide, "big. Maybe eight feet wide, fifteen feet tall, weighs in around three tons. The usual, jaws that can crush steel, claws that can rip open a mountain, and a temper to match."

"Then I'd guess she's slow and stupid," stated EJ.

"Eh, yeah, sort of."

"Easy peasey. We surround her, confuse her, and bag her," he said with confidence.

"Maybe it's so easy we can skip her?" snarked Sapale.

"Come on," EJ retorted, "we can take my ship."

"We will use mine," Mirraya replied firmly.

"What? You don't trust me?"

"If we take my ship I don't have to," she responded flatly.

"Lady's got a point," he conceded. "Let's go make the world a better place."

CHAPTER THIRTEEN

Suderbak was basically a blimp with legs. Not lighter than air though. She was heavier than most surfaces could support. When she walked the ground didn't just shake, it caved with each ponderous step. Though it would not be hard to track her, one would never want to, because if one did catch up with her, one would have her to deal with. Not a pretty prospect.

She was gleefully trampling the forest floor of Ruchbah A-1b. She was also trampling a goodly number of the inhabitants. Their screams and cries for mercy would have been unbearable to most creatures who understood them for what they were. Such was not a restraint for Suderbak. She reveled in the anguish and delighted in the squishy feeling of the recently deceased oozing through her cloven hooves. Counting the additional seven planets she freed of the burden of supporting sentient life, she was well on her way to enjoying the hell out of her current victim-world. Life could not, in her estimation, get any better.

The inhabitants of Ruchbah A-1b never evolved to the level of any significant industrialization. A few steam engines and water wheels were about it in terms of technology. It was apparent they never would advance much further, due to their impending demise.

Suderbak especially cherished the conquest of these simpler civilizations. Inevitably, word would circulate that some form of divine retribution or demonic invasion was underway. The natives feared her all the more, since she was the tool for what they were certain was their impending damnation. Good stuff, she reflected. Fun for her, and double the mental torment for the pestilence she was clearing.

There were once large cities on Ruchbah A-1b, or The Mother, as the rapidly dwindling number of locals called it. Mostly constructed of wood, they burned with an intensity and speed Suderbak almost lamented because it was too fast to be enjoyed for any length of time. But it was perfect nonetheless. Once a good old firestorm initiated, there was no stopping the absolute destruction of the structures and the total immolation of the population.

Suderbak charged out of the thick charred tree cover and up a steep hill. Soon she could see for miles in all directions, and all was a sight of beauty. Acrid smoke, boiling rivers, and flames rising to meet the clouds above. But she couldn't help noticing a small patch that seemed spared from her wrath. Oh, my, she thought angrily, that would never do. She ran as best she could in the direction of the anomalous normality. Given her bulk, and the smattering of lingering souls fleeing every which way who required stomping, it took her almost half an hour to reach the green island of trees. But she was pleased that by that time, she was good and angry. She felt *marvelous*.

Suderbak hurled her frame toward the virgin turf. Icing on the cake, she saw five juicy pre-victims just standing absolutely still, waiting politely for her death blow. She almost—*almost* being the operative word—felt guilty for her excess of good fortune. Her bliss came crashing down, as did her bulk. She struck a partial membrane at what for her was top speed. Recalling she was a whale with multiple legs, after ramming her snout she plopped back on her butt gracelessly. There she sat staring at the nothing that had just laid her low.

Her joy transitioned to blue-hot rage in a flash. She charged forward again because she was both furious and not all that smart. Bang, she hit the invisible wall again. Switching tactics, she sped to her right before advancing. Again, she ended up rump-on-the-dirt and confused. A strategic retreat was in order. She made a one-eighty and steamed away to regroup. *Kaboom*! Crash. She realized she was trapped inside some form of bubble.

That was when the five onlookers began advancing on her purposefully.

"Who are you to try to hold a god?" she bellowed. She was stunned. They neither answered nor even slowed. "I will stew each one of you in the others' juices. I will eat your bodies, vomit them up, and consume them again for all—"

She fell silent when she realized they couldn't hear her.

The thin male stepped forward. He studied the invisible wall with a hand, then spoke. "There, I've put a pinprick opening in the membrane. We can communicate now. Sorry, whatever you said before couldn't get out."

"Who are you to try to hold a god?" she bellowed for a second time.

"Judging from her body language, that's what she said before. A real one-trick pony, this one," remarked Sapale as she peered in for a closer look.

"Who are you?" Suderbak demanded.

The tallest one, the one with scales unlike the others, spoke. "Who we are is unimportant, Suderbak."

"You know my true name?"

"What do you think, cupcake?" responded EJ.

Mirraya held a hang-on-there palm to him. "I will speak and we will not taunt the creature."

"Cre ... *creature*? I am not a creature, I am an ancient god," she howled in protest.

"You are both," replied Mirraya. "That also is unimportant. We need to perform a few tests on you. I am sorry in advance for any suffering you might experience."

"Woah doggies," exclaimed EJ. "Why are we being nice to this monster? She ravaged this planet probably beyond any potential recovery. This is *war*. In war we don't apologize in advance for pain, suffering, or inconveniences imposed on war criminals. We kill them."

Suderbak looked between Mirraya and EJ. "You are in charge here?" she asked of Mirraya.

"Yes."

"What a *relief*," breathed Suderbak.

Mirraya's face hardened. "Only a temporary reprieve, I fear. Now, as I was saying, you are our prisoner. We will run a set of tests. Since you are captured and not engaged in combat, you are owed certain considerations. We do not victimize a captive lightly. That would be wrong of us."

"I couldn't agree more," Suderbak responded quickly. "Ah, what sort of tests? Perhaps I could cooperate and be done sooner?"

"We wish to estimate your resistance to various assaults. We also want to determine your lowest threshold for death."

"I formally withdraw my offer of cooperation." She narrowed her snout into a wedge shape and slammed into the membrane with all her might.

"Fascinating," remarked Toño. "She put a temporary ten-micrometer dent in the membrane."

"Impressive," agreed Sapale.

Suderbak rammed the invisible wall repeatedly, each attempt a little less energetic than the prior one. Finally, her nose bloodied and her head throbbing, she rested back on her butt. "How'd I do?" she asked, a bit dazed.

"Um, at first well. Toward the end there you failed to cause a perturbation in the membrane," replied Toño. "Understandable, I presume."

"When I get out I shall pulverize you last," she remarked.

"Thank you?" Toño responded with uncertainty.

"Can we get on with this?" demanded EJ.

"Yes," answered Mirraya. "Fetch the gas cylinders."

Within a minute a tube passed through the membrane. It was then attached to one of five tall metal cylinders.

"We are testing your response to caustic and toxic agents," said Mirraya clinically.

"You forgot one thing," said Suderbak quietly.

"I doubt that," replied Mirraya.

Without further notice, Suderbak hurled herself at the point where the tube passed though the membrane. "You forgot *this*," she squealed in triumph. She then bounced off the second smaller membrane set up like an umbrella to protect the pinhole opening from Suderbak's anticipated escape attempt. Sitting again on her rump, dazed and confused, she remarked, "I guess you did *not*. My bad."

Without acknowledging Suderbak's comments, Mirraya announced, "This first one is chlorine gas. Please breath normally."

"*Normally,* I'd curse you at this type of juncture," replied a subdued Suderbak.

"I appreciate your restraint."

After five minutes it was clear the chlorine gas had no effect on Suderbak. The gas was vented off and hydrogen cyanide infused. Again, it had no effect. Hydroflouric acid fumes similarly showed no effectiveness. A one-hundred percent nitrogen internal atmosphere didn't asphyxiate her. She didn't even breath harder. Finally, a mixture of anesthetic gasses, including halothane, sevoflurane, nitrous oxide, and desthuroflate, was tried. She didn't even get droopy eyes.

"Well, I'd say she was impervious to all inhalants and corrosives," concluded Toño.

Suderbak perked up visibly. "Are we done?"

"Not hardly, moronovich," replied EJ. "*You're* not done until *I'm* done. And at that point, trust me, you won't be paying attention."

"We will now try a few physical interventions," said Mirraya.

Through a small pulsed opening she shoved in a large satchel. When the bag hit the ground fifty falzorn burst forth. Those were the ravenous vipers that were universally feared. The pack instantly homed in on Suderbak. She backed up cautiously, lowering her head. As if shot from a cannon they burst upon her and began writhing. She tossed and bucked. Falzorn flew off every which way but immediately dove back at her. For several seconds it was unclear to the observers who was winning. Then Suderbak jumped as high as she could. When she hit the ground, all the falzorn were shed to the dirt. With unexpected speed she stomped every one of them a foot into the dirt. None resurfaced.

"Hey, that was fun," she beamed. "What were they? I need to get some."

"The next test is possible due to the, um, *resourcefulness* of Mr. Ryan here," stated Mirraya.

A large crate was pushed up to the membrane limit. A window pulsed on and off in a microsecond. When it did EJ and Toño shoveled the wooden crate in and backed out quickly.

Suderbak looked at the box uncertainly. "What have we here?" She sniffed the container. "Don't recognize the smell, but boy is it strong. I thought I smelled bad."

She swiped at the box and one side splintered. Five Berrillian war cats burst into the open. They wielded traditional swords. As a team they set on Suderbak with ferocity and abandon. Fur flew and a cloud of dust rose. Within ten seconds all that was left of the oversized tigers were their mangled corpses.

"I preferred the snaky things myself," observed Suderbak in an offhand manner.

"So far, pretty much what we anticipated," Toño remarked generally.

"Let's try something harder then," responded Mirraya. She stepped forward. Suderbak didn't realize it at first, but Mirraya was then inside the membrane. She raised her arms and spread her wings. "Haras uter *badum*," she shouted. Then she backed away, behind the safety of the membrane.

Red and green flames erupted all around Suderbak. They were so intense the massive beast couldn't be clearly seen. After five seconds the flames snuffed out.

A crazed Suderbak lunged forward and impacted the membrane. Her skin was charred and her tail was singed off at the tip. She howled in pain.

"Well *finally*," snapped EJ.

"Yes, but all that heat and look how little it affected her. I'm surprised and disappointed," responded Mirraya.

Suderbak rolled frantically on the ground, either not aware or not certain the flames were out. After a while she stood and lumbered to where Mirraya stood. "Do not ever do that again. Do you understand me, defiler? I will suffer such punishment on you, you will wish you'd never been born."

"Oh yeah, tough gal," quipped EJ. "Wouldn't that first involve you getting out of *jail*?"

Suderbak took two steps back. She closed her eyes and mumbled some unintelligible words, possibly in some unknown language. A blinding beam flashed in front of her like a carbon-arc searchlight. She charged out of her containment directly toward EJ.

He knew in a heartbeat she was free. He whirled his arms in the air with practiced confidence. Suderbak literally froze mid-stride. A crackling frost quickly formed on her skin and a mist rose off her, wafting in the soft breeze.

"*That* was intense," remarked Toño.

"Crap," muttered Mirraya.

"What?" snapped EJ. "I was damn impressive."

"Yes, but it took magic to suppress Suderbak. I wish some *conventional* force would have been effective."

"Yeah, and I wish I was taller," EJ replied. "But I ain't. If magic's all we got, it's all we got." He shadow-boxed the air. "I'm ready. Bring 'em on. Bring 'em *all* on."

Sapale shook her head and looked to Daleria. "Yeah, bring all one *million* of them on. Hell, bring them on all at once. Captain Delusional here'll smite them, but good."

CHAPTER FOURTEEN

The attendance at the conclave was impressive. Cleinoids of every shape, size, and body type spread out as far as the eye could see. All were anxious to hear how and when Vorc was going to get them to Prime. Also, and probably even more passionately, to an individual they wanted to know how and when Gáwar would be sent away. He had not worn out his welcome, since he had never been welcome in the first place. But every day he made his kinsmen more and more miserable. Gods didn't like that. Gáwar was nice only to his one friend, Tefnuf, and the profound oddity Zastrál. He was the only one who could summon Gáwar. The god of demons *had* to be nice to Zastrál or he'd remain in limbo forever.

Otherwise Gáwar had made a royal pest out of himself in the land of the ancient gods. He didn't drink alcohol. No, he blenderized and drank any drunken gods he encountered. He didn't pine about not being able to go to Prime to pillage and maim. No, he did so locally and often. Bodies were stacking like cord wood in the Lower Chambers' morgue. In fact, he was so contrarian that when a couple asked him to please *not* kill their firstborn, he did. And when another couple asked him if he would please kill *their* firstborn, he refused. He said something to the effect that there was no sport in being helpful. Any way one looked at it, Gáwar was unpopular. That his presence was singularly associated with Vorc did much to further sully the center seat's already foundering public approval rating.

Vorc rose to call the assembly to order. The front row, usually populated by Vorc's friends and supporters, was occupied exclusively by Gáwar. The god of demons wished to make it clear to Vorc he was paying very close attention. No one else dreamed of sitting with or near Gáwar, so the entire row was otherwise empty. Even Zastrál wanted no part of Gáwar when he was in his murderous rapture. He sat somewhere anonymously in the crowd, toward the back.

"Let us come to order. Much has happened since our last meeting. I would like to—"

"Fall on your sword?" shouted someone near the front.

"No, that would require more skill than this stiff fish possesses," yelled another, off to one side.

"Please, come to order," demanded Vorc. "Petty name-calling and insults will help with nothing."

"*Correct*," screamed a female. "Only your head on a *pike* would."

"I brought a pike," exclaimed Jacularus, a warrior god. He held his massive pike aloft as a clear threat to Vorc.

"Pass it here," cried out the female voice. Aamera stood with her arms extended toward Jacularis. It seemed she was quite serious in her desire to skewer Vorc. The god of womanly spite even pushed in Jacularis's direction until a pair of golems lifted her up and plopped her back in her seat.

"I said *order* and I will have *order*," howled Vorc. "Anyone who wishes to test my foul mood will regret it. I promise you that."

Naturally Gáwar stood and held a clawed arm high in the air.

"Is this really necessary, Gáwar?" pleaded Vorc.

"You said *anyone*, didn't you?"

"*Again*, is this really necessary?"

"Are you going to make an actual announcement I will care about?"

"Yes."

"Then it's not necessary that I test your resolve at this particular moment." He rested back.

No one else was foolish enough to follow up Gáwar's performance with further posturing or pestering.

"Thank you," scoffed Vorc. "Now, we will forego the usual benediction and procedural mumbo jumbo. We're all on edge and no one really wants to hear that rubbish, anyway."

Loeedor, god of accountants and obsessive compulsives, waved an arm frantically calling for attention.

"No, Loeedor, just *no*."

His arm went down slowly and reluctantly.

"For those who might not have otherwise heard, as best we can tell Dominion Splitter is dead."

A rumbling thunder of murmurs erupted.

"*Order*. Don't make me kill anyone today."

The crowd reluctantly and slowly quieted.

"I have no reason to believe another similar transfolding vortex exists. Hence, none of us here will be going to Prime via that method, the traditional manner of conveyance."

"Are we going to close our eyes and *wish* ourselves there, then?" taunted Tantrulus, the god of petty grudges.

Vorc let that quip pass. "As you may also know, I have identified the criminal who killed DS as Ryanmax. He falsely represented himself and his friends to be Cleinoids. He infiltrated our society to specifically keep us from entering Prime. He was bad to the bone right from the start."

"How could you be so stupid as to mistake him for a god? Didn't I *tell* you he wasn't?" badgered Tefnuf.

"Now is not the time for blame and recriminations."

"When is? I'll make sure to be front row and center for that," she responded.

A chorus of laughter arose. Vorc hated many things, but he hated nothing more than being laughed at.

"*Golems,* seize Tefnuf and confine her. I will punish her severely after this conclave."

"Let her stay," Gáwar said softly. "She is with me."

Golems were animated clay with no functioning brains. But even moving mud knew better than to mess with Gáwar. They retreated to the entrances where they had been stationed without asking permission.

"As I was saying, the criminal Ryanmax set about to destroy our culture and traditions. He is dead, thanks to Gáwar here. His companions are to be killed upon sight. Is that clear?"

"How can we see them in their own universe?" asked Gáwar with a chuckle.

"I mean, if they ever return, they are KOS, okay?"

"Wait. How do they, mere mortals, ferry back and forth to Prime, when we mighty Cleinoids can't?" asked Beltrmaint, a minor god of record keeping.

"They seem to have a technology that allows it."

"Why don't *we* have such technology?" shouted Quisstin, a redundant god of the perfectly obvious.

"Because we don't," snapped Vorc. "In case you haven't noticed, we're not that big on technology. Never much needed it, because *we're gods,* moron."

"I wish to formally retract my support of you as center seat," returned Quisstin.

"*Your* support? You were my only challenger for this stupid job," railed Vorc.

"Can we get back on topic?" shouted Olitopis, god of orderly processions. Yes, there was one for those, too. Go figure.

"Yes," thundered Vorc. "I am here today to ask for your help. The help of each and every Cleinoid god. I want to announce formally that I have no plan to get us to Prime. I also have no idea how to get our people home from Prime when they are finished. But I want to remind you that we are a great race. We are *gods.* I am asking that if anyone has any idea how to solve our isolation issues, please share them with the rest of us."

"You have *failed* us, Vorc. You must resign. We must elect a *competent* leader," shouted Giwiriwa, god of mobs and large angry protests. Vorc knew her involvement couldn't be a good thing.

"If my stepping down would fix matters, I would do so gladly. But if there is no solution identified, creating a power vacuum at this critical junction would serve no purpose."

Gáwar stood. "I agree. And if you resign, I will run *unopposed* for the center seat." He plopped back down limply.

Well, that extinguished the movement to oust Vorc in a flash. Gáwar as center seat was incomprehensibly bad. Perhaps that was Gáwar's intention, to quell dissent. Or maybe to stir it up further. No one had any clue as to why he might have said what he did, but no one was about to ask him for clarity.

"Again, I call for any ideas," cried out Vorc.

"What about the aliens's tech. Can't we steal it or duplicate it?"

"No. The only example of it is gone. Our science is a very long way from allowing us to have similar technology of our own."

Murmurs sloshed through the assembly, but in the end, no one spoke publicly.

"I assume the lack of input reflects the fact that I am not alone in failing to find a solution," Vorc concluded in a low tone.

"Then are we done?" growled Gáwar.

"Yes, I suppose so. Why?"

"I was just thinking how good those seated in Row 5 looked. I thought we might catch a bite together."

CHAPTER FIFTEEN

The JCIDC Senior Security Subgroup met only when important decisions needed to be made. Trying to get a mixed bag of intergalactic politicians to agree on anything significant was impossible in any of the JCIDC's General Sessions. It was a wonder that mass murder and mayhem weren't the common norm at those get-togethers. The only consensus seemed to be that every *other* representative was both ignorant and wrong. Politicians. Where would life have been without them? Yeah, no telling for sure, but it would have been somewhere a whole lot better. A lot more citizens would have survived to enjoy that superior place, too.

Admiral Counter Van Alt of the Pleiades Federation was the chairwhatever of the subgroup. His home world Deplaciow was one of eleven sentient systems in the open star cluster. If one asked him, Van Alt would state with pride that his particular species, for there were three independently evolved sentient species on Deplaciow, was the most advanced on the planet. The other two naturally proclaimed the same standing. But that would not be relevant in the narrative at hand, so it need not be a center of focus. The admiral's race, the Quantsor, were the only terrestrial sentients of Deplaciow. The other two were oceanic.

Quantsors were very small and improbably constructed creatures. There were four sexes, two male and two female. Seriously. The details of that physiology were obscure and changed frequently, so were best ignored completely. A mature Quantsor was like a Russian nesting doll. A Male-1 was constituted as one each of the other three sexes joined inside him, though technically separate. To be consistently confusing, a Male-2 had the three sexes that were not the same as his inside him, and so forth. See, very confusing and malleable. They clearly existed, so their bizarre system worked. But don't even ask what happened or was culturally opined if, say, a Male-2 had three Female-1s inside him. Oh the blasphemy. But that would not be relevant in the narrative at hand, so it need not be a center of focus.

The important point concerning Quantsor anatomy was that all other members of the JCIDC Senior Security Subgroup were physically much larger. The tiny admiral had to stand and sit atop a tall tower at meetings. Behind his tiny back the other members referred to the elevated platform as the Napoleonic Pedestal. Politicians, right? Admiral Counter Van Alt's additional challenge to his credibility was that he needed to speak into an amplification system to be heard. Also, when addressed with any significant volume, his body, filled with three others as it was, would rattle like an infant's toy. There was little wonder that outwardly he was a male of very little humor, and he brooked no disrespect.

A final note would be helpful in placing Admiral Counter Van Alt and his race in their proper perspective. Though they *brooked* no disrespect, they never *received* one iota of respect. That was not xenophobic, racist, or inappropriate on the part of all other alien species. No, the Quantsors were repugnant, effete, and fully condescending to a unit. *They* were xenophobic, racist, and inappropriate. But they possessed two factors that made their participation in the galactic community tolerable. First, the Pleiades cluster turned out to contain most of the Helium-3 created in the Big Bang. No one had any idea why that rare and useful isotope chose to concentrate itself there. But if a creature were to exist that floated in Helium-3, it could have swum from one side of the cluster to the other with ease.

The second factor was that Macher lay inside the Pleiades Federation's space. To control Macher was to control the divine. It was a stable wormhole with properties that bedeviled belief. If an unmanned probe was sent in to Macher and the AI instructed to return, the probe always did. It would report various findings depending on how long it was allowed to explore whatever realm existed on the tunnel's other side. Stars, planets, and lots of empty space were documented. The usual suspects. But if an expedition of living, breathing organisms went through, they never returned. Their crews were never found by the unmanned probes, nor were any signs of the spaceships. No matter what races went in, none came back.

There were two reasons generally agreed upon as to why such an unclear outcome might happen. One was that a mechanical device could survive the round-trip journey. If, however, living matter was in contact with the mechanical system, the combined unit was annihilated in transit. The party would never make it to the far side to leave traces.

The other notion was that there existed something so wondrous, so transfixing in that new cosmos, that any and all visitors experienced an immediate and perpetual rapture. Those then-blessed souls not only never reported back to those that sent them, but they made it a point to be absolutely invisible, fearing that their enduring bliss might be interrupted by visitors from back home. It was interesting to note that no evidence, theory, or remains were ever discovered to support the second theory. The second theory, the so-called Serenity Always Proposition, or SAP, was, however, so alluring that an endless stream of paying customers passed through the star cluster to assess Macher. The unlimited wealth of the Pleiades Federation could not be overlooked by any society in possession of functioning brains. Thus, the federation had indelible influence.

The bottom line? When the Pleiades Federation announced that they wished for *their* representative to be given the rank of admiral and that he or she be the permanent head of the JCIDC Senior Security Subgroup, it easily came to pass. Quantsors were fortunately so self-absorbed and narcissistic that they never involved themselves in the workings of the subgroup. To lead it and garner self-proclaimed respect was their single endgame. The JCIDC was free to plunder the Helium-3 and shovel out their treasury while still being in complete control of the subgroup's critical functioning. The arrangement *defined* the concept of win-win.

"The *Kaljaxian* female who formally resides on *Azsuram* but who lives on *Kalvarg* wishes to address the subgroup," boomed from the speakers amplifying Admiral Counter Van Alt of the Pleiades Federation's voice. He did that a lot, the turning up of the volume. Pissant. "If there are no objections I, Admiral Counter Van Alt, firstborn of Hathorbas the Significant, will permit her to do so, if only briefly." It was hard to tell from any distance, but Van Alt then sat down.

"I ... if only—," stammered Sapale. "The living of the universe are about to die. I have *critical* information to share. And I ... I must be *brief*?" She began to rise. She wasn't certain if it was to storm out or crush the chairwhatever. Possibly it was to do both.

"Be assured, honored guest," began MumMunMur. "*Our* time is *your* time. You may speak as long as it pleases you." MumMunMur was vice-chair and actually did all the steering of the committee after Van Alt made his opening hostile and universally offensive remarks.

Sapale recalled that she was warned in advance of the politics involved, and she forced herself to sit and calm down. It was very much against her nature.

"Thank you, Commandant MumMunMur. Your words are reassuring and most welcome."

MumMunMur bowed her long thin neck. She was Pred. They were an avian-like species with the outward appearance of a stork or crane. The Pred were renowned for their thoughtful, kind, and inquisitive nature. Only the Quantsors were on record as despising them.

"As most of you know, I spent a while in the universe of the ancient gods. My brood-mate and Dr. DeJesus were with me, as was our ship *Blessing*. Since my return I have assembled a team to help in our struggles with the Cleinoids. That is how they generally refer to themselves, by the way, not as ancient gods. That term is meant only to frighten their victims."

"I believe it does," replied MumMunMur, with her species' version of a wry grin.

"Yes," hissed Van Alt. "I have come to learn that you brought a sex slave back with you, one of these Ancient Cleinoids. She's a *spy*, I say. You are *both* spies." He then returned his full attention to his handheld unit. He was in the middle of watching holos of dubious moral integrity. *Why* he chose to speak an unprecedented second time during a meeting was never determined.

All others present repeated in their minds the sustaining mantra. *Helium-3 and money, money, money.*

"Is the JCIDC aware of any victories or even partial defenses against our enemy?" asked Toño.

MumMunMur swept her small head along the horizontal. "Nothing of note. Naturally, we cannot know where in the infinite universe they may or may not have struck. Our scientists have documented a good correlation between their activities on a large scale and significant quantron-radiation bursts."

"What's quantron radiation?" asked Sapale. "Never heard of that one."

"Er, it's an extremely energetic form released when larger atoms are basically crushed into their constituent parts. Mesons, bosons, protons, theoretically even quarks if the fission impact is great enough," she replied.

"Translated into *non*-technonerd?" Sapale chided.

"It forms when a lot of matter is being pounded out of existence," Toño replied.

"Since we already knew these guys were badasses, what does this observation of quantron radiation add to our database?" Sapale asked with mild annoyance.

"It can suggest where they are active," replied a neutral MumMunMur. "Monitoring stations set up widely detect it and the information is sent to us by subspace data pulses. That way we have real-time information of their activity."

"Um," grunted Sapale. "And what have we learned?"

"That we are in big trouble," answered Pow-Don-22, one of the three representatives from the planet Oberon. Liptalisions always did things in three. Three mates, three jobs, three meals a day, and three deaths. The last was assumed to be allegorical, but outsiders were reluctant to press the Liptalisions for details on account of their foul and hyperaggressive general tendencies. Their famous joke, which no off worlders found humorous, went thusly. *Someone asks you what time it is. Your response? Time for you to die.* It was then customary to try and kill the individual asking the time of day. Odd race, and one best avoided in most social contexts.

"Didn't we already *know* that?" snapped Sapale, who was only vaguely aware of the Liptalisions' ill temper.

"So what we say in answer to her highness's question was a waste of our effort. We are stupid and out of touch? Maybe our species is so much stupider than yours that we just can't keep up? Well, lucky for us all we're good at dueling. You choose, bitch of Jon Ryan. We slay you here and now, or we duel outside where we slay you then and there."

"Hmm. May I have three seconds to think of a funny answer?" Sapale shot back with a war growl.

"Now, Sapale, please," pleaded Toño. "Let's leave the killing for the Cleinoids."

She gestured to the three humanoid Liptalisions seated in a row. "Yeah, sure. But a little practice will help keep me sharp."

The toleration of the challenging Liptalision and his two associates evaporated. They leaped up onto the table and sprinted toward Sapale.

For her part Sapale sat passively with folded hands, seeming to barely notice their charge. When the line of Liptalisions was a meter away, Sapale's probe fibers burst out in bundles of three. Each set wrapped around the head of an attacker. She then slammed the heads against the ceiling very hard. So there they were, suspended and dazed, legs flailing and muffled curses struggling to enunciate themselves from overhead.

"Sapale," MumMunMur asked respectfully, "was that necessary?"

"Probably not."

"But you enjoyed it?" MumMunMur added.

"Oh yes. Very much so."

"Then let me know when you're ready to release them. I'll summon some guards in the meantime."

"This happen often?" Sapale asked matter-of-factly.

"Every single meeting. Every damn single one," the vice-chair bemoaned.

"You'd think they'd learn," Sapale responded, staring up at them.

"One would hope. Actually I think they *have* learned. They simply cannot resist their lesser nature."

"I'm happy to help. This is what I do." Sapale beamed back.

Five minutes later Sapale not so softly dropped the Liptalisions onto the floor at the legs of six guards. The Klackmass males were basically two-legged snails that walked upright. Their shells had evolved to be more like a turtle's but the rest of their anatomy, all four hundred pounds of it, was pure escargot. In place of individual arms, they sported a circular muscular membrane that was able to manipulate objects with excellent dexterity. That particular species was routinely used to restrain the Liptalision representatives, because the slimy residue they left behind drove the OCD race crazy.

The three representatives were wrestled into their seats and then held in place with significant force by the guards. Before they could say a word, however, Sapale extended her probes a few inches. "Now, boys, before you go threatening me or promising revenge, I want you to know one fact. I've been killing people who said shit like that to me for two billion years. Let's not add the names of three more idiots to my ever-growing list of those who tried my patience, shall we?"

Though the Liptalisions scowled and hissed, none said a word.

"Back to the threat on all of our existences," announced MumMunMur. "I have placed a map of the areas of current Cleinoid activity that we are aware of on your screens. As you can see, their presence is over a fairly wide swath of the universe, perhaps a bit more concentrated near this galactic cluster." She shined a laser pointer on the region she was describing.

"Likely the area they first entered is in or near that cluster," observed Toño.

"Man they spread out quickly," marveled Sapale.

"Any respectable pestilence would," replied Toño.

"And there are no peskier pestilences than the Cleinoid gods," added Daleria.

"How can we even begin to fight them?" asked the Gorgolinian representative. They were the fish-tank sentients of Sotovir. "We know no fear, but to attack them surely would bring a swift and pointless death."

"We begin by beginning," replied EJ, who'd been conspicuously silent up until then. "You throw a dart at the map and we go there and kick some booty. Any questions?"

"You we do not like," responded the Gorgolinian.

"Right back atcha. Oh, and who cares, what does what you say matter, and why even bring it up, bubble face?"

"We are an orderly species. Declaring one's contempt is orderly."

"Do you mind if I get that tattooed on my ass? It's ... it's so *profound*."

"Madame Commandant, he mocks me."

"EJ, please stop mocking our valued ally."

"Do you *have* to call me that stupid name, mumumumum?"

"No. But Mirraya-Slapgren specifically asked that I do. The chair chooses to respect their request."

"Can we adjourn this farce and go kill something?" asked a frustrated EJ.

"I will determine which target we hit and who will join our assault force," stated Mirraya firmly.

"You do so with the full blessing of the JCIDC. You needn't clear any action with us beforehand, but we do request a full update when it's practical to provide one."

"Thank you, Mum. We shall."

Mirraya gathered up her stuff and left without further comment. Her team followed quietly.

It was go time.

CHAPTER SIXTEEN

In a place of no palpable substance, the thin air gusted and blew randomly. There was no matter and there was no time. Neither had ever existed. No one and nothing inhabited that state of being. No one and nothing ever would. It did not exist sufficiently to be occupied. No universe contained it. It was so outside of reality as to make any such connection both impossible and meaningless. The domain was neither light nor dark, happy nor sad. It *was,* albeit barely, and that was about all that could be said of Camelot.

No, this was not the Camelot of King Arthur and Merlin and love unrequited. It was named Camelot by its sole inhabitant, though to actually consider that which resided in the realm an *occupant* was to abuse the intended meaning of that word. Fate had always been there. Fate knew of all other places and times, but knew no time or place for itself. And Fate did not care, worry, or dwell on its state of being. Why should it? How would it? That which always *was,* always would *be,* simply *was.* Fate had no wants or desires, because there existed in Camelot nothing to desire, aspire to, or to need. Fate possessed but two things. Camelot and the indirect control over all forces in all universes. Fate therefore owned nothing, and it owned everything.

If a visitor could visit Camelot, they would see it as a place of wonder and unlimited fantasy. Dials were attached to all the surfaces. Some ran forward, some backward, and some had never run at all. Lights of infinite colors and frequencies flashed and swirled at their pleasure from and to wherever they pleased. If anyone was there to witness Camelot, they would conclude that it was beautiful and mystical. But visiting Camelot was more impossible than all other unattainable impossibilities. No, being there in Camelot with Fate was infinitely harder to achieve than other mere implausibilities. To make a fair maiden love you. To live as a youth forever and never know pain, never know loss. To know God, to understand God's ways. To be the best person you could be while harming no *one* and no *thing*. Those quests, and all other lofty undertakings, were so much less infeasible.

But dreams did exist in Camelot. Yes, Fate dreamed. Well, that was to say, Fate dreamed, *if* Fate wanted to dream. But Fate wanted nothing. So dreams were relegated to the state of possibility; they *could* come to Fate, they *might* pursue and afflict Fate. But Fate never *wanted* them, never *courted* them.

However, the fact remained that no force of will can stop a dream that *would* come. Fate was at dream's mercy, as much as any lord in any high castle, any pig in her mire, or you in your bed tonight.

And what dreams forced themselves on fate, where fate quasi-existed in Camelot, a land of no palpable substance?

What dreams, indeed!

CHAPTER SEVENTEEN

Gomenchorum, Hilazz, and Compico were not really friends. Back home, they rarely hung out together. But all three were assigned to Fury. Since arriving in Prime, they quickly formed a bond. Over two years, they'd had quite literally the time of their lives. They destroyed planets. They consumed everything in their path. They burned any flammable material until the skies grew black and anything that needed to breathe couldn't. Like kids in a candy shop with fists full of cash, how happy they felt! And it just kept getting better. Nuances of torment, mastering the finer points of dismemberment, and the true art of affliction were slow lessons to learn, but were well worth the time, based on their improved experiences.

Hilazz became the leader of the pack. That was natural, him being an especially large dire wolf and the god of wild fury. He was also the fastest afoot, most of the time having to stop and wait when his companions fell far enough behind. He enjoyed his role. Once they found a stable planet, it was he who ferreted out the best hunting and the direction they would destroy in.

Gomenchorum was not exactly a follower, but at least for a

while he ceded the role to Hilazz. It rubbed his bristles the wrong way, but times were so good, it was hard to complain with any heartfelt conviction. So, for the present, the god of lost souls would follow that of wild fury. Plus, the souls his trio were liberating were anything but lost. No, they were accounted for, one and all, before they were desecrated, desiccated, and disintegrated. One, two, three, they were no longer going to be. *Puff.* In defiance of any natural presuppositions, Gomenchorum didn't look his part. He was no hooded and robed grim reaper or a wispy-lilting manifestation. He was a hedgehog who'd made his nest too near a nuclear reactor. His body was asymmetrical, heaped up in random chunks and lumps. The unsightly mess was covered in irregular-length bristles ending in sharp metal tips, each one capable of delivering a jolt of electricity strong enough to kill a water buffalo. Standing ten meters tall when on his three front and back legs, he looked very much like a bad dream's nightmare.

The silent partner in the group was Compico. Literally. He communicated only by mental simaging and rudimentary body posturing. Why? Because a three-tailed metallic scorpion had no voice box with which to generate a sound. Plus, topping the scales at just over two tons sort of meant he didn't need to speak to have himself understood. Compico's message was always the same. *You are about to die.* There was absolutely no need to repeat that certainty over and over again.

Somehow the three Cleinoids made amiable traveling companions. They did share a similar vision and set of goals, so that wasn't too surprising. They surely made an impressive mess of any and all planets they visited. Their latest selection promised to be the richest yet. It was the play world named The Answer Is Yes. In the distant past the planet was called Visuewa. It was home to a thriving, industrious, and profit-loving society. Think Ferengi but a tad brighter. Over time, the inhabitants discovered the quintessential, surefire, time-tested, lead-pipe cinch way to make even more coin. The pleasure industry.

All restrictive puritanical laws were stricken from the books.

Everything was made legal, even items not specifically known to the lawmakers when they penned the what they deemed the “adaptive moral imperatives.” Yeah, you want it, you got it. So over centuries the entire economy switched to a hospitality footing. If it wasn't an aphrodisiac, an amusement park, or a gaming establishment, it wasn't funded. Visuewa became wall-to-wall knock-yourself-out fun. And the people, or whatever, came. Enclaves dedicated exclusively to either wholesome fun or absolute debauchery sprang up, designed to accomodate any species so inclined. It became Las Vegas/DisneyWorld/Sandals/Sybaris/Caligula/Hugh Hefner on steroids. Then they changed the name to The Answer Is Yes. In time, people mostly called it just *Yes!*, always with that exclamation.

What titillated Gomenchorum, Hilazz, and Compico most about *Yes!* was that it had zero defensive capabilities. The entire economy was based on pleasure. The only provision for weapons of any kind were where they were required in role-playing forms of, ahem, *interactions*. And *Yes!* was always packed to the gills with a mind-boggling variety of species of all ages too intoxicated or otherwise distracted to concern themselves with sudden and gruesome death. Yes, *Yes!* was the icing on any evildoer's cake of lustful desires.

As had become their routine, Hilazz led the attack wedge. The other two monstrosities flanked him to form a triangle. Once they made solid contact with a concentration of playthings, they split off and went nuts privately. They always liked to strike a population center in its densest section first in order to achieve maximal horror-impact. So it was to be with Naked City, a megalopolis of over four million revelers and employees all buck naked, all the time. Nudity was actually a strictly enforced law. Talk about being defenseless. Nowhere to hide so much as a Swiss Army knife, let alone a good-sized blaster. No, easy pickings had a poster child, and it's name was Naked City.

A large central square, Lecher's Lookout, was bounded by tall buildings and small parks. The square itself was completely open. That allowed lots of those casually strolling to have unobstructed views of a whole bunch of other gawking individuals. Reaching out and touching others, by the way, was considered a must.

Hilazz took aim as he hurled down from on high. When he was a hundred meters from the lookout he hit the ground running. Homenchorum and Compico set down simultaneously but fell behind quickly due to their inabilities to match pace with the wolf. That dispersal was very much appreciated by Mirraya. She stepped into the clear of the naked mannequins set up in Lecher's Lookout. She spread her massive wings and murmured an incantation. A sparse amber light leaped from her extended arm and struck Hilazz in the chest. He immediately tumbled limply at high speed. When he finally came to rest he was as still as a corpse.

Mirraya jumped on him, sunk her talons in, and seized flesh. She tore ferociously at his exposed belly. Large chunks of Hilazz flew everywhere. Blood spewed and was cast up like a public fountain dedicated to exsanguination.

Then Hilazz rallied. He rolled side to side with what little energy he could muster. But he could not dislodge Mirraya. She continued to rip and tear at him. Slowly his resistance waned. Soon he was still and lifeless. By the time Mirraya jumped off, there was more of Hilazz in tiny scattered pieces than left intact.

Meanwhile, EJ addressed the overgrown hedgehog Gomenchorum as he lumbered into the square. The assailant was only becoming vaguely aware that something was rotten in the state of *Yes!*. Instead of retreat he chose only to slow down. That way he slammed into the membrane EJ deployed less forcefully than he might have. Still, he flipped over and struck the force field again with his back. When EJ dropped the membrane, Gomenchorum had staggered back to his paws. His singular focus became the man that hurt him. Gomenchorum charged EJ in a blind fury.

EJ raised his right hand and formed a power bolt. He cast it at the beast. It sailed threw him like he was formed of jello. Gomenchorum howled in pain and even greater rage. He kept charging.

EJ waved his hands like he was rapidly polishing separate mirrors. Two walls of invisible energy slammed Gomenchorum on either side of his head like a closing bear trap. He skidded awkwardly to a stop and pawed at his neck. His panic grew furiously. Soon he was ripping long strips of pelt and skin off in his attempt to free the crushing of his windpipe. Gomenchorum fell onto his back and his hind legs kicked insanely. He spun like he was playing a game. But soon the game, along with Gomenchorum's worthless life, came to an agonizing end.

Quittle and Domitra were assigned to Compico. If there had been additional Cleinoids involved
in the attack, similar pairs of Deft brindases would have been tasked to kill those. Quittle and Domitra were Mirraya's oldest and most capable students. They were also both battle-hardened by long service against the Adamant. Unfortunately for them, Compico was the most deadly of the trio. He, being by far the slowest, was fully aware that he was sprinting into a well-laid trap when he took aim at the Deft dragons.

When he was several meters away each brindas cast separate spells. Quittle melted the ground under the god's feet so it became like intensely hot quicksand. Domitra pounded down on his back with a ramrod of energy. Compico's claws faltered into the muck. His heavier front end sank the fastest and his hind end bucked up and twisted to one side. He stabbed two of his tails ahead of his roll and steadied himself. He jabbed the third tail on the other side of the quagmire and slowly levered himself free. Without hesitation he raced at the dragons.

Domitra sent a dispersal spell at his flat head. That would, if effective, split her target open. It caused him to shake his head and clap his mandibles open and shut, but no part of him dispersed.

Quittle tried to bind his legs with ropelike mystical manifestations. One would catch, then fail, while another found purchase. Compico lurched slightly but was not slowed appreciably. He was on the brindases with the impact of twin locomotives. Both dragons heaved backward. Quittle took flight midway along her arch. Domitra tumbled clumsily to the ground and rolled out of control.

Compico pounced on her before she came to a stop. With his massive pincers he pinned her down. All three tails took rapid-fire turns pummeling her. The tail with universal toxin struck her face. The stinger of unquenchable acid sniped at her chest. His barb of unending fire whacked her sides. She began to smoke and then she began to burn.

Quittle leaped onto the back of one of Compico's tails and sunk her talons. She struggled to lift him. He was too heavy. She only stopped that appendage from striking her friend. His merciless assault on Domitra with the two other stingers didn't slow.

Once the brindas was fully engulfed in flames the god scampered away, pulling the attached dragon with him. He stabbed at Quittle, but his weapons were never designed to fight off an attack from behind. He spied a tall tree and raced toward it. Halfway there, Quittle reasoned he meant to pound her against the tree until she was knocked loose. She pushed off as hard as she could and rose above Compico's range. He nonetheless flailed at her as he screeched madly.

Compico never saw Mirraya coming. She flipped him on his back with one wing and drove her beak into his abdomen. His tails were again useless in her direction, but his pincers were not. He clawed frantically at Mirraya's neck and wings. She flapped as hard as she could to drive her head deeper and deeper into his midsection. Finally, in a show of immense strength, she punched her head through him and lifted Compico into the air. He oozed over her neck and back and cried out in agony as he slowly and painfully died.

When he was limp Mirraya dropped to her knees and wiggled out of his dead carcass. She hopped two steps back and stared at the lifeless Domitra. Mirraya then threw her talons into Compico's face. She ripped at it until it was unrecognizable as having once had form or function. At one point Toño considered trying to pull her off but decided the effort was not worth the risk. Her rage was justifiable and he was unlikely to shorten her wrath.

Hours later, a cleaned-up Mirraya rested, back against the wall aboard *Blessing*. Sapale, EJ, Toño, and Daleria sat at the mess table not even touching their mugs of coffee.

Finally Toño spoke. "Well, at least we proved they can be stopped."

No one, most noticeably Mirraya, responded. All eyes were concentrated on the cold coffee. All but Mirri's. They were staring off into some distant, unknowable private hell.

"The three we faced are among the tougher of the Cleinoids," remarked Daleria, trying to sound upbeat. "That's something to take into account."

"I supposed," replied EJ with an exhalation. "But it was not easy. It was hard, in fact. *Too* damn hard."

"But they *are* dead," responded Daleria.

"And so is Domitra," said Mirraya in a hollow voice.

"She died well," responded EJ. "She died fighting for the best of causes."

"But still, she's dead," whispered Mirraya. A few seconds later she continued morosely. "Run the numbers. Four of us to kill three of them. One in four dead. Multiply by one million. Oh wait, you can't. We don't have four million brindases. Five hundred, maybe. So we can rid the universe of six or seven hundred of them. Then they're free to do whatever they were going to do in the first place."

"Maybe we can find the antigods and enlist their help?" remarked Daleria with absolutely no conviction.

"Or maybe the antigods'll save their own asses and never give the remainder of life one single thought," muttered Mirraya darkly.

"Well what the heck else are you going to do?" snapped EJ. "Barbecue wharf rats and sell them to passersby?"

"That's nauseating," replied Toño.

"Then let's not. Let's kill as many as we can and plan on dying in the process." He harrumphed. "Universe won't be missing us old tin automatons, I can tell you that for nothing."

"I'm certain we'll think of something," reassured Toño softly. "We always do."

"No," Sapale said as tears streaked down her face. "*Jon* does. We follow him, but it's Jon who always thought of some harebrained scheme at the eleventh hour."

"Well, thanks for nothing," quipped EJ, "And you can forget that coming from me, because it ain't gonna happen. His magnificence is apparently not in our shared DNA."

CHAPTER EIGHTEEN

I was no *where* and I was no *thing.* I drifted in nothingness. That, unreassuringly, was all I knew. Around me was the perfect void. No light, no matter (or annoying neutral matter), not even any cosmic microwave background. I was immersed in the absence of existence. I could not see, because I had no eyes and because there was nothing *to* see if I did. The same went for sound, smell, and touch. You name it, I didn't have it. But since nothing to do with Jonathan Alan Ryan was clear-cut or reasonable, I somehow *knew* I didn't know, see, smell, or fart. Wash, rinse, repeat. If there was a pile of unresolvable doggy doo-doo riddle anywhere to be found, yours truly stepped in it one hundred percent of the time. Ah well. Lucky for whatever I was or wasn't at that moment, in the center of my reality, and until there wasn't any me left to ponder mysteries, I was a fighter pilot. Instead of floating there—or whatever—I was motivated to do something.

In the distance I noticed a light. It was weak, fragile, and wavering uncertainly. I moved toward the light. Of course, the minute I did, I kind of freaked out. I'd spent forever hearing tall tales concerning the recently departed *moving toward the light.* The finality of that process gave me the willies. Nearly stopped my in my nonexistent tracks. But again, as always, #fighterpilot kept me moving toward the damn light.

The closer I came, the more I took in what it was I approached. Thank goodness it did *not* appear to be a tunnel or portal. No motes of sparkle being drawn in and Granny Miller standing beyond the opening, extending toward me a lemon meringue pie in one hand and a cold beer in the other. There was no TV right behind the non-Granny with the Super Bowl about to kick off. What a *relief*. I wasn't about to dock with Heaven.

I neared a structure of light. Puffy clouds of light stacked to look like, I don't know, maybe the Parthenon. The form was rectangular with a definite opening and purposeful form in the columns of stacked clouds. The whole thing looked like a strong breeze would end it but good. I thought to myself, if self I actually was, who designs buildings in the void that can't stand up to a light breeze? JPS, if you ask me. Just Plain Silly.

Finally, I stood—or whatever—before the entrance. Gut check time. I'd read enough science fiction to know there were rigged passages out there. One-way traps you could enter but from which you couldn't depart. *No going back* leaped to mind. Then again, my day calendar was otherwise empty, so I drifted in. Honest to goodness, using the retrospectoscope, I'm not entirely sure I made the correct decision. Fortunately, Jon Ryan never suffered from remorse over decisions made. Oorah.

Inside I saw the reverse side of the cloudy blocks. They were—alert the media—the same as they looked from the outside. The vast nebulous interior was otherwise featureless. Not exactly welcoming or promising, but what the heck. In for a dime, in for a dollar. I proceeded. Naturally, as I did, forms, shapes, and walls began to materialize out of nothingness. Sure, made sense. Inexplicably bizarre needed to be punctuated with the stupefying. They went so well together. I passed chairs, tables, and a particularly uncomfortable-looking chaise lounge or British-made Chesterfield sofa. Bingo. I knew one thing now. Place was designed by a woman, female touch present and accounted for.

Just when I began to wonder why there were no residents zapping into existence—you got it—one zapped into existence not three feet in front of me. Talk about gender-neutral. The figure was humanoid; of course, in LaLaLand here, it wore a robe with a hood, and had facial features that were bland, generic, and hairless. This was not God à la Michelangelo as represented in the Sistine Chapel. That was an immediate relief. I was disembodied and disoriented, and hence not at my best. Whenever I faced God, I needed to be on my A-game. Yeah. Lots of *'splaining to do,* don't you know.

"Hi," I said cheerily. Not sure how, by the way, since I lacked the body parts to say anything.

"Hi back at you, Jon. It is a Jon Ryan I address, is it not?"

"Think so. Hang on a sec." I patted my non-body with my non-hands to see if I had any ID. Yes, I know, but in my defense I *was* disembodied and disoriented. "Beg pardon, are there more than one of me?"

"*Is* there more than one. No plurals in play, my friend. And yes. You yourself know of *two,* if memory serves."

"Yeah, technically, I guess."

"So, where the blazes am I?" said my possible host.

"Ah, Houston, we have a problem. *You* don't know where *you* are either?"

"No," it said with a faint grin. "I was anticipating the next words to exit your mouth."

"Ah. I see. You ... you get that often?"

"Often is relative here. Let's just say I've heard it more than other potential points of conversational departure."

"Conversational departure, eh? Look, is this a grammar place?"

"Nearly out of the gate you ask what zero have asked before. I'm impressed. And no, this is not a grammar place, though I would be loathe to accept bad grammar in any context."

"Okay, grammar place it is."

"You stand, Jon Ryan, in the Pillars of Creation."

I stared at him a bit. "No drumroll?"

"You've lost me already."

"No, it's just when someone proclaims *you're in the Pillars of Creation,* there should be deep echoes and thunder. Drumrolls may substitute, if the others are busy at the time."

"I'll bring that up at our next roundtable."

"You're welcome."

We both stood there silent a while.

I went first. "So, em, you got a name?"

"Pravil. My name in your frame of reference is *Pravil.*"

"Hmm. What's your name in *your* frame of reference?"

"There I do not have a name. I don't need one."

"What about in the context of your semi-regular roundtable discussions with your peeps?"

"Not certain this is a fruitful direction for our conversation to go, but I will, as you say, *go with the flow.* In our semi-*irregular* meetings, my name is whatever it needs to be."

"But not *Pravil?*"

He shrugged. "*Could* be Pravil."

"I see your point about fruitfulness."

"Thank you."

"And I never say *go with the flow*. Hate the expression. It's what high-school guidance counselors and inspirational talking heads say. And one's mother. Yeah, mothers everywhere tell their kids to *just go with the flow, Arthur.*"

"Your mother called you *Arthur?*"

"I'm probably not the one to ask that question."

"I see your reputation has correctly proceeded you."

"What's that supposed to mean?"

"It's supposed to mean, can we move in a *cogent* direction in our encounter? A rational, logical, non-Jon Ryan one?"

"I'm game."

"Now you're going to ask what you're doing here."

"I am? I was going to ask where the little boy's room was."

His once calm demeanor seemed to briefly stiffen. Wuss. "I doubt that very much."

"Okay, I'll bite. What am I doing here?"

"I have no idea."

"Gee, Mr. Wizard, I'm sure glad I asked."

"I am being *as* forthcoming as I can generate."

"*Grammar* place," I mumbled, pretending to make it a cough, fist covering my mouth and all.

"What did you say?" He seemed intensified if not hot.

"Say?" I coughed. "Ah choo, you know, pollen count's up and you sneeze."

"Hmm."

"So, how is it I come to be in *the Pillars of Creation* and a local employee does not know why?" I kind of boomed the place name. Seriously, if I could have controlled myself, I might have.

"You heard me when I said I didn't know. Your subsequent peppering me with questions has yet to alter my state of understanding."

"Let's take this one step at a time. Pravil, you work here, right?"

"If you can call it that, yes."

"I'll let that partial evasion slide. Pravil, you live here, right?"

"If—"

I cut that crap off. I was not in the mood. "Second obtuse answer accepted. Pravil, are you a religious icon, personification, or divine being? The designations *angel, god, demon,* or *politician* dance at the top of my list."

"*No.* That one I can answer emphatically."

"My gosh, headway. An easy, direct answer. Okay, what's your role here?"

"I'm ... from your reference point I'm a *facilitator.*"

"From *your* frame of reference, does Pravil translate into my language as *vague?*"

He started to respond.

"Rhetorical only. You are a facilitator. *What* do you facilitate?"

"Into the Pillars of Creation comes nothing and out goes something. I aid in that process."

"Nothing into stuff?"

"Yes."

"Do you have a boss, a supervisor, a majordomo?"

"Hmm, tough one."

"You're kidding. Stupidvisor, micromanager, slave driver with a Napoleon complex? You gotta have one or ten of those."

"In your frame, no. In my frame, least you overstress and ask, no."

"Then isn't the answer simply *no*?"

"Um, I could answer that, but I don't think doing so would advance your happiness."

"Let's roll with that. More angst I don't need, but okay. Here's a fascinating question. Into this domain comes nothing and out goes something."

"I believe we've established that."

"*Ah*," I snapped, "but here's the rub. I am *not* nothing."

"Let me say, without the need for further comment, that I would've preferred you not using a double negative. That said, your point is as stunningly obvious as it is true."

"Follow-up question. Do other not nothings occasionally enter here?"

"Hmm, kudos on a well-played logic series. No, from your reference frame, it has essentially never happened."

"Then why, Pravil, my good man, do you suppose that is the case?"

"I have no idea. I neither set the boundary conditions I labor in, nor govern what may or may not enter here."

"Excuse me. I heard sounds but no answer. To play back what I heard, I'd summarize blah, blah, blah blah blah, blah. Want'a take a second swing at that pitch?"

"It's not my job to know why you're here."

"That's more like it. The next question will require you to speculate. I insist you do so. Why do you *suppose* I'm here? If you respond that you don't know, I'll pin you to the floor and tickle you into submission."

"You lack arms to tackle with and fingers to tickle with. Yours is hardly a credible threat."

"Don't test me, Pravil. Many have and many have been unpleasantly surprised. Start speculating for all you're worth."

He wrung his hands briefly. "You appear to have been subjected to death."

"You should have seen the truck that hit me."

"Gáwar? I've not seen him and would rather not."

"You know of the beast?"

"I may reside in the Pillars of Creation, but I do get out occasionally. If I might continue?"

"Please do."

"After Gáwar pulverized you, you drifted in here. As you would in no way be able to drift, let alone persist in a conscious state, I can only conclude some force desires for you to be here."

"Some force? God? My guardian angel? My bookie to whom I owe a lot of scratch?"

"I'm going to leave it at *some force*. As neither of us knows, that'll be best."

"Okay, Sherlock Holmes, if some force wants me here, why might that be? What value can you provide me with?"

His arms spread widely. "Hello. Pillars of Creation. We offer ... all things."

"*Hot* damn," I exclaimed impiously.

"I insist upon your pardon."

"Oh, sorry. It's just that I get a do-over. Not every day you get one of those. Well, technically, I've had a few, four, five depending on how you count them. But, dude, I'm stoked."

"Is that a serious condition, this *stoked*?"

"It sure as he ... heck is if your name happens to be Gáwar." Although existing just then in an indistinct state, I nonetheless did a happy dance. I think.

"I tend to agree with your assessment. It is certainly within my power to reestablish you in your android form." He then grunted a laugh.

"What?"

"I guess I could regenerate you in any form, couldn't I?"

"You're not seriously asking me, are you?"

"I could even place you in your original human body if you'd like."

"No."

"That was a snap decision."

"Of course."

"Ah, yes, this fighter pilot thing I've heard tell of."

"No, goofball. Gáwar easily defeated the android me and would stomp the human one even quicker. I need bigger, stronger, faster."

His face shined like a lighthouse beacon. "You want the Six Million Dollar Man."

"You do get around, don't you?"

That brought a proud shrug, kind of an *oh-shucks* maneuver.

"So I need a body that can't be beaten. I need invulnerability, and I need it now."

"You want me to make you look like Gáwar but maybe give you, I don't know, a dart gun on your forehead that he lacks?"

"Have you seen a picture of Gáwar? I want to save the universe, but I don't know if I want to save it *that* badly."

"I'm kidding, Jon. Gáwar's power doesn't lie in his form."

"Oh yeah? He ever pound *you* into dust and debris?"

"His is an *inner* strength."

"Lord, you sound like a two-bit self-motivational speaker."

"No, I mean his strength rises from what's inside him. It is thus with all living things."

"*Thus*? Have you ever paused to hear yourself speak? People ... people haven't talked like that since Queen Elizabeth I."

"I'm not people, and can you please get over the obvious envy you have concerning my erudite form of speech?"

I wanted to punch his lights out. If I only had fists, arms, torso, and legs I would have, too. I'd erudite his butt.

"Before time expires universally, may we proceed?"

"What, now time's in danger, too? When am I going to catch a break?"

"I was speaking from frustration. Jon, if I made what you are in Gáwar's body, you'd stand the same chances as you did before."

"I find that challenging to lend credibility to." I'd show him.

"If you want to sound smarter than me, try not to end your sentences in prepositions. It's something up with which I shall not put."

"Who's drifting off target now, golden throat?"

"You're right." He sighed. "You do bring out the oddest side in people, don't you?"

"A gift's a gift."

He shook his head slowly, just the way Doc did way too often.

"Jon, I could return you to your reality in the form of an apple and you'd be able to defeat Gáwar. It is not how you *appear* but who you *are*. How you're perceived is important, too. But true power rises from the soul."

"An apple? Like a regular old Red Delicious apple? About yea big?" I held my cupped hands near each other.

"Yup."

"Is your supervisor present? I'd like to proceed with another head consultant."

"I'm not crazy."

"Crazy? Who said anything about you being mentally incompetent? I didn't mention dense, unschooled, out of touch with the real world, or stupid either. I just want a second opinion."

"Second opinion?"

"In the near term, please."

"I already explained that in your frame of reference, I don't *have* a supervisor."

"Oh yeah. Pooh. Okay, back to the apple. I could kill that monster even though I had no arms to strike him with? No legs to run?"

"Perhaps an apple wasn't the *best* analogy."

"Ya think? And what if I did win by making him laugh himself to death? Then what? I'm going to spend the rest of my life as an apple in the fridge? Waiting for fruit flies, worms, and Granny looking to whip up another pie? Not a bright prospect, dude."

"Forgetting altogether the apple analogy, let me press ahead."

"Okay, but if you suggest I reincarnate as a parrot or a hammer, I'm outta here."

"Where do you come up with these things? A parrot? A hammer? I do believe I'm getting a headache."

Served him right, wanting me to be an apple.

"Let us first decide what form you would *like* to take. Then we can get into specifics as to functionalities."

"And my options are?"

"Limitless. I wouldn't suggest Jack Benny or Popeye. The former's not imposing enough and the latter's a two-dimensional animation."

"Where do *I* come up with stuff? Sheesh. Look in the mirror, buddy. Ya see, this is easy. I want to return as I was. Good old android Jon. Only not refurbished. No, I want to be like I was right off the assembly line."

"All right. So just as you were when Dr. DeJesus first transferred you?"

"No, not even."

"Huh?"

"I didn't have all my toys and I didn't have my life experience. I want to retain those."

"Then what are you exactly asking for? If I guess, it might be you want an elephant trunk and then you'd go off on me. I don't need that."

"Calm yourself. No trunk. I was just thinking, if it was possible ... I'd—"

"It *is* possible, but not if you don't say it. So help me if you don't tell me pretty quick, I will put a trunk right where your nose used to reside."

"Do you drink coffee?"

"What?" he snapped.

"No, but if you did, maybe try enjoying decaf."

"What are you not—"

"I want my *sperm* back."

That shut the freakazoid up. He crossed his arms, pointed at me, and then recrossed his arms. Then he snickered. Such disrespect from a supposed professional. Within thirty seconds he was doubled over laughing. I seriously thought he was going to bust a gut.

Finally I had to defend my dignity. "You know I'm still here, right?"

"I ... I ... I do. It's ... it's just—" He broke into loud, uncontrolled laughter once again. "I can't im ... *imagine* what a two bill ... billion-year-old robot would want his ... his sperm b ... back for?"

"Are you *trying* to belittle me and hurt my feelings?"

"No, but it's pretty *damn* hard not to, with a request like that."

Yeah, fool collapsed back into a giggle fit.

"I'm not entirely comfortable with you swearing," I said to try and shut him up.

"Me, neither, but ... but ... y ... your *sperm* back. What, you want me to go through all past *epochs* and retrieve them one at a time?"

"That will not be necessary. A full complement of new sperm will be sufficient."

"Gosh, I mean *thanks*." After he snorted unbecomingly he asked, "Seriously, and no question about it, your wish is my command, but why that specific requirement?"

Make me say it. How uncouth. "A guy feels better about himself if he's firing live rounds, that's all."

"Okay, never thought I'd live to hear that, but no problemo. Anything else? A little taller? Maybe a chiseled chin or a Kirk Douglas dimple?"

"Now you're being sarcastic."

"I *am* not. I'm having fun at your expense, sure. But I'm not being intentionally *cruel*."

"Only accidentally so."

"Yes."

Son of a ... "Back to Gáwar. How am I going to be able to defeat him? I know you said inner strength and a dart gun, but I'm looking for specifics, not useless options."

He was serious again. "You must tell me?"

"Why. You're more ... more worldly."

"Why can't you simply say smarter?"

"I can. I just wasn't sure it was the best adjective."

"I'm so looking forward to not missing you."

"So I've been told. Why do I have to guess?"

"Those are the rules."

"No way. You just made that up this very second."

"No, honest to goodness. It's in the rule book. I can show you it if you really care."

"What can kill Gáwar?" I asked.

"There has to be something."

What would harm the big oaf? A pure heart? Faith? Bad breath? What would work when thermonuclear weapons, lasers, and brute force didn't? OMG. I freaking *had* it. I hoped I got a shot at Gáwar again. There was a tremendous gulf between the two of us. I had no idea if we could ever reconnect. But if and when we did, man-o-man, was he going to be surprised.

I looked at myself in the mirror Pravil whipped up for that sole function. I looked good. Even my hair was perfect. And he took the liberty to freshen up my jumpsuit to give it a more moderny feel, sexier.

"Pravil, you've done the Pillars of Creation proud."

"I'll make certain you get a survey so my boss knows how valuable I am to the team."

"You're the bad boy. I knew it." I wagged a finger at him.

"So, if there's nothing else I'll show you to your destination."

"Funny you should mention it. Say, Pravil, have you ever been on a business trip?"

"No, I can honestly say I have never been on a business trip. Why?"

"Well, when a guy's away on a business trip and he comes home, he has to bring his wife a present."

"Fascinating. But since you've been dead, not here on business, I'm wondering why you bring that cultural pearl up?"

"Well, I fight for a living. I died fighting. So, in a very real sense, this *is* a business-related trip."

"If it'll get you out the door that much sooner, I'll agree with you."

"Great. So the presents I had in mind were really easy-peasy ones, I mean for you that is."

"I can hardly wait."

I gave him my requests. He said he wished he could somehow forget my requests but he knew he could not.

"So, one last question," he said to me quite seriously. "I can send you anywhere, any when. But I can do so only once. Where shall I send you?"

Where indeed? If I went back to Godville to even the score with Gáwar, I could be marooned. Sapale and the others might have survived and made it home. Or maybe Gáwar killed them, too. In that case who cared if I was marooned? But if I went after Gáwar and my friends were back home, I'd never see them again. They'd never know what became of me. Wait, what was I hemming and hawing about? There was one and only one correct response.

"Send me to where Sapale is."

And I was gone.

CHAPTER NINETEEN

After their depressing debriefing following the fight with the three Cleinoids, everybody sort of went their own ways. Daleria said she needed to get some fresh air and left alone for a long walk. Toño busied himself at nothing in his lab. Tinkering helped soothe his wounded mind. EJ went to an unoccupied room and watched 1950s black-and-white TV shows. Mirraya-Slapgren went home with a final message to contact them if anything came up. *Blessing* and Al, well, who knew what they did, but they were silent.

Sapale stayed at the mess table. She clutched her long-empty coffee mug so tightly her fingers were numb. But she didn't notice. If she had, it wouldn't have mattered. She had never felt so alone, so sad, and so hopeless in her very long ...

There was a knock on the hull.

One, Sapale flashed on immediately, the portal was open. No one who needed to enter needed help doing so. Two, there was zero possibility of a stranger come a-calling. They were in the most secure isolation. Three, who knocked on a spaceship's front door? No one in their correct mind would. It wasn't Halloween, and door-to-door sales were a thing of the extinct past.

Sapale rose to see who or what was tapping at the portal. Add anger to her prior emotions. Yeah, she was going to flay someone in about three seconds.

I have absolutely no idea why I thought it was a good or proper thing to do. Why was I knocking at my own vortex's door? Dude, it was *my* vortex. But, in for a dime, in for a dollar. Why wasn't anybody answering? Someone had to be inside. I counted at least three thermal images through the hull. I knocked again, harder.

"Hang on," came the voice of my one true love. "I'll be there quick as I can to kill you several times ov—" She trailed off when she saw me. Then her face grew dark, very dark. Scary dark. "Why the hell did you change clothes, sneak out, and knock on the door? That is the *stupidest* lamest stunt I've *ever* seen you pull, and we traveled together two *billion* years, asswipe."

"Hi," I said uncertainly. "Honey, I'm home." I waved like an idiot. "It's me."

"Oh really? You are you? Thanks for the 4-1-1. There I was thinking *you* were *me*."

"Have I come at a bad time?" I mumbled.

"No. You came at all. I know Mirraya thought we needed you, but for the record I was dead-set against it. Thank you. You just reinforced the validity of my dissent." She attached her probe fibers to the hull. "Close portal."

"Yes, Form Two," responded *Stingray*.

The opening sealed instantaneously.

It then reappeared instantaneously.

"*Blessing?*" snapped a pissed wife of mine.

"Yes, Form Two?"

"I thought I was Form *One* now?"

"You were, up until now. By protocol, you are Form Two now that Form One has returned."

"Form One has returned?"

"Yes. Can you not see him? He stands zero point six five meters in front of you."

"He's returned from the dead?"

"That is not a speculation I can currently support or refute. I can only report that he is back."

"You might try saying *hi*," added Al.

"You're EJ, right?" Sapale said as her jaw dropped.

"I don't think so. Should I be?"

"You were a couple minutes ago?" She nodded her head over her shoulder. "Back in your quarters."

"EJ's here? Why the devil—"

"That *twice* I've heard my name used in vai—" EJ, like Sapale before him, trailed off. He stopped dead in his tracks, too.

"*Jon?*" asked Sapale in a whisper.

"I think so." I extended my probe fibers and retracted them. "Yup, it's me all right."

"But, but—"

"But I *died?*"

"Oh, you more than died. Way I heard it, that maniac Gáwar ate the tiny pieces left after he crushed you." EJ spoke with unmistakable relish.

"Ouch," I said reflexively.

"Tell me about it," he responded.

"Jon?" asked Sapale with a trembling voice. Then she jumped up and wrapped me up in a most pleasant knock-down bear hug.

"That'd be my cue to skidoo," said EJ with a one-eighty pivot.

"You replaced me kind of quickly, didn't you?" I teased as we tumbled on the ground.

She bit my ear—actually quite hard.

Five minutes later we were at the mess table with hot coffee. I took a sip. "Wow. Peet's Major Dickason's Blend."

She set her mug down. "It's a special occasion, Lazarus."

"I won't go as far as saying it's worth dying for, but I will say yes to a refill." I held out my mug.

"Pot's right over there," she responded without moving anything but her thumb over a shoulder.

"And thus endeth the tender homecoming," I bemoaned playfully.

"Oh, I'm not done celebrating with you yet. I just am not your handmaiden."

"Ah, no prob. If you could just point her out, I'll ask her to refill my mug."

She shook her head. "And to think I was glad to see you back. Silly girl."

"Hey, that reminds me." I reached into a deep pocket of my bitching new jumpsuit. "I got you this, you know, as a present."

She accepted the ornate box questioningly, with a dubious glance. "What's this?"

"A present."

"You have got to be kidding. What was your first clue?" She slowly tore the ribbon off and opened the box. She pulled out the figurine. "What the f—"

"It's *me,*" I said quickly, to cut her off.

"No. It's a tiny *statue* of you, which, by the way, I like more than the real you."

"It's in case, you know, I get killed for good. It's something to remember me with."

She glared at the porcelain. "I don't know what to say."

"Thanks?"

"I was thinking more along the lines of *I want a divorce.*" She set it down. "Then again, it is a gift from *you.*"

"Bar's pretty low, isn't it?"

"*Pretty,*" she agreed with a smirk.

I slid a golden locket across the table.

She picked it up and inspected it. "Exploding jewelry?"

"No." I smiled. "Open it."

She did. Sapale stared at the contents a good long while. "I don't get it. Two hairs? The statue was lame, but two hairs? You going for the world record here?"

"They're our real hair. One lock of yours. One lock of mine."

"Where did you get honest to goodness hairs from us? We've both been dead forever."

I frowned. "Hard to explain. I think you might want to drop it for the time being."

"For the time being? Why?"

"I thought I heard you say something about you not being done celebrating with me yet."

"Oh yeah. That I did."

An hour or so later the entire team was in the galley. Everyone had badgered me repeatedly to tell them how I could possibly be back from beyond the veil. I told them all I'd explain it once when we were all together. After I told them the story about Pravil and the Pillars, boy did I draw blank stares.

"Look, sport. If you don't want to tell us, fine," snapped EJ. "But even I wouldn't try and pawn off a cock and bull story like that one."

I shrugged. "What can I say? That's what happened." I fluttered my eyelids. "Which kind of leads me to the topic of *what in the name of sanity are you doing here?*"

"Unicorn skewered me and deposited me here against my will," he scoffed.

"Ah. Perfectly understandable."

"We needed him," said Mirraya as she strode through the portal. "Otherwise, he'd still be under his slimy rock."

"*Mirri,*" I exclaimed. "This just gets better and better."

We hugged as best one could with a golden-metal-scaly-ten-foot-tall dragon.

"Sorry, Uncle. There is no joy in Mudville," she responded.

"Where's Mudville?" asked Daleria.

"It's just a saying, kiddo," replied EJ. "She's letting him know gently we're up Shit Creek *sans* paddles."

"What? Does that run through Mudville?" Poor girl was idiomatically incapacitated.

"How bad is it since I've been gone?"

She looked me squarely and coolly. "Worse than that."

"That being?" I pressed.

"Whatever bad you envisioned before asking."

"Okay. We got a plan?"

"Yes," Mirraya replied.

"And it is—"

" The plan is to wait for you to tell us," Mirraya responded flatly.

"Oh, crap," I replied.

"You could say *that* twice," quipped EJ.

Mirri gave me the *Reader's Digest* version of their battle with the Cleinoids and whatever else I needed to know.

"I think my plan is to return to being dead," I mumbled to myself.

"Happy to help," beamed EJ cheerfully.

"Give me about half an hour. I'll get back to you," I said hollowly.

"*Mi tiempo es tu tiempo, amigo,*" he reassured.

CHAPTER TWENTY

"Verazz?" shouted Carol as she entered an empty cave somewhere in the Milky Way galaxy.

Aside from an impressive echo, her cry returned no acknowledgement.

"Where *is* that useless male when I actually need him?" she fussed out loud.

"I don't know," came a voice from behind her. "But I'd be willing to help you locate him, if sex was involved in the reward."

She spun to see Verazz there with a massive grin on his face. He was in an erect humanoid form. So were his genitals, she noted with some displeasure.

"Must you always?" she chided, rattling her forehead pebbles at his groin.

"Must I? *Nay*. Must I when you are about? Yes, I proclaim—"

"Put a lid on it. I'm here for an *important* reason."

He bobbed his eyebrows. "Can there be any other more critical to *life*?"

"You are so close to emasculation you would not believe it," she growled.

"Promises, promises."

She rattled her rocky bulk to the ground. "It would appear you're going on for a while. I'll sit, if you *don't* mind. I'll sit if you *do* mind."

"Poof," he said, casting his palms into the air. "There went the mood."

"I'm pissed."

"At me? How novel."

"Let me start over. I came to find you because I'm pissed. Please note temporally that I was in a foul mood *before* I made contact with you. Now, for the record, I'm doubly pissed."

"Do tell," he said, taking a seat on a nearby boulder.

"It's those damn Cleinoids."

Verazz said nothing. He did sigh loudly.

"I repeat. It's those *damn* Cleinoids. You have to do something about them."

He pointed a finger skyward. "Ah ah. You added to your thought content. And why is it *I* have to do something about them? Hmm? Are your offensive powers *broken*?"

"One, do not take that tone with me. Two, pray I remain only pissed at the rat gods and not *you*. Three, you are the *man* of the house. It naturally falls to you to deal with the invasion of pests. Everyone knows that. Four, I'm pissed."

"Excuse me, eternal bliss. How does point four factor into your argument?"

"It helps clarify how quickly and definitively you must act."

"Ah." He thought a moment. "What is it that they have done to vex you?"

"*This* time?"

"This time."

"You know that garden I planted a while back?"

"The one with," he waved his hands in the air, "all those sentient fungi?"

"Yes, that one. You know the forked toadstools were developing *quite* the sense of humor."

"That's not the way I heard tell. *Query: What's the smallest room. Response: a mushroom* is *not* funny."

"*I* giggled."

Verazz shook his head slowly. "What about your sentient garden do you wish to tell me?"

"The Cleinoids destroyed it."

Verazz stiffened. "They *what?*" The walls of the cave trembled with his booming response.

"Yes. They ruined *four* excellent days' work."

His face turned to stone—literally. "How *dare* they trouble you in the slightest."

"Then you will act? You will smite them?"

Verazz's face melted back to flesh. "Yes, I will."

"Then you do love me."

"Such was never in doubt."

"Shall I await your return here?" she asked with great anticipation.

"Er, no. I did not say *when* I would deal with the Cleinoid infestation, only that I *would*."

"Why is now not the best time to act?" she asked menacingly.

"Because ... because I'm busy ... otherwise occupied. *That* is why."

She craned her head side to side. Pebbles clinked. "You do not appear to be otherwise occupied."

"Well, I am. I just haven't thought of the *with what* part yet."

"Why are you stalling? I have been *wounded*."

"I know and I acknowledge your pain. It's just ... well, it's the damn *smell*. Once you kill a few of those Cleinoids, the stench stays on your fingers for *ages*. They smell like rotten cheese fermented with obridge droppings."

Verazz spun when he heard a pack of screeches behind him. It was a dozen flocks of terrestrial obridge, and they were all relieving their bowels as one. That is when Verazz noted that the floor of the cave beneath them had suddenly become Roquefort cheese that was oh so long in the tooth.

He turned back to Carol. She was gone.

"Oh, bother," he said to himself...and the obridges.

CHAPTER TWENTY-ONE

"You want to *what?*" barked EJ.

"Hey, y'all said you were waiting with bated breath and whispering humbleness for me to come up with a plan."

"Technically, *yes,*" responded Toño. "However, I was hoping for at least a non-insane plan."

"It's not crazy," voiced Sapale.

I proffered both hands in her direction. "See, my brood's-mate supports me."

"Crazy called and said it had an injunction. It will sue if its bad name is associated with Jon's lamo *so-called* plan."

"Okay," I replied, totally miffed, "then one of you haters tell me how *you're* going to save this universe."

"I don't have a solid idea as of now, but I know this much," spat EJ. "It will involve me staying in *this* universe to save it."

"I'm not sure I see the wisdom in returning to the Cleinoid base," Daleria said thoughtfully. "Can you convince me?"

"Wow, at least one team member can muster civility," I wheezed. "Look, you guys tried to fight them here. Ya barely succeeded. It's a proven fact in my book that if we dig in here and go toe-to-toe with the ancient gods we *will* lose. Ergo, the only logical choice is to fight them back on their turf."

"I'm not certain that's logical," responded Daleria. "Even if we wiped them out to a god back there, it would do nothing to stop the ones already present in this realm."

"Honey, a plan has ... phases. You execute part one, then part two. It's a logical progression."

"First off, Mr. Spock, stop using that word logic in the context of whatever comes out your piehole," slammed EJ. "I think the little lady's getting at the point that you can't complete phase *two* and then hope you develop a viable phase *three*. You get dead while standing there with your teeth in your mouth."

Daleria stood. She wasn't tall and she was thin, but she rose with authority. She jabbed a finger at me. "I am *not* honey." The digit swung to EJ. "And I am *not* a little lady. I am a Cleinoid demigod and I am angry. I am also an equal member of this whatever it is, so you will both show me respect or I will show you exactly what a Cleinoid demigod is capable of inflicting." She sat.

Sapale clapped loudly. "You *go,* girl. Right down their piggy little throats."

"Daleria," I said, lowering my head, "I'm sorry. You're right. I spoke in anger. Just because everyone I care about and respect was lambasting me, I shouldn't have struck out at you."

"You have the annoying habit of turning an apology into a victim-spiel," observed my wife of forever. "Return said gift for a full and complete refund."

"I know this much," I said, changing the subject back to serious, "if we give the bulk of the Cleinoids enough time, they'll find a way to get here. Then it will be curtains for sure."

"But why do you theorize we can kill them better *there* than *here*?" posed Mirraya. "They're just as strong there as they are here."

"Yes, and no. There, we have the element of surprise. Plus, we were able to use some of their magic against them. I'll bet we can do it again."

"Wait," said Sapale. "Now I get it. You just want to get another shot at Gáwar, don't you? It sticks in your craw that he killed you and you want to return the favor."

Wow, was she clairvoyant all of the sudden? "I will admit that taking Gáwar out would be the first order of business upon our return. *But*," I raised a finger in hopes it would distract my wife from being so spot-on, "that is only because he is so powerful. When *we* take him down it will demoralize *all* the Cleinoids."

"What, you think they'll offer their unconditional surrender when they see Gáwar's dead?" snapped EJ. "Your plan just gets thinner and thinner. If you keep talking much longer, it'll be invisible."

"*Man*, you are a Negative Nellie," I returned.

"Ouch, that really hurt," he replied.

"Boys," thundered Toño, "that will just about do it. We have no time for Jon-Ryan pettiness *squared*."

We both gave him such sour looks. Identical sour looks, in fact. Go figure.

"Let me take this step by step," said Daleria. "We return to their home. We somehow kill Gáwar. We fight more effectively and cull through the Cleinoids better then we can actually hope to do. What's next?"

"I do not know," I replied frankly. "I honest to goodness don't. But we'd have the wind at our back and we'd be making forward progress."

"Oh ca-ca-ca *crap*," sneezed Sapale.

"What?" I returned weakly. I didn't know where she was going, but I knew it was going to be Jon-unfriendly.

"Whenever you are reduced to your *football* analogies, I know we're in deep doo-doo. Most often *preterminal* deep doo-doo."

"Hey, football analogies efficiently convey enhanced meaning," defended EJ.

"So spoke the remainder of the peanut gallery," responded Toño.

"Okay, this is the point where I as leader call for a vote," I said resolutely.

"And then you do whatever you wanted to do anyway. Yeah, I'm familiar with the drill," responded Sapale.

"And who exactly anointed you leader?" pressed EJ.

"He *is* our leader. End of discussion." Mirraya spoke with passionate conviction. "We do not require a vote, Uncle Jon. We will follow your instincts. They have never failed us."

EJ recoiled visibly. Then he responded with vitriolic bile. "Well, he sure as hell isn't the boss of me. You want to go die in some foreign universe for no possible gain, then *screw* you all."

He walked out of *Stingray* and was gone. Where, I could neither guess nor care.

"Good riddance," said Mirraya angrily. "He fights well but is a net negative in spite of that."

"I only just met him and I agree," added Daleria with disdain. "La-hoos-*sher*."

"Uncle, you have already tainted the poor woman's speech. Surely her soul will follow quickly in kind." If Mirri could have grinned, I knew she would have.

"Who knows?" I responded. But quick enough I was down to business. "Als. You mentioned there was a finite limit to the number of passages we could make from our universe to theirs."

"Correct, Form One."

"What percentage have we expended?"

"Approximately sixteen percent. Perhaps as much as twenty."

"Plenty of wiggle room then," I stated confidently.

"Plenty?" questioned Mirraya. "I'd say *some*. When we're down to zero percent we're trapped one place or the other."

"Worrywart," I teased. Stuck out my tongue, too. "*Stingray*, put us in the same cave we hid in when we first met Daleria."

"No!" Daleria snapped.

"Belay that order, *Stingray*. Why?" I asked her.

"Just a hunch. I have to believe Vorc is pressing hard to find us. He may or may not know we left, but he will worry we'll do exactly what we are doing. If so, he might have found traces of your presence in the cave. There are many gods quite skilled at homing in on that very thing."

"Good point. Any suggestions?"

She thought for a few seconds. "Somewhere far from that region."

"*Stingray,* set a course for the Lower Chambers."

"Whoa, whoa," chided Sapale. "How's *that* safe?"

"Remember their society's in turmoil. No one's doing their jobs as before. The Lower Chambers is the last place any god would want to be."

"But what about the time differences? It may be long enough from now that Vorc has restored order," she responded.

"No, the time is fast here compared to there. A day for us is minutes, *seconds* for them. It'll be empty."

"Or at least we'll save them the trouble of shipping us there after we're caught." Sapale grinned grimly.

"See. Plus plus. Everyone's a winner," I shot back with a raising of my arms. "Calgon," I shouted, "take me away."

Nothing.

"*Stingray,* we're still here."

"Affirmative, Form One."

"Why? I said *let's go.*"

"No, Pilot, you asked a detergent no longer in production to sweep you off your feet. Sounds pretty twisted and kinky if you ask me." That Al. What an Al.

"*Stingray,* take us to the Lower Chambers now, *please.*"

A little nausea, then a lot of nausea later, we were there.

"I'll take a look around. The rest of you stay here," I said as I extended my probe fibers.

"Does that include me?" asked—you guessed it—Casper.

"How the devil did you find us so quickly? And do not say because you were always with us, because you weren't. We were in a different universe, a ghostless universe, which was *nice* for a change, by the way."

"If I can't say, you know, *that,* then I think I'll just say nothing."

"Uncle Jon, please introduce me to your associate," asked Mirraya with grace and courtesy.

"Mirraya, Casper. Casper, Mirraya."

"Very nice to meet you, ethereal spirit," said Mirri. "I hope we become fast friends."

"I'm sure we will. Say, did you know you're nicer than him?" Casper moved part of himself in my direction. Darn ghosty was still morphing. He'd come all the way from a nebulous cloud to a walking cigar, and now he almost looked humanoid. Almost. He was still disproportionately plump here and there.

"Why, yes, I did."

"Most people are," added Sapale.

"Casper," I said authoritatively, "the roast is over. Is anyone around in the Lower Chambers?"

"Just Tefnuf."

"Crapazola," I hissed. "What's she doing here?"

"She *lives* here."

"Figures," I responded. "Creepy ogre lives in a creepy dungeon. Is she nearby?"

"No."

"Good. Lucky break," I sighed.

"She's directly outside."

"*Membrane,*" I shouted. "Now."

The vortex thudded once.

"She got off one energy blot before we cloaked," reported Al.

"Damage report," I snapped.

"None."

"Place her inside a full membrane, then drop ours."

"Done."

"Now what?" asked Sapale. "She might be able to get out like that bitch Bethniak."

"Nah, Tefnuf's not that powerful. Plus she won't be around long enough to put a dent in her coffin."

"What do you mean?" asked Toño.

"I mean to kill her," I replied. "She knows we're back. Can't have that."

"What if she's already sent word?" asked Daleria.

"Then she'll be just as dead."

Daleria had a funny look on her face.

"What? Is there a reason I shouldn't cross her permanently off my Christmas list?"

"She will be missed," she responded.

"Not hardly," I tried to joke.

"Jon, listen to her," snapped Sapale. "She knows the locals' behavior."

"I can't release her. If she hasn't betrayed our location, she sure as hell will." I turned to Casper. "How about you? Any thoughts?"

"Vorc will know if she's dead."

"*And*?" I pressed. "I care because—?"

"He will know, Uncle. That is divulging useful information."

"But if she's inside a full membrane, won't he miss her anyway?"

"No, I don't think so," said Daleria. "I don't think that's how it works."

"How *what* works?" I said, with exasperation.

"The god thing," replied Casper.

"Okay, fine. You win. Als, seal her in a membrane, make it perpetual, and place a sensor to indicate if she's able to break out."

"Done, Captain," responded Al.

"Are the chambers otherwise clear, Casper?"

"Yes, I believe so."

I rolled my eyes. Belief I did not need. Hard intel, that's what I wanted. I officially hated working with ghosts.

"Come," said Mirraya, "let's get going."

Toño opened the hull and I stepped out first. Tefnuf's semi-invisible prison ball was off to the right.

I pointed at it. "*Stay*."

"Where are we going?" asked Sapale.

"First, we secure the building. In the meantime, Als, you two catch up on the bugs we placed. See what's going on. I especially want a 10-20 on Gáwar."

"10-4, Captain," responded Al.

"Could you ease back on the testosterone-talk?" requested Sapale. "It makes me crazy. Just say where's Waldo."

"Who's *Waldo*?" asked a confused Daleria.

"10-22 that," I peppered in. I watched Sapale cringe when I said it. Sweet. Not sure why, but it was.

It took us twenty minutes to clear the Lower Chambers. No one else was present. "Als, place monitors at all entry points. If anyone comes in I want to know about it."

"Roger that," replied Al.

"Any location on the big bad?"

"Not yet. We can report that things are basically the same as when we left. Dominion Splitter's still dead. Vorc is suffering withering criticism from all parties. Gáwar has been playing poorly with others and that further chafes the general population. It's looking like Vorc's reign will end soon and unfavorably for him."

"Good. Instant karma's going to get him," I responded.

We had a secure base, an unwanted prisoner, and not much else. Since there was zero tactical advantage in laying low, I made a quick decision. We were going ... somewhere.

"Mirri," I asked, "I'm not super clear on this. Can you still shapeshift?"

"Ah, goodness sakes, Uncle. How can you ask personal questions like that in public?"

"Huh?"

"We are ... joined. We are a visant."

"Huh?" I repeated.

"Uncle, it's sexual. We're ... engaged."

"Can't you disengage?"

"Yes, of course. But ... oh, you're impossible. It's very very private."

"Ah, *hello*. War zone here. No private secrets. Split in two or whatever now."

"Everyone turn your backs," Mirraya said softly.

"I don't think I have one," responded Casper.

"Give it your best, please," she said even quieter.

Thirty seconds later I heard the all-clear from Slapgren.

Yup, there they were, my two kids. They were old and graying, but they were my kids nonetheless. And naked. Nice.

Without my asking, they headed for *Stingray* to dress.

"We're going outside. You two need to look like Cleinoids," I said to my kids when they were back. "Between you and Daleria it'll provide us some cover. The rest of us'll have to rely on old faithful. Robes and hoods. Come on people, let's move."

"I think I'd look ... odd in a robe," said Casper. "Not sure it'd stay on either."

"Okay, you disguise yourself as a ghost."

"I can do that," he replied cheerily.

What a maroon.

We headed out. Mirri was a humanoid female while Slapgren was the funniest-looking quasi-octopus I could imagine. We made our way casually toward the staging area where Dominion Splitter had hung or whatever. I needed to make certain with my own eyes he was good and gone.

The promenade and field where DS was suspended was completely empty. Gone were the myriad of guards and onlookers. What a relief.

"I want to reconnoiter the lab where the neutral matter is fabricated," I announced.

"Do you think we can steal some more?" asked Toño dubiously.

"Probably not, but it sure would be useful."

"Good point," he mused.

I found out where all the guards that used to encase DS were. Yeah, they were swarming the fabrication building. Once bitten, Vorc was twice shy, it would seem. Crap.

"We've had a busy day," I said from our safe distance from the mass of Cleinoids. "Let's retreat to the chambers and set a plan. Daleria, you probably need some sleep, right?"

"Soon," she replied apologetically.

"Hey, I used to be the king of sleep. God I miss it. I consider you lucky," I replied wistfully.

It turned out Mirraya and Slapgren jumped at the chance for some rack time, too. We androids let them sleep all night long. We went over reports from the Als about the inside scoop concerning the Cleinoids. An interesting picture was developing. I think we actually knew more about the goings on than anyone else, including Vorc.

The current center seat was not just unpopular. No less than three factions were actively planning his removal from office with extreme prejudice. Two groups wanted to assassinate him quietly and privately, quick and clean. The third wanted to make a public spectacle of his gory death. They had an itinerary of horror laid out. They would start by locking him in a cage and subjecting Vorc to taunting and thrown objects. Act two was to be flogging until his skin was gone, then boiling him in some as yet undetermined liquid until he was done. They had imaginative notions of what to do to his remains, but those were too sick to even pass along. Man, I prayed I'd never be on the third faction's shit list. Dudes were seriously twisted.

The bottom line was that for the foreseeable future, no ancient gods were making the trip to our home. That was a relief. The Cleinoids, self-indulgent and detached as they were, actually hadn't recorded where Dominion Splitter came from or when he was acquired. So they had positively no idea how to obtain the services of another. Idiots were stuck waiting with their thumbs up their butts hoping a magic bus would show up to transport them. No educational system, no sense of history, and no interest in culture. These guys were sorry indeed.

The last report on Gáwar's location was several days old. He'd torn the crap out of a settlement not too far from the capital. The local gods apparently united to fight him, but still they lost. I guess I knew Gáwar was tough. He creamed me in zero time at all. But not the next time. I could hardly wait.

Once our sleepyhead members were bright-eyed and bushy-tailed, we had a powwow. I relayed what we knew at that juncture. Daleria had an unexpected question. "Who's involved in the three conspiracies?"

"What, you mean their actual names?" I asked.

"Yes. As many as you know."

I listed the names we'd gleaned by group. When I was halfway down the list on the second faction, she threw a hand in the air. "Festock? You said Festock, right?"

"I believe I did, yes," I replied, puzzled.

"Can you be more specific? There might be more than one."

"More than one god with the loco name of Festock?" I remarked aghast. "You gotta be kidding."

Al chimed in. "He is a three-legged spherical creature that can levitate. A bowling ball that flies."

"Yes, that's the one. I *know* him," she said energetically.

"And that matters because?"

"I know him. He's a good guy."

"The floating bowling ball?"

"Yes, *Jon*. Why is that so surprising?" she shot back.

I shrugged. It just didn't sound plausible.

"I've known him for a very long time. We basically grew up together. Then he chanced to move near my restaurant. Became a regular. Good guy."

"I know. You said that. Aside from being fascinating, do you have a reason for educating us as to his personal worth?" Maybe—*maybe*—I was being a little hard-nosed.

"Jon, I think I see where she's going here," said Sapale. "Lighten up, Francis." She raised a warning finger. "And don't anyone ask who Francis is. If you *don't* know you *won't* know."

"I need to spend some time with my old friend," said Daleria thoughtfully.

"Any conspirator against Vorc is a friend of mine," said Mirraya.

"Excellent idea," basically shouted Toño.

"Hang on," I began to say. "I think—"

"That someone else came up with a great idea and you're jealous," Sapale interrupted.

"I second that notion," added Toño. He had the most unwelcome smile.

"Shall I call the roll for a vote?" layered on Slapgren.

"Hang on," I defended quickly, "I want to hear where this plan of Daleria's is going. Dinner and drinks, or something that advances our cause?"

"Okay," she responded, "very reasonable, boss."

I gave her a look. "I'm not the boss. I'm the mission commander."

"The difference being?" asked Toño.

"I've never had a good boss. Never heard of such a thing. But all mission commanders are top shelf."

"Anyway," emphasized Daleria, "my notion is this. Festock hates Vorc so much he's risking overt insurrection. That's big here. I want to feel him out. Maybe we can work together against Vorc."

"I thought that's where you were heading," I responded. "Two big problems. One you probably thought of, and one I bet you didn't."

"Okay, smart mission commander," challenged Sapale, "what's the first?"

"Obviously Vorc knows that all of us are tied for being public enemies number one. I'm assuming that's a result of Gáwar's summoning. The fact that Vorc employed Gáwar to kill us reinforces that assumption. I know Gáwar doesn't have the civic commitment to take us out for the team."

"True, but I doubt very much Vorc told anyone else about his epic screwup. Gáwar wouldn't tell anyone, because his lifestyle is I-could-care-less," responded Daleria. "I do not think Festock knows anything about us. Plus, you're dead, Ryanmax. Use a different name and no one'd know the traitor was back, unless you ran into Vorc or Gáwar themselves."

"If I did, either one'd be dead before they could sound any alarm," I said flatly.

"So I chat up my old friend and see if he knows about the foiled rebellion. Either way, I win his confidence and we cooperate."

I nodded. "Sounds doable."

"That's a pretty terse assessment," said Slapgren.

"That's because of the second issue."

"Come on, you old goat," snapped Sapale. "What?"

"Sooner or later our mission will conflict with our possible cooperation with this Festock fellow."

"How so?" asked a concerned Daleria.

"One of us'll have to kill your old friend turned coconspirator."

Daleria paled. "Kill him?"

"He's a Cleinoid god. We need to kill all of them save one."

"Me?" she said feebly. She looked like she was about to hurl.

"If we succeed fully, you're the only one left alive. It's them or us, period." I let that sink in. "So when the time came, if it fell to you, could you slip a knife in his back?"

Daleria was white as a bleached sheet.

"She would," said Sapale. "I know her. If it fell to her she'd complete the mission."

"Let's hope it doesn't play out so we need to find out if you're right," I said as cold as ice.

"Jon, are you trying to frighten the girl?" pressed Toño.

"Because if you are, you're doing a good job," she scoffed weakly.

"This is war, bilateral genocidal war. I've fought in those before. The coming storm will bring out the ugly in everyone. That's a lot of not pretty. We'll all do things we never dreamed we'd have to, and there will come a point where each and every one of us'll not be sure we're capable of what needs to be done. Messy mess is on the doorstep." I quieted a second. "Daleria's a rookie. Those are generally the first to snap. No offense intended, peanut, that's just a fact. So I want you to picture yourself slitting your pal's throat in the middle of a pleasant conversation or leaving a satchel bomb in his home, knowing his kids are there romping with daddo on the carpet. Er, you come to a point where you don't think you can do that type of thing, tell one of us. It's better to abort a mission than to fail it. Either way people who weren't going to die will, but the numbers'll be less the sooner you act. You got that?"

Daleria's nod was barely perceptible. Good. She took what I'd said to heart. This wasn't a holo game with power crystals and reboots.

"So tomorrow you make contact with Festock. If he gives off any signals that don't pass the whiff test, we let the lead go. You clear on the parameters of engagement?"

"Yes."

"You and a few friends are planning to open a restaurant/club in a new area. Happens to be near where he lives now. Funny coincidence. You wondered if maybe he wants a piece of the action. Lead investor so far is me, Magilla. Tester," I pointed to Doc, "Headcase, Slick, and Scruffie are the others in the group." I'd indicated Sapale, Slapgren, and Mirraya. "You, you're still Daleria. Got that?"

She nodded. The color was returning to her face.

"Since Scruffie's a pro and easy on the eyes, she'll go as your BFF. She can get you out of trouble hasty quick if need be."

Mirri cracked her knuckles. "You don't want to piss *this* alpha bitch off."

Slapgren whispered a quiet, "Can I get an amen."

"Those that are staying behind are the backup team. They'll monitor the whole interaction. If it gets hairy, they'll bust in and set the record straight."

"Set the record—" Daleria began to ask with confusion.

"Backup'll kill everything that moves. Hopefully that doesn't accidentally include you."

Daleria's eyes saucered huge.

"War, peanut. They say it's ugly for good time-proven reasons. You ready?"

"Y ... yes," she replied.

"Then let's do this. Simage your old friend."

CHAPTER TWENTY-TWO

Vorc was reasonably confident he'd finally chosen an acceptable assistant. Since his (in retrospect) regrettable decision to fry Dalfury, he'd struggled mightily to find a replacement he could live with. *Live with* in this context was a euphemism for *not kill in anger almost immediately*. Hizzar might have been saddled with several less than optimal personal characteristics. But he was a hard worker, he was punctual, and he had no sense of humor or irony, qualities that plagued Dalfury up until his demise. The fact that Hizzar was technically a zombie accounted for those laudable traits. It also, less fortunately, brought along the issues of the smell, the ceaseless moans and groans, and the flies. The flies were really bad. Perhaps it was Cleonoid magic at play, but even if Vorc singed a massive swarm of the blood-sucking insects, another swarm appeared almost immediately. Maybe there was just a long queue of hungry pests waiting to get close to Hizzar. But he even took shorthand. It was amazing. Yes, Vorc would call the outer office and ask Hizzar to come copy down a dictation, and Hizzar would detach a hand and it crawled in to do the job. The rest of Hizzar was then free to continue to work at his desk. Plus, one hand drew many fewer flies than the entirety of the long-dead humanoid.

There came a squishy knock on Vorc's wooden door.

Vorc couldn't help himself. He cringed. What a nauseating sound. "Come."

Hizzar spoke, but he did so neither clearly, at a normal cadence, nor dryly. "There is a live body to see you, ssssir." Hizzar, as intensely as Vorc might coach him, could not suppress the interminable hiss when saying *sir*. When Vorc instructed him to lose the appellation—you got it—he replied *yes, ssssir.* What they said about old zombies and new tricks was a fact. The same applied to the live-body thing. It seemed to be a defining feature for zombies.

"Who is it?"

"I don't know, ssssir. Shall I ask?"

Approximately one thousand times Vorc had answered that query in the affirmative. Vorc foolishly hoped that if he did so, it would impress upon Hizzar the need to get the party's name before announcing them. A saying concerning *that* aspect of zombie intellect was still pending.

"Nooo," Vorc sighed, "just send them in."

"*Them,* ssssir? I counted only one."

"Then send them *in.*"

"Them, ssssir? I counted only one."

"Send the one live body in, pl ... please."

"Ssssir." He turned slowly so as not to disarticulate any parts or appendages and went to fetch the live body.

A full two minutes later Hizzar reappeared. "Your live body, ssssir."

Hizzar backed away to allow Nephelt to enter. The feline god of triumph did not take her keen eyes off Hizzar until the door was securely closed and then some. "Why did you send for a live body, Vorc?" she asked with piqued concern.

"I didn't. My newest assistant is fixated on the living, that's all."

"Little wonder. You know it's a zombie, right?"

"*He's* a zombie and yes, of course. Good help is hard to find. I'm going through an extended vetting project."

"So I've heard. You have killed more assistants than any center seat in memory. You are to be praised on your commitment to history."

Vorc tapped his fingers nervously on the table. Big mistake. Fast-moving little objects drew instant attention from any cat. Nephelt nearly leaped on the desk.

Vorc quickly set both hands under the table. "What brings you?"

"We need to talk."

Vorc growled in a low tone. Rapid-fire mistake number two. Cats respond poorly to low growls. She nearly leaped for his throat.

Vorc reflexively snapped a hand in front of his windpipe. He instantly regretted the rapid-movement thing again.

Nephelt slowly cooled. "Gáwar is out of control. As you know, he continues to ravage our land, as if it were Prime. You summoned him. You are center seat. You must end our suffering."

"Or *what*?" Vorc rallied to ask darkly.

"What do you think, brainless? You will be lucky to leave office alive, let alone in one piece. You will then become the newest, largest, and *ugliest* monument at Beal's Point. Any questions so far?"

"Are you threatening me?" He stood to his full height, clutching Fire of Justice in one hand.

"No, I'm apprising you to a reality you seem not to have noticed."

"Do you know of any specific threats to me or my administration? If you do, you had better tell me at once."

"*If* I knew of any and *if* I told you, I'd end up as miserably dead as you're looking to be."

"I'll warn you but once. If you withhold information, you will live to regret it."

"Possibly, but by my read of public sentiment, you won't be around to witness my regret."

"So that's it. You came to cast veiled threats at me?"

"I came to demand action. I came to impress upon you how passionately the rabble in the streets are feeling. Vorc, it's damn ugly out there. I've never seen it so bad, and I'm a very old cat."

Vorc looked down. "I know there are widespread calls for me to step down."

"No. There are calls to widespread your body like liver pâté." A thin wisp of saliva escaped her lips.

"And you have come for what reason? To taunt and lord it over me? To kick me when I'm down?"

A growl flared deep in her throat, then eased back. "I came to tell you. I want to go to Prime. I want Gáwar preferably dead but definitely gone. Many feel the same. If you do not act soon, others will act." Without a further word or courtesy, she whipped around and sprang out through the still-closed door. She wanted to leave a reminder of her passion with her idiot center seat.

CHAPTER TWENTY-THREE

Daleria indicated that Festock's immediate reaction to her message was a lukewarm cordial type. Since the stakes were so high, I pressed her as to the possible ramifications of his less than ebullient response.

"So he used to be more open, more friendly?" I posed.

"Oh, yes. That was a subdued Festock."

"Any hint as to why?"

"No, and I paid close attention to just that aspect."

"As to getting together, he agreed, but was it a friend-location or really neutral open ground?"

"I'm not certain. When we were younger, we'd carouse like kids do. Later he came to my restaurant. We never agreed to meet anywhere, so I'm not sure if this is a defensive move on his part."

"Are you familiar with the club?"

"No."

"Then I'm guessing he's being cautious. He either suspects your motives, or he's just hyper-vigilant because he's up to his ears in conspiracy juice."

"I'm hoping it's the latter."

"You know what my pappy always used to say."

"Stop that, Jon, you'll go blind," interjected Sapale.

"Besides that. Hope for the best but plan for the worst. We'll set this up like he's going to double-cross you but leave him plenty of room to warm up to your sudden return to his life."

"That sounds ... ah, difficult," responded Daleria.

"No, don't let it be. You be charming and engaging. If he hiccups incorrectly, Mirraya will incinerate him. No big deal."

"I am not *fond* of incinerating strangers, Uncle."

"Practice makes perfect. It's only the first few rash acts that give one pause. Pretty soon you'll be as callous and reflexive as me."

"Oh, now there's a non-goal to cling to," Mirri responded.

"In this first meeting, make certain you don't mention Vorc, Gáwar, or disenchantment with the political realities facing the Cleinoids."

"Why?" Daleria asked.

"No subversive of any worth would tip his hand on so life-threatening a secret. If he dangles it, he's fishing."

"Fishing?"

"Seeing if you'll take the bait. If he mentions it in passing and you profess an undying passion to make Godville a better place, he'll know you're trying to set him up."

"Than *he'll* do the incinerating," added Mirri.

"You'll never see it coming," I agreed.

"Okay, this sounds like fun," replied a nervous Daleria.

"If at any point you experience a feeling of fun, Mirraya here'll kick you under the table."

"Even more to anticipate with glee," she responded.

"You'll do fine. The first few meetings'll be a breeze. This only gets interesting if he decides to take you into his confidence," I reassured her. "The best way to see that he does is to express no interest in the politics while seeming concerned about Festock's well-being."

"Won't he be suspicious if I reappear from his past and demonstrate a significant and consistent concern for his well-being?" she pressed.

"No way," I grunted. "He may not be a man, but he's male. When a pretty girl is blowing smoke up your butt, no male ever reaches for a fan. There's no cure for testosterone poisoning."

"I do believe Sapale's correct," Daleria responded with a frown.

"Yes," my mate added quickly, "he *is* a pig."

"A realistic and seasoned pig. Okay, you two get going. Remember, no politics and don't sleep with him on the first date."

"You are an *intolerable* pig," Daleria added.

"No, just sayin'. Stringing him along is the best way to get him to open up to you. Remember, he's male."

"And on that note, they left, while throwing up in the backs of their throats," announced Mirri. Gotta love that dragon.

CHAPTER TWENTY-FOUR

Festock sat in the center table of the expansive nightclub/bar he asked Daleria to meet him at. Her first impression was that it was, by far, the most conspicuous spot in the room. Obviously, Festock wanted to have their reunion be most public. That already betrayed a bit of paranoia. Not, she reflected, a good sign. She was happier than ever to have the very lethal shapeshifter along riding shotgun. Daleria flirted with aborting the entire mission, but then calmed herself down and went ahead.

Festock raised one of his three pencil-thin arms into the air and waved her over. "Dally, over here," he called out in his nasal voice.

He once told her his species was the Lud. Their origins were from a planet named Sessalian. It was a slimy, hot, jungle world, hence their spherical shape was ideal. Falling was common, so having no angles or sharp edges helped minimize injuries. He aways said his voice sounded funny to others because the atmosphere of Sessalian was more dense than most places. That made the pitch unnatural when he spoke in thinner air. Hearing him again, she was reminded how hard she had to try not to laugh at his speech when they were kids.

"Festock," Daleria said as she leaned in and pecked him on one cheek. His round mouth was huge. That made Daleria aim carefully so as not to seem to be romantically kissing him on the lips. "Good to see you, old friend."

He set all three arms on his chest. "Old? Why I'm *half* your age, old lady."

They both chuckled at his remark.

"Sorry, Jiju," she said, resting the back of her hand on Mirraya's, "that's an inside joke. Festock here is so old no one actually remembers his age. He might even be from the early times of our universe."

"Ah," Mirri replied neutrally.

"Festock, this is my good friend Jiju. She's the one Clinneast referred to as Scruffie. When I told her I was going to meet you, she said she simply had to come along."

Festock extended two arms. Mirraya bumped him with both hers as Daleria had instructed her. "A pleasure to meet you, Jiju. That name is not familiar to me. What are its origins?"

"My actual name is inexcusably long. I've long since contracted it down to just Jiju. Trust me, I'm doing the world a favor."

"Ah," he responded with some stiffness in his tone.

"Dally, are you two lovers?" he asked pointedly.

"No, you big beach ball. You're still always trying to marry me off, aren't you? Can't I just have a *friend*?"

"I suppose. But you're not a child any longer. It's time you settled down, got married and squirted out a family."

"Yes, *Mom*, so you've told me for the past millennium. I'm simply not ready." She nodded her head. "Maybe I never will be. But you know what?"

"You're happy, and that's all that counts," he replied approvingly.

"Yes." She turned to Mirraya. "That's what I have told the busybody for years. He says the words but doesn't mean any of it."

"You a fan of marriage, Festock?" Mirri asked with little interest.

"Why, yes, I *am*. I have fifteen wives and three hundred twenty-four loin-spawns."

Though he was totally alien to her, Mirraya saw the proud look on his face. "Wow, that's ... that's a lot of loin-spawns," Mirraya sort of gasped.

"And even more loin-*spawning*," teased Daleria.

"Really, child," he responded, "such talk in public." He gestured around the almost empty room. "What rumors you will start."

"No, the rumors I start are much juicier than that mundane aspect of your life," she replied with a grin.

"Last I heard you had a restaurant up north," he stated, changing the subject.

"I still do technically. I'm on an extended vacation."

"The two of you," he said, pointing an arm at Mirri. "On a long *non*-romantic vacation?"

"You are *such* a slime ball," Daleria snarked.

"Yes, I am. Why do you feel the need to say it?"

"Because where I come from a slime ball is a bad thing."

"Where I come from it's the *typical* case."

They chuckled in a restrained, polite manner.

"And you, what are you up to nowadays?"

"Me?" He again rested his arms on his chest.

"No, the centaur standing behind you. Of *course* I mean you." He was way too en garde for Daleria's liking.

"I guess you could say I'm semi-retired. Yes, that's it. Semi-retired."

"But you never *did* anything to retire from, you lazy-assed globe."

"Hey," he protested with some vigor, "I'm an artist. That's *real* work, I'll have you know."

"An artist? Since when?"

"Since always," he responded, miffed.

"What art form are you the master of, if I might ask?" Daleria was truly interested to learn.

"The art of living well. In my case it's elevated to the art of living *perfectly*."

"That's an art form now?" she responded incredulously.

"Yes it is."

"Any of your work in a gallery or available for purchase?" asked Mirraya politely.

"No, my art is internal, not external."

"Might you give us an example or two of your artistic prowess?" asked Daleria with a wicked grin.

"Yes I might. For years I've taken a nap at four o'clock every afternoon."

"That's lazy compulsion, not art," shot back Daleria, playfully.

"No, that's not where the magic comes into play. Now I nap at 4:05 every afternoon."

"Uh huh?" throated Daleria.

"Don't you see? I used to stress over finishing whatever I was doing by 4:00 p.m. on the dot. Now, since my nap's not scheduled until 4:05 p.m., I don't stress. I mean, I'll nap a little after four. If I don't check the time I won't know I'm off schedule."

"And you call that art?" asked Daleria dubiously.

"As they say, it's in the eye of each beholder," responded Mirraya.

"See," he pointed to Mirraya. "*Some* people are art lovers."

"Yeah, whatever," dismissed Daleria. "So you loin-up spawn and nap. That's it? How can one retire from such inactivity?"

He tapped his head/body near its top. "It's all up here, my dear. That, too, is art."

"Oh my *gosh,* you're amazing," Daleria wheezed.

"Thank you."

A golem came and took their orders. Mirraya and Daleria ordered first. They requested some small plates and delsta, a sparkling light intoxicant along the lines of prosecco. However, Festock requested only a small drink, suggesting he wasn't planning on lingering very long.

After the waiter left, Daleria asked, "So what do you do with your retirement time, when you're not creating great art, that is?"

Festock passed from stiff to openly fidgety. He repositioned his napkin several times and rearranged his cutlery twice before responding. "Not much. I try to take long walks. They say those are good for one's general health."

Good for the health of an immortal? Mirraya recognized that as an evasion, not an answer. "What rank were you slated to egress with to Prime?"

Daleria shot her a quick questioning glance.

Festock seemed to melt a little. "Beg pardon?" he managed to groan.

"What rank in the egress were you supposed to join? It's a rather straightforward question if you ask me," Mirri responded coolly.

"I ... I don't recall asking," he replied almost inaudibly. He pulled out his handheld device, nearly dropped it, then set it back in his pocket. "Will you look where the time has gone. Dally, I hate to eat and run, but I must." He stood so quickly his chair toppled backward to the floor.

"I was scheduled for Torment," stated Mirraya.

Strain was evident on Festock's face as he labored to understand why she felt the need to mention that factoid.

"I'm actually quite upset," she added when it was clear he was not going to respond.

"I'm ... I'm sorry to hear—" He leaned his entire body to one side. "I'm sorry, why are you telling me this?"

She gestured to the recently vacated chair on the ground. "Have a seat and I'll tell you an interesting story."

"No thank you. I really must—"

"My brother departed with the first, and it appears to be the only rank to be able to leave."

"Your brother?" he mumbled.

"My dear brother. He's an idiot. That's why I feel the need to pass along my sad story."

Festock visibly trembled. "I'm sorry yet again. Your *dear* brother's an idiot?"

"Yes, top-notch."

"Ho ... how does that reality intersect with my plane of existence?"

"Perhaps you know him. Gorpedder?"

"Everyone knows him." He looked uncertainly at his chair, then back to Mirraya. "Your brother?"

Mirraya angled her face. "See the family resemblance?"

"I suppose so, now that you mention it."

"Here's my point," Mirraya said as she stood, uprighted his chair, and gestured that he be seated.

He sat reluctantly.

"Gorppy has as much functioning brain matter as one would presume an aggregation of boulders to possess. I asked Vorc if I could switch from Torment to Rage, you know?"

"I didn't ... excuse me, *how* would I know that?"

"You might have heard the rumors. Anyway, Gorppy and I have always gone on transheavals together. Every single one. Do you know why?"

"No, I clearly do not."

"Because he's an idiot."

Festock toiled with that seemingly impenetrable non sequitur.

"Don't you see? I accompany him to protect him. A fool like my dear brother is quite likely to get himself killed rampaging and wrecking."

"Ah."

"Since I am clearly present, you can see that Vorc denied my request. He offered some gibberish about pace and order, fairness to the whole not the parts. In any case, my brother is almost certainly going to die and I sit here idle, waiting for the bad news." Mirraya's face became steely with anger. "Do you know how that makes me feel, friend Festock?"

"How does it make you feel?"

"Uncharitable toward our current center seat."

CHAPTER TWENTY-FIVE

Our universe was infinite. By definition, no one place was distinct or unique from any other. That said, if there was a backwash, a lost cause, the actual middle-of-nowhere kind of spot, the planet Drivel was that exception to the laws of nature. It was a hot, barren world with little water and only a thin atmosphere. It was also the residence of the most dull, inarticulate, and foul-smelling race of sentients ever. *Ever*. The locals called themselves the Drivel. Yes, the creatures were so unimaginative that they took the planet's name for its own. And mind you, the reverse was not the case. Such a sad, inadequate lot.

After the Drivel evolved from the muck, they naturally entered their version of the Stone Age. Though it took them fifty-five times longer than any other comparable species to do so, they finally passed into the equivalent of the Bronze Age. For the dreary Drivel, that was the living end. They put down cultural stakes so deep and so numerous that they never even conceived of, let alone welcomed, an Iron Age. Thank you very much, they'd have said. Bronze was way better than stone and we're good. Don't let the societal-stagnation door hit your butt on your way out.

Similarly, they never advanced from the hunter-gatherer

nutrition scheme like any respectable fellowship. Drivel imagination, as paltry and sparse as that oxymoronic term was, didn't allow for the expenditure of effort if immediate results were not rewarded. As long as there was anything edible out there, no Drivel of Drivel was going to plow a field or milk a cow. The very thought was abhorrent to their DNA. Work hard for food one might produce down the road, at a later time? Mental vomit, that was what they'd label such a notion. In fact, the proof, the nail in the coffin of the Drivel's lack of motivation and industry, was their reproductive rate. Genetically, the females could produce an offspring every six months, give or take. But many females never gestated. Copulation was too much bother for both them *and* the males. Even, and please excuse the potentially mature nature of the anthropologic disclosure, they rarely masturbated. Yeah, even that was too ... laborious.

Imagine, if you will, the introduction into that pallid civilization of three ancient gods. The brothers Trace One and Trace Two, along with their companion Bingo, chanced upon Drivel during their extended romp of pillaging and destruction. Trace One was a god of excessively poor taste. Think velvet glow-in-the-dark Elvis paintings [https://goo.gl/Jb2reR] or 2 Columbus Circle, New York [https://bit.ly/2DsPtJb]. Blame Trace One. Trace Two was *the* god of anything sent by public conveyance that became lost. His picture should have been in every dead-letter office in existence. Bingo was the god, not of a game favored by elderly ladies and played in church basements, but rather of forced labor. Go figure. Of the trio, he was the surliest and most disagreeable, by far.

As the team approached Drivel, they collectively salivated. This was a planet so disorganized and unsophisticated that the only resistance would be with rocks and sticks. Well, those and a handful of bronze swords, but those took industry to produce, so were in short supply. All other worlds they had ravished put up a decent defense. There were even a few occasions that they were lucky no god lost his life. But Drivel and the Drivels were a complimentary dessert buffet.

They stuck together after landing. They generally split up, but the pickings were so blatantly rich they actually suspected an ingenious trap might have been laid. No culture could be so incompetent, so inept as this one seemed to be. Boy, were they mistaken in their cultural over-generosity.

The three walked tall, shoulder to shoulder toward the nearest grouping of hovels. As basically stick people, for Trace One and Trace Two the tall part was easy. What they lacked in visual presence they made up for in meanness and ill-will toward others. It wasn't until they stood in the center of Village that anyone seemed to take note of their anomalous presence. The name Village was given to the place because it was too fussy and laborious to name any village as anything other than Village. All of them were so dubbed.

Trace Two raised his pencil-thin arms and shouted, "Fear and worship us, mongrels of Drivel."

Slowly that announcement drew a sparse crowd. Perhaps a third of the adults in Village bothered to answer such a seemingly provocative summons.

Bingo screamed in rage. "Who among you is the leader? That person will be the first to die." He then laughed the laugh insane gods were supposed to laugh.

The assembled rabble looked amongst themselves.

"Speak, worthless scum. Who leads you?"

Clumbford, the least witless resident of Village, responded. "No one is actually the leader here. Er, we once had one, they say, but no one seems to recall the specifics. I certainly don't."

"Well I guess that makes *you* the leader," snarled Trace One. "*You* will be the first inbreed to suffer our endless wrath." Trace Two stepped as threateningly as a stick figure could toward the hapless Clumbford.

As he neared his prey, someone called out, "Now hang on."

Bingo located the objector. He pointed a stick finger at him, for he was a stick figure, also. More a stick-wolf than a stickman like the brothers, but inexcusably thin, nonetheless. "You beg for mercy for your kin, you lumpen? Well, there will be none. His soul is mine and yours will soon be mine." He sounded actually quite evil and credible.

Trace One advanced again.

"Ah, wait, what are you thinking?" responded Forlor. The second least witless Drivel spoke up again. "I have no objection to you desouling brother Clumbford there. It's just that if he gets to be our leader so easily, *I* want to be the leader instead. It ain't fair appointing him boss over me without my getting a crack at it. By the by, what are the perks of the office?"

"You get to be the one who dies horribly *first*," replied Bingo.

"That's not much, but it's something. Any other less consequential benefits?" asked Forlor thoughtfully.

Bingo looked to his brethren in confusion. He shrugged at them.

"No, you base fool. We kill you, we eat you, and you are no more. What bonus could you possible imagine as a result of our consumption of you?"

"Are you *kidding?*" yelled Babbél, a younger male of Village. "There's lots of gravy associated with you eating Clumbford. Forlor, too, for that matter."

The brothers three began to shoot each other furtive, nervous glances.

"Name *one* dividend, citizen," challenged Bingo.

"Citizen, is it? How dare you. I'm as uninvolved and complacent as the next guy. *Citizen* my mother's grimy ass."

"Huh?" said all three Cleinoids as one.

"But that's a separate matter, you insulting me," snapped a haughty Babbél. "If you eat old Clumbford, he gets one over on the rest of us. Yeah, what, you three so stupid you don't think we all know you all know why?"

Due to weakness in his knees, Trace Two sat down.

"You have tested the patience of an ancient god and you have lost. You will *forever* suffer because of your impiety," screamed Bingo. The veins on the sides of his head swelled to a larger diameter than his neck. He charged Babbél.

"No, you have to *stop* him," howled Grandles, an elderly female of Village. "Eat *me*, not these lazy males."

That stopped Bingo dead in his tracks. "I am confused," he wheezed. "I hate being confused. Why does *everyone* want to be eaten instead of *anyone* else. Are you all daft?"

Forlor stepped forward. "You serious?"

"I ... I think so. Yes. *Yes,* I am. Why do you welcome death?"

Babbél looked to Forlor, who glared at Grandles. She opened her arms in confusion toward Clumbford. The population as a whole was incredulous.

Forlor continued. "Look, none of us welcome death. What ... what kind of slackers do you think we are?"

Bingo, ever vicious of the tongue, was about to ask how many types of slackers there were, but fortunately thought better of it in time.

"If you eat, say, Forlor there," he gestured to which Forlor he was discussing, "he doesn't have to go hunting and gathering to eat."

Bingo sat next to Trace Two, mute as a rock. Trace One was able to stammer, "I ... if I ea ... eat th ... th ... that male, y ... yes he need not ... not labor t ... ttt ... to eat. I will gr ... grant you tth ... that."

"See, you *do* get it," beamed Forlor.

Trace One crumbled to the ground by the other two.

"If anyone's getting a pass from gathering bitter nuts and unripe fruit, it should be *me*," exclaimed Grandles. "I'm the oldest and most withered occupant of Village. I forbid you scoundrels from favoring *anyone* over me, you scalawags."

Trace One was able to respond weakly. "What if we promise in advance to eat every single one of you. Will that be okay? Is that fair?"

"Yes," agreed Bingo. "No one will be left alive when we're done horrifically demolishing Village and stuffing everyone, *in their proper turn*, down our throats."

"No," decried every resident present.

"What would it take?" pleaded Bingo.

"Well, I suppose you could eat us all at the same time. That way no one would have a leg up on anyone else." That was Forlor speaking. Second least witless, remember?

Trace One staggered to his feet. "Now *that's* just unfair. It's unreasonable, arbitrary, and frankly preposterous."

"What?" Grandles asked snidely. "You young fellows look like you have proper appetites. Are you some of those analrexic people we heard tell about?"

"Auttie, I keep telling you it's *anorexic,* not analrexic. The condition has nothing to do with rectums. Get over rectums," chided Sallas, heretofore silent but overburdened by the elderly female's misuse of language and potty preoccupation.

"No," protested Trace Two. "Why, just last planet I ate six *thousand* groveling trolls in one *day*." He smiled at his companions.

"So eating us all together, so as not to show favoritism, will not be a problem," stated Forlor.

"Come *on,*" Trace Two whined. He slipped fingers on alternate sides of his mouth. In as funny a voice as one would presume given the contortion of his lips, Trace Two said, "Wook at my mouf. How bib do you shink it is?"

"Look, the young and the moronic," snapped Grandles, "my patience with your excuses and physical inadequacies is over. If you can't do one little act so as to make our hideous consumption bearable, I suggest you get on your high horses and leave."

The threat piqued Bingo's sense of wrath. "Or what, old female with such a small brain yet large a mouth?"

"Or else? Lords and *lice,* you three are dense. If you don't agree to eat us at the same time and you don't bug off we will, to a male, female, and child, kill ourselves." She allowed that warning to sink in. "Yeah, sure, you can pound down rotting corpses all day long, but it won't be bothering any of us."

"*No,*" scoffed Forlor in agreement, "we'll all be dead so who'd care, you big bullies?"

"B ... bu ... but you ... you'd all b ... be dead," Trace One stuttered yet again.

"What kind of pitfall is that supposed to represent, losers three?"

shot back Clumbford. "We're dead and gone, so could care less, and we're all relieved of the burden of hunting, gathering, and listening to fools like you."

As straining of credulity as it might have been, the inhabitants of Village gathered there together in a semicircle facing a trio of monsters and performed an act in concert. They all turned, bent over, and displayed their bare rumps to the Cleinoids.

"I think we should leave," said Trace One to his brothers.

"Yes, definitely, and soon," agreed Trace Two.

"Me first," shouted Bingo. "If we ate any of these wackos it might get into our brains."

They popped to their skinny feet and exploded from Drivel, never to return to it, but cursed to never forget it.

So much for the mighty Cleinoids.

Or, wait, maybe the Drivel of Drivel were not the societal incompetents they might have had you believe?

CHAPTER TWENTY-SIX

"I always knew you had a pair of steel cojones, but hot diggidy dog, you're a badass," I exclaimed.

"Anyone else accusing me of having testicles would already be dead, Uncle Jon."

"Then I'll assume you love me good," I responded with a huge smile. I pointed at Mirraya as I looked to Sapale. "My little girl made the round ball blink. She forced him to accept her."

Sapale rolled all four eyes. "I know. I was sitting here with you when she told us what happened."

"But I mean, *dude*," I marveled.

"Uncle, it was not that bold a move," Mirri replied. "If I scared him off, I scared him off. It wasn't like he was going to turn *us* in."

"Yeah, but I'm glad I sent someone who could think on her feet. That was brilliant. He's about to blow you off and you crack open his shell."

"He actually *has* a shell," said Daleria. "Please don't be so gross. I may want to eat again some day."

"Learn at her feet, Dally. I said keep away from politics, and Mirri here bends the bull's horns by doing just that."

"First off, don't call me Dally. Festock does and I hate the name.

Second, it's kind of like you don't give me any credit. I might have secured his allegiance my own way in my own time."

"Daleria," I began, "it's okay to learn from a master. You don't need to defend yourself."

"I suggest you drop it," said Toño to Daleria. "It's impossible to alter the course of his mind normally. When he's agitated, as he is now, it's even harder. Let it be."

"I will. You were impressive, Mirraya," agreed Daleria. "You molded his behavior like a clay urn."

"One does not grow to my age after having been schooled by Uncle Jon without learning to master the art of imposing one's will on others." She nodded toward me.

"Roger that," I said, mostly to annoy Sapale with more military slang. "So you secured a second meeting. Where and when?"

"He said he'd simage me."

"You sure that's not a don't-call-me-I'll-call-you?"

"No, he was serious. Serious and cautious," replied Mirri. "I say a couple days, three at the most. He'll want to seem in no hurry, but I know he would love more support. He was needy that way."

"You think —" Daleria started to ask. The question evaporated under Mirraya's withering stare of incredulity. "A couple—three days tops. I agree."

"In the meantime, we'll listen in on Festock's every movement, including bowel ones. You got that, Als? I want every detail of his life. If he's a double agent I don't want to walk into a trap."

"You're coming next time, too?" queried Mirraya. "Might that be too much too soon?"

"Time's critical. We're fighting a war on two fronts, in two universes. I want maximal pressure applied wherever possible."

"What if the fellow balks?" asked Toño.

My response was to drag my thumb across my neck. "No second thoughts, no witnesses."

Three days later, Daleria got word to meet Festock in a different pub than before, not particularly near our mutual location. He said to be there in an hour. Dude was taking no chances of us laying some kind of trap for him. He was undoubtably there already with eyes watching every possible angle. I'd have done the same. When it comes to one's own death, one can't be too careful.

Before we sat down with him, I had compiled a detailed and completely cohesive picture of Festock the sphere. He was what he purported to be: A serious conspirator inching his way toward the elimination of the leader his group hated. As for the names of his coconspirators, I was fairly certain I knew all of those, too. He naturally had to clear it with them before bringing anyone new into their cadre. There were five others working with Festock. Four of them checked out fine. The fifth one, a woman named Bellicity, was a bit too nebulous for my liking, and no, she wasn't a cloud-being. I just couldn't pin down many details on her past or her present. I didn't welcome that obscurity. I told the Als to really dig deep into her situation. I would have used the expression *drill down,* but, seriously, I've always hated that group-think term. George Orwell's soul preserve me.

Festock was seated at the most obvious, public table in the pub. Totally front and center. He wanted to be plainly seen and potentially heard. Smart move for an arch-conspirator. His eyes did bulge a bit when he saw I was with Daleria and Mirraya. His pulse picked up briskly and he began sweating. Good. Amateurs reacted that way under pressure. But he remained seated and kept a pleasant expression on his face.

"Festock," Daleria began very directly, "this is Clinneast. He is a very old and very trusted friend of mine."

He extended a thin arm. We shook.

"Nice to meet you, I hope," he said obliquely.

"No hope or prayer required," responded a confident Mirraya. "Clinneast is both a powerful man and like-minded, as we all are."

"What kind of name is that?" he asked. "I don't believe I've ever met a Clinneast."

Oh, it's a contraction of Clint Eastwood, dumbass. "It's an old family name," I actually replied. "My father was a Clinneast and his mother before him."

He got such a cute dazzled look in his eyes. Nice. Always keep the enemy off balance.

"Ah," he mumbled. "So, *Clinneast,* why is it I've never heard of you?"

"That's a question I can't answer," I replied as smugly as I could. "Why is it *I've* never heard of *you* until a week ago?"

That brought a nervous grin to his oval-shaped mouth. "Point taken. Perhaps we are both simply private individuals?"

"Seems that way," I answered unhelpfully.

"I assume you are a kindred spirit, based on what we three discussed the other day and your appearance today. Are you their leader?"

"Let's call me first among equals. All three of us have lives to lose and families to endanger. Hence we all have a similar say in what we do."

"Very prudent."

"Festock, I'd just as soon not beat around the bush, if you take my meaning. We have been planning a rearrangement of power in this glorious land of ours. We will do so by first rearranging the atoms currently ordered in Vorc's body. There. I've said it. Are you similarly inclined?"

After a significant pause, he spoke in a hushed tone. "I am."

"And when the center seat is vacant, whom do you envision occupying that sainted spot? *Yourself,* maybe?"

Another long silence. "No. I do not seek power, not in that sense, anyway. Since you ask, do *you* see *yourself* at the center of the table?"

"Most definitely not. I hate Vorc. I want him ... I see forced *retirement* as a pleasant prospect for the jerk. Past that, I'm happy to follow. *We,*" I gestured to the women, "are all followers to a fault."

"To a fault? Hmm. That doesn't sound promising."

"How so?"

"If no one seated at this table wishes to sit at that one either, who *will* fill the power vacuum?"

"I assume you're not working alone," I said while studying my glass. "Perhaps someone you trust *does* covet such an important position?"

"Perhaps?"

"How many are you, your band of like-minded citizens?" It was time to see if he'd openly lie.

"Several."

"As there are plainly several of us," I bantered back.

"But there might be more who couldn't make it on such short notice?" Festock remarked.

"I will be completely honest. Our cell numbers *six*. Us three, her mate," I pointed to Mirraya, "mine, and my oldest friend."

He studied my face. Lots of luck with that undertaking, fella. I ate and shat out people like him for brunch.

Finally he responded. "I work with *five* others. I'm certain you'll understand I can't mention names or positions just yet."

"I did."

"Yes, I suppose you did, didn't you?" That gave him pause. "But I don't know their actual names or locations, do I?"

"Clinneast," I patted my chest, "Scruffie, Daleria, and Headcase." I indicated the women. "Tester and Slick round out our play group."

"How odd it would seem that I've not heard any of those names, aside from that of my old, dear friend."

"You know what? I'll give you the names as a sign of trust. You keep yours as a sign of respect on our part."

He fumbled nervously with his glass. "Fine, fine for starters, that is."

"Do you have any specific plans that are in any way active?" asked Mirraya.

"I'd rather not ... er, *no*. Not presently."

"Neither do we," said Daleria. "Obviously, at some point action will need to take place. Can't have a coup d'état without a head on a pole, now can we?"

"No. Obviously." He was right about done at that point. Physiologically and mentally the dude was spent.

"I suggest we part company for now," I said softly but forcefully.

"One of us'll contact you in a few days to firm up some actual details based on our individual intelligence."

"*That* is agreeable," Festock replied with relief. Stupid rookie conspirator. Who needed them?

"Until then," Daleria raised her glass, "to success."

Silly old Festock was too drained to respond. He just returned a weary half smile.

CHAPTER TWENTY-SEVEN

Vorc sat behind his desk and he worried. No, he ruminated, he obsessed, he languished in vexed cogitation. He had lost control, respect, and was about to add his mind to that list. More importantly, he had come to the rational conclusion that if he were anyone but Vorc, he'd kill Vorc, several times over, if possible. He'd done that bad a job as center seat, as a Cleinoid, hell, as a living breathing lump of flesh. The fact that he was still alive indicated to him he served a society of absolute incompetents. Yes, any wise and concerned citizenry would have long since assassinated Vorc. Why had someone not? What was *wrong* with his people? Maybe, instead, it should be *Vorc* killing all of *them.* They were so unworthy of existence, it sickened him. *Someone please blow my brains out and do it quickly,* he railed in his troubled head. One almost had to feel sorry for Vorc, were he not otherwise so unredeemable and contemptible an individual.

Ni, his latest assistant, entered without knocking. Ni was literally the bottom of the barrel in terms of office helpers. She was a slime mold. She layered a few inches up from the floor, spread over two or three feet, depending on her mood and the room temperature, and she was of a surly disposition. How could one blame her? She was not given one of the easier assignments in life, in terms of physical gifts.

"Today you have accomplished nothing," she began in her bubbly, oozy voice. "Yesterday you accomplished less. You performed negative work yesterday. I am ashamed to work with you, if what you avoid so adeptly could be called work."

Vorc set his face in his palms. "You work *for* me, not *with* me. You are not a coequal. You are a gopher."

"I am not a rodent. I am a fungus."

"No, I meant *go-for* in that you get me things and do tasks. A *gopher*. Everyone knows that. Where were you raised? Under a rock?"

"Yes."

He peeped through his fingers at her. "Why are you here?"

"I work here; sad to admit it, but there you have it."

"No I meant here, as in *in my office berating me at this moment?*"

"Ah. You have a visitor."

"An *appointment?*" he attempted to clarify.

"Not to the best of my knowledge. You don't have any."

"A friend?"

"Not to the best of my knowledge. You don't have any."

"A drop-in?"

"I'll show them in and we'll find out. Won't that be fun."

"No, wai—"

But Ni was gone. She quickly returned with Bethniak. The child was not wearing her typical garb. No frilly dress, no multiple petticoats, no parasol. She was in a one-piece black body suit and her face was rubbed in charcoal. She looked like a play-toy version of a Navy Seal.

"Are you armed?" he asked.

"Do you see a weapon, moron?" She twirled to show there was no hiding anything in her clingy outfit.

"Isn't that a bit ... I don't know, wanton and lewd an outfit for a child to wear?"

"I'm not a child, pig fart. I'm older than you. If anyone so much as smiled at me wrong, I'd pound them to mush. Any further questions or thoughts?"

"Not a one. What can I do for you?"

She shrugged. "Die?"

"Then you are here to kill me?"

"Not worth the bother. No, I'll let everyone else claw over the others for that dubious honor."

"Then why are you here?"

"Hmm, let's say that I'm here to say goodbye."

"Are you going somewhere?"

"No, pinhead. Vortex is dead, thanks to you."

"Am *I* going somewhere?"

She shrugged again. "I'm guessing hell, and I'm certain about Beal's Point."

"And since I have nothing to lose, I'll just ask. *Why* are you wearing ninja garb?"

"Ready for a rumble." She shook her torso. "Easier in this getup than a girly dress."

"I'll take your word for it."

"Or I could lend you one. Might be small but, heck fire, you'd sure turn heads."

"No, thank you."

"Suit yourself." She rested back quietly.

"So you came to wish me ill as I involuntarily head into the afterlife?"

"Yeah, I guess so. You're not nearly as dumb as you look, you know?"

"Thanks."

"Don't mention it."

"Ebib."

"Say again?"

"Ebib. I mumbled something meaningless, born of frustration and depression."

"Ah. So, see you never, loser." She popped to her feet and started for the door.

"Seriously? That's it? You actually came to taunt me so morosely?"

"Yeah, I guess so."

"That's beneath even you."

"No it's not. *Nothing's* beneath me. Oh, say hi to your idiot mother and idiot father when you get to the bottom of the pit of fire, will ya? Tell 'em I don't miss them one little bit."

"Nothing *is* beneath you."

"One last thing, sweetie. I haven't changed these clothes for two weeks."

Vorc recoiled. "That's revolting."

"And I'm not wearing any underwear."

"That's the grossest thing I think I've ever heard."

"Mention it to the parents when you hook up with them. They deserve holding that thought forever, too, because they spawned you."

CHAPTER TWENTY-EIGHT

The more I learned about Bellicity, the more I grew suspicious. The Als didn't uncover anything incriminating, but they also didn't find anything that didn't smell of a good scrubbing with a powerful detergent. Squeaky clean plus. Either she was the god of the Girl Scouts, or she was covering up an important set of truths. Either way, I was going to find out her story. If she was playing any kind of game, I'd delete her from the Cleinoid gene pool faster than you can say Darwin. I knew I had a past history with getting very dark when the killing got too intense and frequent. That said, I was going to see this fight through to whatever end fate held in store for me. If my sanity was yet again a casualty of war, so be it.

"Al, you're a tricky and despicable jerk," I chided him one afternoon. "Why can't you find out what Bellicity is hiding? No way she's more clever than you, right?" Yeah, goad him a tad. Might help motivate the overpriced tape recorder.

"Pilot, we have several thousand bugs tailing her, with her, and ahead of her wherever possible. I am honestly coming to the conclusion that her poop does not give off a foul odor."

"TMI, Al. What about her contacts? I'm talking family, mailman, butcher's next-door neighbor—everyone she touches."

"My word, Captain Obvious, why didn't we think of that? Your circuits once again top ours. We cry a mental uncle."

"Sarcasm is the last refuge of an unprepared mind." What did I just spout? Drivel.

"Yes, we know. We're hoping to stoop down to join your level of intellectual bliss. With practice and application, we'll make it this century."

"You're as funny as a crutch, Al."

"Ouch. My wound, it will never heal."

"Is this mental diarrhea of yours interfering in any way with your main and mission-critical task, moronovich?"

"At our combined compilation rate, no. At one one-thousandth of our joined speed, not even close."

"I'm so impressed. May I be your friend?"

"Are you two simpletons about done?" Sapale harpooned us. "This is by far the most pathetic banter you've offered up in forever. It's *lame,* on anti-steroids."

"Hey, I resent that," I defended weakly. "I don't think I've ever been sharper, more eviscerating."

"Yes, but that only adds to my aggravation. Your best is weak cheese, meat."

My but she was rude. I had half a mind to tell her just that.

"Maybe we should make a separate contact with Bellicity?" Sapale asked, changing the subject to rational.

I rubbed my chin. "Nah, too risky. If either Festock or she learned we were new buddies to the two of them, they'd bolt."

"So?" she challenged. "I think this operation is looking to be fairly low yield. If we screw it up and are forced to clean a small mess, I doubt it would matter."

Interesting take on her part. What was the maximum gain I hoped to pull down? If our combined forces took down Vorc, were we much further along in our war against the Cleinoids? Maybe. If we were taken into the confidence of the new world order, we'd be privy to any new attempts to egress to Prime. That was something. We'd also be in a position to disrupt their plan. Then again, realistically, the cabal was more likely to fail miserably, and we'd be lucky to escape with our hides. Until I eliminated Gáwar, we could be exposed at any point. Even that useless Bethniak knew me on sight and hated me enough to out us by attempting to kill me. I let Sapale know my thoughts.

"We can see where this leads us for now," she concluded, "but keep in mind we need to keep our roots shallow and our ears open."

"Agreed."

"As to Bellicity, we're going to have to live with some uncertainty as far as she's concerned. Hell's bells. This is a murderous conspiracy. Those are never without high intrigue, right?"

"Lord, you're sounding literary today."

"And?" she snapped back.

"And that can't be a good thing. Just saying."

"You ... you like those teeth in your mouth?"

"Yes. Why do you ask?"

"Then don't ever say that again." Ah, the war growl. I loved that one of hers the most.

A week later I had Daleria message Festock we needed to meet. This time I set the time and place. I made it very isolated and two days down the road. I wanted to see how he'd react to those uncertainties. Hell, I kind of hoped he wouldn't show and we could be on to whatever our next move might be. Sapale's uncertainty about this entire gambit was growing in my mind. But, he arrived on time and with one of his partners in crime. I'd asked him to bring one as a further test and on the off chance he'd bring Bellicity.

No such luck. Festock brought along a truly funny-looking compatriot. Yeah, in this screwy universe, that's saying a whole heck of a lot. Aaaverd was not male or female. Aaaverd was *trisexual*. No, I didn't press Daleria as to what that actually meant. It sounded bad enough, without a full anatomical explanation. Anyway, Aaaverd's pronoun was not he, she, or it. Nope. Too easy. It was *we*. Jerkwad spouted off like royalty, an editor, or someone with a mouse in their pocket. I needed neither of those in my life. Of course, the fact that *we* looked like a pregnant capybara with bat wings didn't jump *we* to the head of my gotta-be-buddies-with list. *We* smelled as funny as *we* looked, to complete the grim picture. Now, my mama always told me not to judge a book by its cover. But my mama was never confronted with Aaaverd.

After quick introductions, I spoke for Mirraya and Daleria. "So, does your group have a specific plan, a realistic way to eliminate Vorc and seize control?"

"My, you don't beat around the bush you referred to last time, do you?" replied an unwelcoming Festock.

"Don't rightly see the point," I said in my best Captain Malcolm Reynolds imitation. It ... it just came out, so help me.

"What if the tables were reversed?" Aaaverd hissed through his overbite. Whistled way too much like Mr. Busy the Beaver in Disney's 1955 animated feature *Lady and the Tramp.* [Curious? *https://www.youtube.com/watch?v=vNDFy3zoBGE&t=104s*]

"Meaning?"

"My associate wonders if *your* alliance has any specific plans as of yet," clarified Festock coolly.

"I seem to recall asking first," responded Mal's channeled spirit. "That counts for a consequential amount in my estimation."

"I'm sorry," Festock responded. "What did you just say?"

"You blink first or I'll arrange things so you don't do much more blinking ever."

"Is that ugly creature *threatening* us?" squealed Aaaverd.

Festock started to reply. I stopped him with a hang-on-a-second finger. "Friend, a threat's what might happen if you don't react properly. What I announced was a statement of fact. Be advised that considerable is the difference between the two in terms of your short-term well-being."

That's when Mirraya kicked me very hard under the table. She apparently was not a huge *Firefly* aficionado. No accounting for one's taste in 21st century Earth video.

Festock fortunately rallied. "I take your point, Clinneast. There's no need to expand the issue into a crisis. We have no specific plans.

Our general intention is to take advantage of Aaaverd's unique skill." He gestured to the large rodent.

Aaaverd disappeared then instantly reappeared.

I could not help myself. I snickered in the back of my throat so hard snot came out my nose. After a quick swipe of my sleeve, I said with considerable disbelief, "That's it? Dude can be *invisible* and you hinge an assassination plot on ... on—" I pointed at the smelly pest. "On him being hard to *see*?"

Festock was not an immediate fan of my critique. He more or less exploded. "That's *enough*, you reprobate. I have never, Daleria, been more disappointed in an old friend or a new acquaintance. Please make certain you never contact me again." He stood to storm/roll away in a righteous huff.

"Ah, care to hear *our* plan before you depart to the promise of quick and complete failure?" I said softly.

That froze him. Unfortunately, it stopped *we*, too. They both begrudgingly sat back down. Cool. Now all I had to do was come up with a credible plan that they couldn't possibly kill us after hearing and reproduce easily themselves. You know, it was at times like these that I become an interested third-party observer as to what the heck was about to come out of my mouth next.

"Yes," Festock replied tersely.

"I do have to say, as an *homage* to my friend here," I flipped the back of a hand at Aaaverd, "it does include, if not fully rely, on invisibility."

He ground his teeth together in what I took to be a threatening manner. Color me scared.

"Yes. I was noodling with using a cloak of invisibility, but, hey, the real deal's even better, am I right?"

"A *what?*" coughed up Festock.

"He said an invisibility *cloak*," responded Mirraya. She mimed placing a sheet over her head and shoulders. "Surely you've heard of them?"

Festock trembled with uncertainty. "Ah, a cloak, you say? I

thought ... I thought he said a *coat*. No such thing. But a *cloak*? Of course I've heard of them. My cousin used to own one a while back."

"Do tell?" marveled Mirraya, who was thoroughly enjoying herself by the way. "Whatever became of your cousin and his cloak?"

Festock giggled like a fool. "They disappeared." He slapped the table lightly, which was George-McFly-body-language annoying. "They ... they *both* disappeared."

"Imagine that," sighed Mirri. "Such an unanticipated twist of fate."

Festock sobered up like he'd been gut punched. "I was speaking in jest. No need to invoke Fate." He seemed genuinely miffed. This universe was officially weirder than mine.

"Back to our initial thoughts," I prompted.

"Yes. Proceed," Festock said, still quite put off. Jerk.

"We have learned the cycles of the changing of Vorc's staff and personal guards." I looked left, then right, then left again. "All twenty-*five* of them."

Festock was stunned. "He has that many guards? We ... we seem to have seriously underestimated that number."

"Per *cycle*, mind you. There are three cycles, and a reserve for public appearances and PTO, naturally. That's over a hundred and fifty total."

"PTO?" Aaaverd whistled.

"Personal time off," I responded incredulously, mixed with a big scoop of scorn. "The individual guard employees will have personal needs for time away from work. Family milestones, medical office visits, and vacations to name a few."

"Vorc's guards need to go to the doctor?" puzzled Festock. "Wh ... why would *immortals* need to go for medical care?"

I tented my fingers on my chest. "Hey, don't shoot the messenger. I have no idea either. I'm just passing along our intel. Any data is good data."

Aaaverd slapped Festock's nearest arm. "Why do gods need doctors?"

"We ... we simply," he pushed all his hands in my direction, "don't know. It's as baffling as it is true."

"There, you see our input has already been of invaluable help to you," purred Mirraya. "And I'm thinking there's more where that came from." She kicked me again, but much softer. It was a *fun* kick, not a *mad* kick. Personally I wasn't very fond of either.

"Anywho," I continued, "knowing the rotation times and patterns has shown us there is a distinct and repeated opening for hostile intrusion into Vorc's—" I stopped abruptly. I looked left, then right, and then left again. "Into Vorc's personal space." I shook my open palms toward them. "His *personal* space."

"We can access his personal space," repeated Mirri proudly. "Can you imagine?"

Festock's thought process was clearly trailing behind ours. "Hmm. I think I see, er, *hear* where you're going." He pointed at the center of the table. "So if you can be alone with Vorc at a predictable time, you could don your cloak and kill him with no one being the wiser?"

"Sure." I shrugged. "Why not?"

Aaaverd was inconsolably pissed. "*Why not?* Is that your plan, or do you mean why *isn't* that your plan?" Perceptive little puke. Spoiled my damn irony. That, I'll have you know, sure pissed me off. Always did.

"Are you attempting to be ironic, my little friend?" I challenged.

"If he is, he'd better be careful," Mirraya said to me, with some panic in her voice. "I've seen you react to irony and rhetorical machinations once too often for my liking."

"I am *we,* not *he,*" protested the buffoon. "Please do not insult *us*."

"But ..." Mirraya trailed off inexplicably. What an improv diva.

"But nothing," I snapped at her. "He's a *we*. Yes, he's a *wee* we, but that doesn't make them a him. *You're* in big trouble when I get you home."

I could tell Daleria was about to wee wee herself, she was struggling so mightily not to burst out laughing.

Odd, seriously. I could be so inappropriate at the most incautious of times.

"Friends," called out Festock loudly. "There is no need to anger ourselves or find contention where there is such a potential for harmony."

What he said, about harmony, wow. Made me hate him even more than I did before. PC-speak was the surest way not to my heart, but to my sidearm.

"Look," I grumbled, "I think we've done enough for today." I glanced at everyone present. Okay, I intentionally did *not* glance at Aaaverd, because I knew *we'd* feel the insult and I loved it. "Let's break for now and pick this up later."

"Sounds wise and prudent," agreed Festock.

Oh, yeah. *Wise* and *prudent* on top of *harmony.* Dude was itching for a double dose of whoop ass, wasn't he?

"I don't *like* you," Aaaverd shouted while pointing at you will never guess who.

Yes, Mirri said it. She was such a shit disturber. Of course, that was one of my favorite qualities in her. "He doesn't like you. I don't like you either." [https://www.youtube.com/watch?v=yVKySA2-47c]

"Please," appealed a frustrated Festock, "let us adjourn before non-retractable words are uttered."

I just glowered at Festock. What he did to language was wrong, plain and simple. Grrr.

CHAPTER TWENTY-NINE

EJ was uncertain where to go or what to do. After ditching the desperado losers who were too damn goodie two-shoes for him, he had no real plans. Good, he reflected. Footloose and fancy free. The way God made him. Of course, then he groaned internally for having in any way invoked that deity. Of late, his opinion of all-powerful beings was slipping from zero to negative values. Who, he reminded himself, needed any of them?

Still, there was something IOJ had said. Yeah, Idiot Other Jon had mentioned antigods. What the hell were those? EJ'd flown from one side of this galaxy to the other. He'd seen a lot of strange stuff, but he'd never seen anything to make him believe there were any all-powerful beings controlling events. There was no mysterious energy that controlled his destiny. It was all a lot of simple tricks and nonsense. He was a trained witch. He'd know, right? Calfada-Joric taught him everything there was to know about magic, and she never once mentioned antigods.

Still, he'd kept her books on his ship after she died and he went his own way. Wouldn't hurt to look the term up. He'd scanned most of the tomes, but some books he'd never actually studied in detail. It beat doing nothing or, worse yet, ruminating on how much he detested IOJ. He put his ship in deep space, far from any possible interruption, and set about to research the antigods.

EJ started with Cala's favorite reference, *Tobin's Mystical Guide*. Tobin was generally unreadable, but Cala maintained he was authoritative. If nothing more, EJ'd get a much deserved nap from trying to go through the material. Of course, he gritted his teeth yet again, the book's table of content and index were useless. Anti-*dote,* anti-*conjuring,* anti-*warding,* and anti-*septic* were cited, but no anti-*gods*. That would have been too easy.

Under "Gods" he found listings of origins, limits to power of, assigned versus earned powers (WTF, he thought), and how to address and reference, as well as relative strengths. There were even citations concerning the Cleinoid gods. But no *anti* ones. Yeah, why make a source book user-friendly?

Then he wondered. If the Cleinoids were afraid of the antigods, wouldn't that mean the antigods were powerful? Tobin did purport to rank potencies. Okay, he'd bite. Under God(s), relative strength(s), there was an almost endless list of obscure or unpronounceable names. Gods or groupings included Figgiform, fragmentary, Harrusametical, non-repeating, Stone Witch, vetimaniacal, war, and, reassuringly, Zeus. Had to list the big guy to be comprehensive. EJ didn't find a simple table of comparative strengths. No, that would have been helpful in sections concerning, ah, *rank-ordering their power.* He was reminded why he never did the book-learning thing like Cala nagged him continually to do. Instead, he had to suffer through multiple separate chapters that might, if he was quite lucky, compare two or three ancient gods' strengths.

Maybe it would be hard to rank them, he conceded. Their powers were often so different, how could the potencies be graded? He learned, for example, that the Becobate Gods active during the Uifery Inclusion were very good at smiting. On the other hand, the mud god Fn-Aneal-To of Kalistra was the best mixer/swirler. Did the Becobates smite better than Fn-Aneal-To blended? Who knew? Who possibly cared? Certainly not EJ. He was ready to blow his brains out. He wished Cala were there so he could kill her for making him ferry these cursed books across the galaxy. Burning was too good for them.

EJ put *Tobin's Mystical Guide* back in deep storage, along with the rest of Cala's precious books. He did so with a glee Tobin himself would have resented. Jon then set a course for the nearest planet with dive bars and loose humanoid females. Lots of both. He needed to work off a bad case of academic overload. Ferrocaril, the lucky planet he was about to support the economy of, was an hour and a half away. No use expending his limited magic or his irreplaceable impossibility-drive to get there any sooner. He could do ninety minutes.

Jon opened his holo files. He'd collected an impressive number of movies, serial shows, and documentaries over the years. Though he'd seen many, there were still a lot left to discover. What was he in the mood for? John Wayne World War II classics? Nah. Porn? Um, no need. The real deal was just about close enough to reach out and touch. Reptilian dance? No, never. He flashed from screen to screen, growing more bored and agitated with each passing suboptimal option.

Stone Witch. He kept coming back to the term. He'd never heard it before that day. Stone Witch. Tobin cited them, but every specific reference ended with *actual facts and characteristics are unknown*. The text mentioned the title a lot, but it was crystal clear Tobin knew next to nothing about the Stone Witches other than their name. How very odd, even for an über-nerd like Hieronymus Gladoid Tobin. To frequently refer to the species, or whatever, yet never say anything useful. A true academic would hide his failures of research efforts, not parade them publicly in indelible print.

Against his better judgment, Jon retrieved *Tobin's* and reread the pertinent sections. Yup, he still knew zilch about the Stone Witches. He dragged out several other massive opuses. Only one even mentioned Stone Witches, and it was in passing. The book reflected as incomplete a knowledge base as Tobin suffered from. Were these witches so ancient, dead and gone that nothing was remembered about them? That was possible, but the library sure went back a long way in time. There were multiple chapters on primordial gods, ones present at or before creation. Perhaps there weren't many Stone Witches. No one knew much because they were so rare. Could be, but nah. Nothing was too obscure for ivory-tower professors. Hell, the more useless the piece of information was, the more those guys got off writing and opining about it.

Jon went to his other research option. He could have called Mirraya, but she was in a different universe and he was still mighty pissed at her. Instead he contacted Phassor Malto. Phassor was almost as skilled and knowledgeable in magic as Cala had been. Plus, he was a mercenary, pure and simple. If he knew something, it was for sale. If you wanted someone to disappear, they quite literally did if you could manage the right price. Phassor was Dulutean, no relationship to the Deft shapeshifters. He had learned his magic in an atmosphere free of ethical concerns and humanitarian limitations.

"Jon *Ryan*?" Phassor screamed into his mouthpiece. "No way. You *have* to be dead. You should, if there is a God and right *purpose* to the universe, be dead."

"No, I can prove those forces do not exist," Jon bantered. "You aren't dead either."

"There is now one matter you and I agree upon. Praised be the day."

"You're too much, you old fool."

"Hopefully so, my old associate. Made so by the successful application of effort to be excessive."

"So what're you up to these days?"

Phassor waited a few seconds before responding. "You call me out of deep space after decades to find out my daily routine? My, my, but you're a curious soul."

"What? A man can't inquire as to another's status? Since when is that a crime?"

"For one thing, I'm *not* a man. I'm a bipedal Dulutean male. For another it's not a crime, just a silly lie to begin a negotiation."

"A negotiation? Since you're now clearly clairvoyant, what negotiation are we about to enter into?"

"One whose price just doubled."

"And if this *is* just a social call?"

"I'll eat half my testicles."

"Half? Crap's sake, how many do Dulutean males have?"

"More than enough. Now what information do you seek or to whom do you wish ill fortune?"

"If you must know, I *was* calling to say hello. I also had an *academic* question, one of a purely historical nature."

"Why do I not believe you? You, Jon, *are* history, but you are not at all *interested* in the subject itself."

"Seems I've changed. Yes, ever since my tutelage by Cala I'm quite the anthropology nerd."

"Name three historical texts not having to do with magic."

"The Magna Carta, the Constitution of the USA, and the Martian Declarations."

There was a long silence.

"What? You still there?" growled Jon.

"Thank you for proving my point. Those are all Earth *source* documents, ones you'd have learned of in school, not independent study. None are textbooks. Moreover, there was not *a* Magna Carta but a *series* of great charters. You clearly know your history less well than an alien. I rest my case and the price has now *tripled*."

"Once I ask, you'll see this is nothing more than intellectual curiosity, not a search for applicable knowledge."

"I shall be the judge. Now ask what you called to ask."

"You ever heard of the Stone Witches?"

If there was a long silent pause before, there was an epic one at that juncture.

"Come on, you drama queen. It was a simple historical question. Either you've heard of the S—"

"Do *not* repeat the name," yelled Phassor. His coy jester-tone had vanished. He spoke with anger and fear.

"Have you lost all contact with reality? It's not an invocation or anything. They're two common words, ones you hear every day."

"Jon," his voice was loud, firm, and commanding, " there exists a word *stone,* meaning rock. There is also a word *witch,* something you and I might be accused of being. But those two words must never—say again *never*—be used in tandem in that order."

"What walked over your grave? What spooked you like a child in a dark room during a storm?"

"Mock me. Fine. It is good that my fright is so transparent. Now I must go. Do not call again."

"Hang on, bucko. Answer the question. Otherwise I'm broadcasting a general appeal for knowledge concerning you-know-who under *your* name. I swear I will."

"You would be about that stupid."

"That's one thing I always rely upon. The abundance of my stupidity."

"Jon, you seriously do not know of them?"

"No. Well, not until recently. I was reading *Tobin's* and ran across the term. But no one, including Tobin, seems to know anything about the sonsabitches."

"Trust me now. It is a lethally dangerous undertaking to learn of ... them. The scholars of old who knew that lived to write nothing about ... them. Any bookworm foolish enough to actually document substance was quickly and quietly deleted from the halls of academia."

"You make *them* sound like bogeymen, the monster under the bed."

"They are nothing so benign or loving."

"So you do know about the ston—"

"*Silence!*" he boomed. "You think I'm joking, don't you? Well I'm not. Do not repeat those words in any context involving me." He sniffed and grunted loudly. "I'd disconnect if I thought I'd be *rid* of you, but I know better."

"Look, Phassor, just tell me what you know, or where to find that information, and you never see or hear from me again."

"Once I tell you and you go looking, I won't have to worry about seeing or hearing of you again. That much gives me great satisfaction."

"My old friend, you underestimate me. Lots of dead folk out there that have. We're talking me here."

"Your famous swagger. Well, if it works on ... them I'll eat *all* my gonads. Yours, too, if you'd like."

"Nah, I'm good. But thanks. So—" Jon trailed off pregnantly.

"I will say nothing directly about ... them. But I will direct you to the Jasminian Monk Library of Peasdoor. Are you familiar with it?"

"Heard of it. Peasdoor's in the Vestibular Galaxy, right?"

"Yes. A long way from anywhere."

"Right in the middle of nowhere."

"That's the place. The head monk in the Cloistered Tower is a Liolipod named Seven Ways. Tell her I sent you."

"A *her* monk?"

"Jon, don't be so provincial."

"My bad. Okay, what am I asking this Seven Ways gal to show and tell?"

"After mentioning me, bring a stone. Show it to her and say the word *witch.* Make sure you say it in Standard, that way she'll place the word stone in the proper context."

"Isn't that a little cloak and dagger?"

"Try it any other way and see what happens."

"Huh?"

"Do you know what a Liolipod female looks like?"

"Can't say I do."

"Since you're a student of Earth's history, think saber-toothed tiger only larger, faster, and less inclined to suffer a fool."

"A rock and a word in Standard. Got it. Jon Ryan never went looking for trouble."

"No, it always finds you."

The connection went dead. Jon rather hoped that was all that would be going dead during this adventure.

CHAPTER THIRTY

Toño sat at the mess table, rubbing his temples in an attempt to ward off the headache that couldn't possibly come. He was kind of frustrated. Yeah, that was the concept. "So you insulted them, threatened them, conned them, and then agreed to meet again to hammer out further details in a few days."

"Yeah, pretty much," I replied as meekly as I could, which wasn't very much.

"And you think in your wildest *fantasies* they will return for any reason in the world, well, aside from coming back to kill you and incinerate your bodies?" He seemed stressed.

"Absolutely. By the way, let's not discuss my wildest fantasies in front of you-know-who Sapale." I bunched up my shoulders. "But ask me later. Promise you will, okay?"

Sapale shook her head. That was it. I was done. She didn't seem to care enough about my taunt to punch me or anything. Ah, marriage after the magic's gone.

"This is a ryperation, Toño," reminded Mirraya. "You know they're like that."

Toño visibly slouched. "I shall hate myself for it, but I must ask. What is a ryperation??

"Doc, come on. A Ryan Operation, a *ryperation*."

"Yes, I must go to confession, I feel so badly knowing," he remarked as he slumped further. Poor guy.

"You going to be okay, Toño?" asked Sapale with a look of true concern.

He waved her away. "Yes, yes. *Lo aguanto. Lo aguantare*." Sure, he could take it. Dude was tough.

"I'm not clear on one point."

Who the hell? I spun and dropped. Then I saw the long lost and never missed Casper. On this occasion I had to ask, even though I knew I'd hate myself immediately after. "Where have you been?"

"I might as well ask you the same question," Casper responded.

"I've been right here. Ask anyone."

"Then I must have been here, too."

That ghost was about to get both barrels. "If you were here why didn't we see you? And you absolutely positively cannot keep your mouth shut. If you were here you'd be jibber jabbering for sure."

He said nothing.

"What?" I snapped.

"I recall having no valuable input and no questions up until now. Yes, that's explains my being taciturn."

"Taciturn," I wheezed. "Okay, forget the hell out of everything. What are you not clear about?"

"You fed the other conspirators a fabrication, a useless plan. They confessed to having no near-term plan either. Your two groups are acting more as insurance policies than threats to Vorc. What the frak are we doing here, team?"

Frak? The ghost of who-knew just quoted *Battlestar Galactica*? Then it hit me. Casper was humanoid, maybe even human, in appearance. He'd nearly completed a transference from thin swirling apparition to a pale man. I did not see that coming. I relaxed a bit when I realized Casper might be *humanoid,* like many Cleinoids, but he couldn't be *human*. There never were any in this universe to die and become spooks.

"We are attempting to see if we can gain any advantage in

eliminating Vorc," I replied coolly. "With him gone, the government, such as it is, will destabilize."

"I realize that," Casper replied, sounding bored. A bored ghost? Yeah, I needed one of those in my life. "But I don't get it."

"Get what?"

"Fine, Vorc's history. Someone takes his place. Where's the upheaval? Where are the streets layered with bodies?"

"Those are best-case scenarios," I defended weakly. "We might achieve only a portion of our maximal goals."

"I think a corporate virus has infected your software, Jon," responded a concerned Casper.

"Very droll," I replied.

"I wasn't kidding."

"Then your insult was only very lame."

Toño had heard enough. "Casper, so we might actually learn something from you, why do you seem to object to our current scheme?"

"For the universe, excluding Vorc will make no difference. Political intrigue, assassinations, and petty egos have dominated this world for a gazillion years. I mean, what do you think power-hungry gods do when they're not ravaging some other poor son of a bitch plane of existence? Political murder is kind of like taking the garbage out on a regular basis, 'round these parts."

Casper was beginning to remind me of someone, though phase plasma pistol to my head, I could not recollect who. Wul? Maybe Harhoff, the only Adamant I actually liked? Oh well, no time to wander memory lane. Worse than anything, dude was beginning to sound like a beacon of correctness in the dense fog of lousy ideas.

"So, what," Daleria challenged, "you suggest we bail on the covert plan, Casper?"

"Yes. Let's move on to something viably lethal to a lot of Cleinoids."

"Such as?" asked Mirraya sternly.

"No idea," Casper quickly replied. "I don't need a better vision to tell you another is piss-poor."

"Aren't we kind of invested in this one?" I whined.

"Only as invested as you choose to be. We can be a million miles away from here by tomorrow," reasoned Casper.

"Ghost's got a point," ventured Slapgren. "Unless something blindingly spectacular appears in a couple seconds, I think we cut our losses and bolt."

"*Like*?" I asked disapprovingly.

"Like I have no idea either. Ditto what the ghost said."

""I say give it a few more days," Sapale weighed in. "If it stays looking low yield, we split."

"I can live with that," I responded.

"So, let's push our new playmates a little harder," said Slapgren, with an oh-so-wicked grin. "Test their mettle."

"Uh oh," cried Mirraya, "I should never have let him escape. Now he wants to have some fun."

"I'n not positive," I winced, "but I *think* that's TMI."

"Oh grow up, Uncle Jon. You've seen us both naked," teased back Mirraya.

I stood and spoke loudly and clearly. "I only saw you kids naked *involuntarily*. Never *voluntarily*."

"There's a moral difference, Jon?" posed a very concerned-looking Daleria.

"In his defense, after we shape-shifted, we always ended up in the nude," said Slapgren. "If he was around, he got an eyeful."

"Is there any way we could change the discussion? Maybe to untimely and brutal death?" I was getting queasy.

"I very much hope so," Toño snapped. "Unless there is a substantial objection, I say we meet with the group of political malcontents one more time. If matters are not looking much brighter, we forget the entire affair."

"Which means we eliminate the witnesses, right?" asked Slapgren.

"Yes. We can't let them know it's coming, and we definitely can't let them escape," I confirmed grimly.

"You know what?" asked an overly quiet Sapale. "I wonder if

they aren't discussing the very same thing concerning us. I'm not certain unique covert cells can even function together. That said, our two sure seem to be having trouble with the group hugs and kumbayas."

My mate was correct. "Then I'd say we're looking at a pretty fun final get-together, eh what?"

"If your idea of fun is fast-paced, close-quarter mayhem with no guarantee of survival." That Toño. Such a thrill killer.

I gave Daleria specific instructions about the next contact she'd have with Festock. It was his turn to pick the spot. I told her it was entirely possible his group was planning to break off contact with us by way of our forced mass extinction. So, if she didn't know the location, the answer was *no*. If she knew it and it was too isolated, again, *no*. She kind of freaked out.

"Jon, if I say no enough times he'll know I'm suspicious."

"So? If he reads that we're getting antsy, he's all that much more motivated to meet with us. How else can he hope to kill us? Kill-O-Gram? Death by vicious and unfounded gossip? No, if he reads you as afraid, he'd be even more intent on meeting. Look, do your best. But I do *not* want to walk into an inescapable trap."

"I'll try," she sighed.

"You'll do fine. You're a natural at this."

She angled her head away. "Not certain *that's* a compliment."

"For an innkeeper, eh, no. For a warrior, yo big time."

I wasn't reassured by the response she made with her face. Seemed to say *WTF have I gotten myself into.* Maybe she just had gas.

Thirty seconds later she opened her eyes and bobbed her head around. "Well, that went weird."

"Did I ever tell you I love weird? Yeah, big fan. Not boring like no big deal."

"Then you'll love this. He said he wants to meet in Farkla Square, near the small pond at the center."

"Shall we bring a picnic?" I asked ingenuously.

"He didn't mention refreshments. Farkla Square *is* public, I'll give him that."

"The problem being?"

"It's right in front of Vorc's administrative building."

"How auspicious," I said uncertainly.

"You mean *sus*-picious," added Sapale.

"That, too."

"We're not meeting them there, are we? You have not slipped inexorably into insanity yet, have you?" challenged Toño.

"We either meet there, or we bolt. If we split without an appropriate goodbye, we leave high-value snitches undeadified. Of course, we meet." I turned back to Daleria. "When?"

"Dusk tomorrow."

"Dusk," snapped Slapgren. "No one meets at dusk. Well, lovers maybe. I'm assuming Festock's not being romantic."

"I don't know about you, but *I'm* bringing flowers," I said with a patented Jon smile.

"I'll agree to the plan, if you promise you will not ooze male hormones and Rambo-speak the entire time we're waiting," said a displeased wife of mine.

"The whole dang time? Come on, that's arbitrary and callous."

"All in favor of Jon not exuding macho pending a likely firefight, please indicate so by raising their right hand," responded Sapale.

Wouldn't you know it. Every hand, including Casper's, went up like rockets. Man, I got no respect.

Naturally, I focused a lot of spy-bots on the city center immediately. I instructed the Als to alert me and show me clear holos of everyone who entered the square. Festock was not going to have a chance to set up an ambush. Not on my watch. Before we headed out that next afternoon, twenty-seven individuals and three paper wrappers entered and left the park. None appeared overtly suspicious, and I included the paper in that assessment. Hey, in the land-o-gods, who knew anything?

At the appointed hour, Daleria, Mirraya, and I stepped out of a taxi and surveyed the park. My first impression? Pretty park like. Trees, pathways, garbage cans, and lawns. It was around a hundred meters to the center. I could just make out the pond Daleria referenced. Festock was presumably in there, but I couldn't ID him yet.

"Let's enter here," I said with a nod. "Slow, casual pace. Nothing out of the ordinary here. Got it?" That was mostly for Daleria's sake. She was kind of jumpy. A deadly trap with a powerful foe on their turf? Oh, yawn. No large deal to me.

Halfway in I made out Festock. He was with the individual currently atop my most barf-on-sight list, Aaaverd. A third person was with them, a slender, tall female humanoid. As we got closer, Festock stood and waved while Aaaverd began slowly flapping his wings. The female neither took notice nor reacted in any visible manner. Cool cookie? Hired gun? Well, I was about to find out.

"Clinneast," Festock called out when I was in earshot. "Over here." When we arrived, he gestured to an empty bench that had been turned to face the one those three sat on. "Nice to see you again."

"Excuse me, Aaaverd," I replied, "speak up. I couldn't quite hear y'all."

What a sourpuss. The expression on *their* plump face was priceless.

"Festock," said Daleria with a curt nod.

"My dear," he said with equal formality. "This is Bellicity. After I apprised her of our last contact, she insisted on meeting you."

"Bellicity," I said with a wave. "Nice to finally meet you." I recognized her, of course.

"Finally?" she asked way too cordially.

"Finally," I repeated obliquely. I did a three count for effect. "Daleria's a big fan. Can't stop telling the story of how you two were introduced years ago." I looked to Daleria.

"Really, child, we've met? I don't recall that taking place."

"I used to run a bar south of Beal's Point. You came through with a large party after your pilgramage. Let me see, you were with Golloporse, FaFaFa, Bodelian, and, oh, what was its name, the one with spiral wings and a red fluffy tail?"

"Sorromar. You have *quite* the memory." Bellicity squinted at her. "You're a demigod, right?"

"Yes I am."

"Hmm. Perhaps that's why I took no note of you." Bellicity must've realized she was being as politically correct as a trumpet player at a funeral. "No offense intended."

"None taken," I replied for Daleria. I wanted to throw this bitch off maximally.

"I don't like him," squealed Aaaverd as he wagged a finger at me. "I told you I didn't like him."

"Yes, you *did*," Bellicity responded condescendingly. "Then again, you like so few others."

"I like you," he replied, clearly hurt.

"Gosh, this is a fun journey down Who I Like Avenue," I said with redlined snark. "I keep forgetting. Is that why we're here today in this lovely spot?" I gestured broadly to the park.

Festock lost it. "Clinneast, you are rude, stupid, and rude. I speak for my group in saying we cannot tolerate you and *refuse* to cooperate with you." He stood up brusquely.

Jon, flew into my head. It was Sapale and she was scared. *You're blown. The park is surrounded by dudes in heavy capes with hoods pulled over their heads. If they had scythes, they'd all look like the Grim Reaper.*

Number and weapons? I asked.

Ten, no obvious weapons but the robes are bulky.

They wouldn't be proper robes if they weren't heavy wool and loose. Stand ready to cover our retreat.

Roger that, she replied.

I looked at Mirraya. That was all it took to let her know. My girl was that good. She transformed into a flaming dragon. Seriously. Six feet of scales, muscles, and fire. "You have betrayed us. For that sin you will die." Mirri drew back an arm and let fly a roiling incendiary cloud.

Aaaverd had just enough time to look at Festock.

Festock had just enough time to scream, "It wasn't—"

They erupted into blue shrouds. Both tried to scream, but all the air was consumed before their lives were. Instead of sound, the last witness to Festock's and Aaaverd's demise was a pantomime of horrific silent torment.

Then Jon noticed an anomaly. Bellicity was not burning. No, she sat with an impassive, almost bored look on her face. She all but yawned. Mirraya's flames evaporated into nothingness. Only then did Bellicity seem to notice there'd been an event. She stood with a practiced grace and bowed to Mirri. "Thank you for doing me the favor of disposing with that traitorous scum. It saves me the dreary task of seeing to it myself."

Status? I said to Sapale.

All ten holding position. Jon, they appeared out of nowhere. They were ... they were just there.

Land of the ancient gods, my dear. Happens all the time.

What's your status?

Mirri just incinerated two of the three conspirators.

Why did she leave one behind?

I'm about to find out. Stand by.

Roger that.

"Bellicity, m'dear. You do not appear to burn? Are you a *water* god?" I asked with a smirk.

She harrumphed joylessly. "Hardly anything so mundane. I'm a god who can move between planes of existence."

"Which would come in handy when all about you becomes a conflagration."

"Witness the results. I was only here in one dimension. You could see me but I could not be burned."

"And that leaves really but one question, doesn't it?"

"How can I pull that off while still looking so marvelous?" she returned with a friendly smile.

"Yes, that, and why it is we are surrounded by men in robes at the very moment you did not combust?"

"Does seem a bit of a stretch, doesn't it?" she replied.

"Place my name in the *YES* column, please."

"Well, there is no coincidence, only kismet. You see, I, like you, was attempting to infiltrate this group of conspirators. I, unlike you, was successful."

"I'm betting *you,* unlike *me,* work for Vorc, too."

"My, but you're the fast study. I do. When that idiot Festock told me the outlines of your plan to assassinate Vorc, I knew you were a player, not a true believer."

"How so?"

"Come, come. Your so-called plan was smoke and mirrors designed to fool a fool. You have no designs on the center seat's life." She reflected a moment. "I'm not exactly certain what your game *is,* though I will find out soon enough."

I twisted my lips. "Hmm. Not likely, actually."

"I admire your bravado, false though it is."

"There's nothing false about me, *babe.*"

That remark wiped the cloy smile off her face. "I've never been called *babe* before. I do believe I detest it. Say it again and you will feel my wrath."

"What, and abort the painful torture to extract the truth from me? That's awfully shortsighted of you, *babe.* No way to run a railroad."

Man. She duplicated the exact same disgusted look it took Sapale two billion years to perfect in an instant.

"My guards surround us."

"I am aware. All ten are holding position at the perimeter of the park. They're wearing holocaust cloaks and scaring little children in an inappropriate manner. Little ones will be marred for life."

"Excellent magical knowledge, Clinneast, or whatever your real name is."

"Puddin' Tame. Ask me again and I'll tell you the same."

"You are insufferable. You know that, right?"

"He knows it," Mirraya responded quickly.

"As I was saying. My guards surround us. In a moment I will have them close in on you. Then we will all go visit Vorc. I'm certain he's anxious to meet you."

"Oh, I'm betting he's not," I scoffed. "But we will never know."

"Why? Because you will not be taken alive? My, how dramatically pointless."

"Sure, let's call it that. You'll never take me alive, *babe.* I'm not going back to prison, never, ya hear?"

"Do you know who the ten guards are under those robes?"

"No, but this sounds like a swell game. Okay, give me one hint, then tell me if I'm getting warmer."

"They're hounding vampires."

I giggled like an idiot. Trust me, it wasn't all that hard.

"That strikes you as funny?" she said with displeasure.

"Well, *duh.* I mean, if they're busy *hounding* vampires they won't have time to capture us,

now, will they?"

"Clinneast," whispered a Daleria about ready to crawl out of her skin. "Hounding vampires are called that because they *hound* their prey until one of them is dead. They never stop once they have your scent. Nine million times to one *they* do the killing. Do not taunt them, *please.*"

"You would be wise to listen to your little demigod friend on that point," Bellicity said, pointing to Daleria.

"Wise? Me. Come on, babe. I got no time for wisdom."

With that I threw up a full membrane around Mirraya, Daleria, and myself. Bet Bellicity didn't see that coming, the smug bitch.

"Great, Mr. Hero," cried out Sapale. "Now we're surrounded by gods you pissed off *and* we're immobile. Sheer genius. Smooth move."

"I got this," I replied, patting my palms toward the ground. "Sheesh. Have a little faith."

"I know this drill. I ask what your next move is and you say you'll tell me as soon as you come up with it. Am I right?" That wife of mine had a mouth.

"Maybe. No, seriously. I have a plan and it's outstanding. It relies on assets Bellicity and her monkeys couldn't anticipate."

"Namely?" she spit back.

"Casper." I gestured to my right. Nothing. "*Casper*," I repeated louder.

"Oh boy," wheezed Daleria.

"Is there another me over there?" asked Casper, who was standing to my left.

"No, thank goodness. Hey, we're in kind of a pickle."

"Kind of? Is there a pickle-like state more pickle-ly than this? I don't think so."

Everybody's a comic. "Look, I'm going to need some outside intel. I need you to slip out and keep me posted as to where the bitch and where the guards are. I'll open a pinhole to maneuver and communicate."

"Sure," he said, and he was gone.

Are they still holding outside the park? I said head-to-head.

No. They're converging rapidly.

Hang on.

No prob.

Remember I held Tefnuf in a membrane? Yeah, I had to bag her when we emerged into this universe. Well, she was still under wraps. I maneuvered that full membrane from the Lower Chambers to the park. I set it right between Bellicity and our current position. Then I did something very cruel to my would-be captor. I released Tefnuf right in Bellicity's face. I waited a couple seconds then called to Casper. *The guards still converging on us?*

Negative, and I'll be damned, no. They're all a few feet from Tefnuf, and boy is she mad. I've never seen her this tweaked. It's .. it's sweet, that's what it is. Uh oh. Now she's slinging power bolts at them all. Oh crap, Bellicity just lost an ear. Bitch couldn't phase out fast enough. Man this is ...

Belay that. I opened the side of the membrane opposite to the action but maintained a shield so they couldn't see or target us. The booming of Tefnuf's bolts was ... well, it was sweet. I waved an arm to direct the other two toward safety. "Move," I ordered. "Along a straight line, double time it."

At the edge of the park Toño and Sapale met us with a damn

magic carpet. He, being a kid at heart, became an instant fan. Anyway, we all jumped on and made for the stratosphere.

"Neat escape, Houdini," said Sapale in a sarcastic tone. "But either Bellicity or Tefnuf is going to tell Vorc you're back. You know that?"

"Hey, once Bellicity unleashed the vampire thingies our cover was blown. If I didn't use Tefnuf, Bellicity would have outed us. Doesn't matter which bitch tells on us."

She shrugged. "I guess so."

"And check this out. If Tefnuf tells him it was me when Vorc knows I'm dead, he'll probably dismiss her as drunk and stupid—*again*."

That got a smile out of my wife.

"And Bellicity can say it was someone, but she can't know it was Ryanmax returned from the dead."

"She could simage him your face, idiot," snapped Toño.

"Not exactly," corrected Daleria. "Simaging is a message. Images are harder and less precise."

I raised my palms in acknowledgement of a minor triumph.

Sapale just shrugged again and looked away.

After multiple evasive maneuvers, we rendezvoused back at *Stingray* with the others. I must admit, I was pretty darn proud of myself.

CHAPTER THIRTY-ONE

The alternate timeline Jon Ryan squatted in an open grassy expanse and fiddled with some wiring. It ran to a set of boxes arranged in a haphazard manner a few feet away. He quietly whistled *The High and the Mighty.* Finally, he was satisfied with the connections. He stood and gave his odd setup a recheck. He was satisfied with the configuration. His next task was much tougher. He had to decide if he was actually going to switch the damn contraption on. There were no do-overs in a gambit that dicey.

In the end, he thought *what the hell* and threw the switch. The jerry-rigged communication device began broadcasting a repeating binary signal on multiple subspace channels. He added multiple conventional frequencies, too, but since they only traveled at the speed of light they were unlikely to reach the ears he sought in a useful timeframe.

The message was a simple one. It was also quite likely suicidal. He set forth into the universe the following invitation.

Stone Witches, you are discovered. Come to the location of this transmission and meet the one who knows of your existence. I will announce you to the world in twenty-hour hours if you do not show up. I wish to discuss an important matter with the antigods.

Then Jon sat and leaned back on one of the larger boxes. He began whistling the same tune again. He closed his eyes and waited. He only wished he could still nod off and nap lightly while waiting. It would have been a nice dramatic accent, the perfect touch.

It would've been, however, a short nap. In less than an hour Jon leaped to his feet at the sound of nearby thunder or a powerful explosion. He scanned the perimeter but saw nothing. Then a second thunderclap vibrated his teeth and shook leaves off several trees. Then his noisy company revealed themselves. Jon couldn't help himself. He began to chuckle softly. Sure, it was unwise to laugh in the face of omnipotent gods and his likely imminent death, but seriously. He was being approached by an elephant dressed as a clown and a fat pile of rocks. They moved with all the grace and ease of fish out of water.

The two figures stopped a few feet away from Jon. The pile of rocks spoke first. "You are the fool who would call the wrath of the Stone Witches on himself?"

"That'd be correct. I'm Jon Ryan. Nice to finally meet you."

"Any pleasant quality of our presence will be as short-lived as you, Jon Ryan," menaced the elephant. "No one dares threaten the antigods without suffering completely and eternally."

"Ah, sorry. I've already been to New Jersey. I was stationed there at McGuire AFB for the longest six months in the recorded history of time."

The elephant glanced over to the rock pile. Jon couldn't be certain, but he thought they exchanged WTF-puzzled looks.

"No one has ever made light of the curse that is our condemnation. You are either the least intelligent or most rash being we have ever encountered," said the rocks.

"Or *both,*" corrected Jon. He held up a finger. "Do not discount the possibility of me being both. By the way. I introduced myself. Isn't this the part where you introduce *yourselves*?"

"Stone Witches do not introduce themselves to insignificant specks like you. We are only here to kill you."

"No, I feel I need to set you straight yet again. If you were only here to kill me, either I'd be dead or you'd be toast. No, you're here to talk, probably pump me for information, and *then* kill me."

The pair exchanged the same quizzical glance as before.

"Did you suggest you might even stand one chance in a *million* of harming either of us?" wheezed an incredulous pile of stones.

"No."

"Ah. That's better," responded the clowniphant.

"I said I might kill the both of you. Big diff there, Peanut."

"Peanut? What does a groundnut seed have to do with anything?" asked the pile.

"Oh, sorry. Inside reference, I guess. Where I come from all elephants are nicknamed Peanut. Well, that or Peanuts. That's on account of the fact that elephants love them some peanuts. Lots and lots of peanuts."

"Are you aware of just how many *times* and how *unimaginably painfully* we are going to kill you?" the elephant challenged angrily.

"I can only imagine. But seriously, as to why I called you here. As you—"

The assembly of rocks bellowed the word *SILENCE*. But to say it did does not encompass the volume, intensity, and fury with which it uttered it. Fissures cracked open in the earth and birds fell dead from the sky. Dude was serious.

"A simple *please* would have made the same point much less painfully, sir," quipped Jon. "So, you probably know the Cleinoids are back in this universe. I want to discuss an alliance between your people and mine. A mutual defense force, if you will. We can draw up a formal treaty and everything if you want."

The rock pile began to gyrate so violently Jon fully expected it to fly apart. Through his quaking he managed to say, "We do not ally with any mortal beings. That the pestilence otherwise known as the Cleinoids have returned is insignificant to the Stone Witches."

"Yeah? Well it's not so insignificant to most lifeforms 'round these parts," returned Jon. "If you haven't noticed, they're sweeping across the universe, killing and destroying with reckless abandon."

"We care *nothing* for the fate of others, either," replied the funny-looking pachyderm.

"Of *others, either*? Man, that's a tortured tongue twister."

Jon got them to exchange a third bewildered glance.

"We feel it's best if we move directly to the multiple killing of your segment of our presence," announced the rocks. "You are clearly insane and deranged. It would be cruel to subject you to further life."

"Don't go to any trouble on my behalf, gentlemen."

"No trouble," responded the rocks.

"In fact, it'll be a dirty pleasure," added the elephant with a snicker.

"Okay, if you insist."

"We do," confirmed the stones.

"One tiny, tiny thought first, if you'll indulge me."

"*No,* and *we will not,*" replied the massive jester.

"Once the Cleinoids have killed every other living being in this universe, they will come for you. Can you be certain they have not evolved, learned, or chanced upon by accident a way of meaningfully harming you?"

"Yes," they both said instantly and without reservation.

"It has always been so and always will be so," amended the rocks.

"So they cannot possibly change? It is impossible for the Cleinoids to manage to eke out an advantage over y'all?"

"It's not fair to place it in that context," protested the elephant. "Technically, anything is possible. But Cleinoids amounting to anything, that's about as close to impossible as impossible can be."

"So you admit there might be a threat to the Stone Witches, unless they ally with the rest of the universe?"

"I didn't say that," protested the elephant.

"Oh, yes you did, didn't he?" Jon asked of the stone pile.

"What Dumblemount said could be *interpreted* in that light, if one was willing to strain credulity severely."

"*There*. You heard it from your own BFF. You need *us*. We need *you*. Let's get together and do some ass kicking."

"No," announced a third booming voice approaching from behind the two antigods. "I knew sending you two was a mistake," scoffed Verazz. He was in human form.

"*What?*" whined Cacucack, the rock pile antigod.

"What?" questioned Verazz incredulously. "I sent you two to annihilate some wiseass upstart and you enter into an alliance with him? Rookie meat. I think it's best for your health to leave now and hope you don't run into me for eons."

"We were about to crush him. We really really were, Verazz. You're always lording this over us or that over us," babbled Dumblemount. "It's not fair."

"Fair? I'll give you unfair. Dealing with you two lunkheads," screamed Verazz. "That's unfair to *me*."

"It's always about you," mumbled Cacucack.

"What did you say?" snapped Verazz.

"Nothing," replied a contrite Cacucack.

"He said if you need us, please summon us back," said Dumblemount, attempting to cover for his buddy.

"Not in *this* eternity," spit back Verazz.

The two antigods skulked away.

"As to you, Jon Ryan. Please allow no worry for the Stone Witches to reside in your mind. The Cleinoids are a petty nuisance at best, nothing more. Go in peace. Know, however, that if you mention our existence to a soul, your death will be as brutal as it is swift."

"What? You're setting me free? No morbid demise as promised?"

"No. You bested my two idiot associates. That is a unique occurrence, trust me. Such an accomplishment should not go unrewarded." Verazz turned and began walking away.

"Verazz, please. All my antics to the side. I'm begging you. The Cleinoids are leveling unholy hell on us. Please help."

"We would never associate with or aid others. Trust me on this also. It is not our way. It is not, as you might say, in our better nature."

"Then we will all surely die."

Verazz considered Jon's words, then nodded faintly. "Most likely."

"How can you sentence us to that fate?"

Verazz laughed genuinely. "Excellently played, Jon. But *we* do not sentence you. The *Cleinoids* do."

"Your *omission* is a *commission*. Don't put lipstick on that pig."

"My what a colorful metaphor. Lipstick on pork. How bemusing."

"Don't you mean *amusing*?"

"Does it even possibly matter, wind-up man?"

"No. I guess I just want to keep you talking."

Verazz turned to fully face Jon. "You *are* unique, robot. You challenge me, if ever so minutely. I'll tell you what. I will part with a gift if you do in kind. How does that sound?"

"A white-elephant gift exchange? Sure, why the hell not?"

"Why the hell not, indeed," confirmed Verazz with a silly grin.

"But I didn't have time to shop. Can I mail you yours?" asked Jon wryly.

"No need. Your gift to me will be your eternal silence on the subject of Stone Witches. Can you promise that?"

Jon wagged his head a moment. "Yes, I can. I promise the secret of your existence is safe with me."

"Forever and a day?"

"Forever and a day."

"Thank you. I accept. And now my gift to you."

"I can hardly wait."

"You seek to end the threat of the Cleinoids?"

"I believe *duh* is the best response I can come up with."

"Then do so by destroying the power that is the Cleinoids."

"Isn't that what we're doing ever so ineffectively?"

"No. Listen. You are fighting the Cleinoids individually. Instead eradicate the source of their power. What, I ask you, Jon Ryan, is an immortal god without power called?"

"I give up. What do you call one of those?"

"Dead."

"That would be convenient. What's the source of their power, you know, so we might destroy it?"

"Must I lead you by the nose?"

"Sure."

"What power sustains and imbues the *Clein*-oids? *Clein,* my simple friend. Destroy the *Clein,* and you destroy the *Clein*-oids."

"Where and what is the Clein?"

"Ah ah, spoiler alert. I've told you more than I should." He raised a finger. "Find the Clein and destroy it, and you will end the threat you face."

Then Verazz literally disappeared.

CHAPTER THIRTY-TWO

I was sitting in the ship's mess staring at a room temperature mug of coffee when Sapale and Mirraya walked in. Great. Two women with long faces looking at yours truly. A finger down my throat and a soap suds enema would have been preferable, in my book. They slid in across from me.

"We think we need to talk," said Sapale tenderly with all the love in her heart.

"You two? Cool, I'll just get out of earshot and you gals have at it." I stood.

"He always acts like this," stated a frustrated Sapale.

"We know," Mirri responded, resting her hand on the back of Sapale's. "Supportive listening and long fuses. Remember, we agreed?"

Sapale looked to the heavens for strength. "I know. He just did it so quick this time."

"*Supportive* listening," I said to my wife. "Remember?"

"Can I kill him and *then* we do the intervention?" pleaded my forever love.

"No. Not unless," Mirraya glared directly at me, "he does it *one more time*."

"Do y'all need me to sit back down?" I asked as naively as I could. I even pointed to my chair. That's how helpful I was laboring to be.

"Yes, Uncle. Please."

I sat with a grunt.

"May I get us all some coffee?" asked Mirri graciously. For the record she detested coffee. Talk about laboring to be helpful.

"Sure. Probably be here a while," I grumbled.

"Not if you're *dead,* my love," responded Sapale. "It will all be over in a flash if you press your luck any harder or farther." She smiled so ingenuously.

I lowered my head in resignation.

"We've noticed you've been in an extended funk of late, Uncle. We were hoping you'd pull out of the nosedive so we let it be. But it's been a week since our escape from Bellicity and you still sulk."

"And do not even *think* of asking which it is, a funk or sulk," warned my mate, who knew me way too well.

I shrugged as if I didn't understand the language she was speaking.

"What's the matter, Uncle?"

I shrugged again, this time more moodily.

"Come on, you can do it," invited Sapale. "I know you're the little engine who can."

"What happened to supportive listening?" I asked.

"I believe it does not *preclude* taunting a reluctant child to participate," she replied with a fake grin. Boy did I hitch my wagon to a spirited filly.

"Uncle, please. We're all in this together. We all want to know the problem."

"To be fully forthcoming, Toño said he should just place you in sleep mode and attach you to the AIs. He felt it was a much more merciful approach from our standpoint," observed my spouse.

Mirri set a hand on Sapale again. "But we said we would discuss the matter and that you would be cooperative."

"Based on what past actions or documented inclinations on my part?" I inquired.

Sapale's hands balled up. Yes! Got her.

"Uncle Jon, behave."

Yeah, I shrugged yet again. I did shrugging really well, I had to say.

The two of them tried a desperate gambit. They sat silently and waited for me to open my heart. They knew I'd see the gauntlet thrown down. They knew I loved being difficult. But, they were the two women in my life and they cared deeply about me. I knew that, too. Plus, worst of all, they were correct. I was in a dark place, had been all week.

"I'm getting a little discouraged," I admitted quietly.

"There, I told you he could," said Mirraya proudly.

"You win. I'll clean the ship for the next week."

"Some supportive intervention," I complained.

"What is it that discourages you, Uncle?"

I hemmed and hawed a bit. "I'm beginning to think we can't defeat the Cleinoids."

"Here or back home?" asked Sapale.

"Both. Everywhere." I swept an angry hand in an arc. "Everyone everywhere."

"It's not like you to give up, brood-mate."

"It's not like I've ever faced an enemy like this before." I sighed deeply. "We know we can't hold our own in our universe. I've learned we can't really affect their numbers here." I shook my head. "It's just a matter of time. I'm betting you two know it also. No matter how long you hold on to a losing hand, in the end you're still going to lose."

"Jon, in two billion years something has always come up. We're lucky that way. Come on, admit it," prompted my dear, sweet wife.

"We took out the vortex but it was already too late. The only thing we managed to do was disappoint the ancient gods who couldn't partake of the fun times."

"Possibly," responded Mirraya.

"And it's only a matter of time until they find, create, or are gifted a new vortex. Somehow they got DS, and somehow they'll get another. Then ... then I don't think I need to finish that thought."

They were both quiet. I almost commented on the two silent women thing, but I let it pass. I was all out of silly.

"If we die fighting, doing the right thing, so be it," declared Sapale.

I could only continue to shake my head. I hated pointless.

"Isn't this the point in the conversation you say your *oorah* thing?" asked Mirri.

"Got no oorahs left in me."

"Then we do have a problem, Houston," Sapale said harshly.

"Huh?" I grunted.

"My brood-mate is not a pansy-assed quitter. If you are then you're not him any longer."

"Supportive listening is officially out the window, I see."

"You bet your sweet ass it is, Ryan," thundered Sapale. "If you're tossing in the towel get the *hell* off my vortex."

I knew way better than to respond. My mate was hotheaded. When she was that pissed, a hunker-down approach was the only survivable response.

"Uncle Jon, hang in here with us. We'll think of something. Can you do that for us?" She turned to Sapale and swung her head in my direction.

"Sorry. I exploded there a little, didn't I?" Sapale responded. "Jon, I love you. Always have, always will. We all do. I *feel* it in my bones, honey. We will win. We will think of something."

"Okay, you two win. I'll stop moping."

"When?" Sapale replied with such a wicked grin.

"Soon," I responded.

"Not soon enough. Grow up now."

If we ever got out of the Charlie foxtrot we were trapped in, I was going to see to it my wife took a supportive listening class. Maybe several.

CHAPTER THIRTY-THREE

Jon sat in the dark cloister he'd been assigned by Seven Ways, the Liolipod monk he'd contacted to learn about the Stone Witches. It took a herculean effort, but he finally got her to agree to let him return to study another topic—Clein, whatever the hell that was. He'd employed his limited charm, threats, incantations, transfigurations, and skullduggery, but he'd won the right to do his research.

That was six months ago. He'd asked every monk, visiting scholar, janitor, and delivery person for help. No one had one clue what the Clein was. Seven Ways was so tired of Jon badgering her for information she'd taken to violently assaulting him whenever he dared ask. He'd lost an eye twice and a hand as reminders not to bother the bitch.

Still, after all that time he found no single clue as to what Clein was, might be, or if it even existed. The Stone Witch could have been playing Jon. That would be in character for the consummate narcissistic jerkwads. But if there was one hope in the haystack of existence of catching that big a break, Jon had to follow up. So desperate was he, Jon even tried unsuccessfully to contact Phassor.

No response even came. Dude had gone to ground like a frightened gopher.

It was finally time for Jon to admit he was going to discover nothing about Clein, not in this universe. There were rare and unhelpful references to the Cleinoid gods, but not one syllable about the alleged whatever that powered them. It was painfully clear. No information about Clein resided in this universe. Most likely, logically, it was located in their universe, the one Jon had so defiantly refused to travel to. Hence he had no clue how to get there, even if his ship could make the jump. If he could access the Cleinoidverse, he could not only seach for the mystical crap, but he could alert the others about it. That native woman, Daleria, she might even know what it was and where to find it. Presumably it powered her, so, duh, she'd be well aware of it.

But thinking about how to go to a universe unknown to him was hopeless. It was akin to trying to think the sun into rising backward. He couldn't send a message either, because where would he send it? Everywhere in this universe and all others? Yeah, no problem. That would require enough broadcast energy to vaporize the surrounding thousand parsecs, not to mention it was multiple times the energy Jon could potentially even summon.

There was no way he could join or aid the others. If they returned he'd sense it, but why would they return? They wouldn't. They'd fight to the death, which was what they probably had already done. If they'd successfully negated the Clein, the monsters ripping this universe to shreds would die. So the great and powerful Jon Ryan had failed. If he hadn't yet, it was only a matter of time. All Jon's magic training was of zero use. Deft magic was limited to just this universe.

Well, it was, wasn't it? It was not designed to send Jon to another universe. But could he use it to contact Mirraya? Sending a complex message was out of the question. Even a short, nonspecific transmission was impossible. But was there a way he could contact her, if only faintly and fleetingly? Perhaps. If there wasn't, all his efforts were for naught.

CHAPTER THIRTY-FOUR

I perked up a bit after my pep talk from Sapale and Mirri. That was good. The problem I began to notice was that for every stumbling step I made forward, Mirraya seemed to tumble backward. She was less cheerful, observant, and engaged. Tonight Slapgren had made an unsuccessful attempt to lure her into an amorous encounter. I could tell by the noise and his rising level of effort that resulted in Mirri leaving their room to share a cup of coffee with me. Yeah, remember how much she hates coffee? For once in who knew how long, he was separate from his mate and wanted to play a little slap and tickle. But she was clearly in no mood to accede to his inclinations. Poor Slapgren. As a dude, I felt his pain.

Well, turn-around fair play was a bitch. That evening it was coming at her in the form of Councilor Jon Ryan. "You seem, ah, kind of down lately. I've recently learned how to be a supportive listener." I gave her my cat-eating-shit grin she always hated to see.

"Oh, you have, have you?"

"I'm a Level-Three Interventionist already. Yeah, did a subspace course."

"Subspace classes on supportive listening? Where, pray tell, do those originate from?"

"Uranus."

She snorted coffee out her nose.

"You set me up pretty good, kiddo."

"Too well. When *will* I learn?"

"So, seriously, what's up?"

"Nothing, Uncle. I'm fine."

"*Fine* would've let Slappy get his rocks off. Poor SOB's *starving* and you refused him a proper meal. No, you're not fine. Never BS a BSer."

"Seriously, Jon, it *is* nothing."

"Ah, then it is a *thing*. If it's a *thing*, it's a thing. A *thing* you can tell me about."

"How can you be so *you* so *quickly*?"

"Practice, practice, practice. Now, about the thing."

"It *is* nothing but it *is* embarrassing. So it will remain uncommunicated."

"Embarrassing? Between you and me, I've seen you naked more than my first wife, Gloria. When you were a child, no less. I was there every time you gave birth or whatever it was. Now we've come upon a taboo topic? Oh, *pshaw*."

"You really are obsessed with the nudity concerns. You should consider counseling."

"Okay, I will, as soon as you tell me the thing."

She closed her eyes firmly. "I knew I should have said nothing and turned you into a toad. When will I learn?"

"You whined that already. Now, before I put you over my knee and spank the truth out, what gives?"

"I have a pain in my ass."

I shook a finger in the air at her. "Don't change the subject with me. Yes, I *am*, but we're talking about you here."

"No, Uncle Jon, I actually have a pain in my backside." She pointed around her hip in the direction of her ... well, her backside.

"Have you told Toño? He's a doctor, you know."

"No I have not told Toño. I don't need a doctor. It's nothing. Just an irritated nerve or something."

"Have you had an irritated nerve in your butt before?"

She shook her head.

"Have you ever heard of *any* Deft having an irritated nerve in their butt?"

Another negative shake.

"Nerves, you know what they do? I'll tell you . They warn you of stuff. Hey, brain, I'm hungry. Yo, brain, your left foot's on a hot coal. Say, brain, I think you might have a serious medical condition I cannot otherwise characterize. You should tell Toño."

"Nerves say I should talk to Toño?"

"Clearly. Hey, I'm not allowed to make this crap up. I'm merely a conduit."

"If I tell Toño, will you promise to drop it and not tell everyone else?"

"Absolutely."

"Then I'll tell him next time I see—"

"What's the medical emergency here, Jon? I only see two people peacefully having coffee," snarled Toño as he trotted into the room.

Ten minutes later Mirri and Toño walked back into the mess.

"There, I told you it was nothing," Mirraya said with excessive pleasure.

"I'm not taking your word. You're a medical-condition concealer. Doc, give it to me straight, I'm the only family. How's my girl?"

"Fine. I find nothing wrong."

"Nothing wrong. My baby's got a pain in her butt. You need to run some tests or something."

"I did. I ran all the tests. Mirraya's healthier than a herd of horses."

"Oh," I mumbled.

"Oh, my, that's wonderful to hear," Mirri said on my behalf. "It also affirms my adult child's ability to know her own body."

"He came as close to saying that as he ever will, my child," lamented Toño.

"Then why do you have a pain where the feathers are the thinnest?" I asked. "Is it a constant pain?"

"No. It's not much more than a tickle and then it's gone."

"Is the pain sharp, burning, needle-like?"

"Ah ... ah sort of tickley-pinchy."

"Tickley-pinchy. Doc, that's got to mean something to you."

"Yes, she's getting older. Soon she'll be as decrepit as you are."

"Mirri, we need to get you a second opinion. This alleged medical provider is clearly incompetent."

"I'm fine, Uncle. Now recall your promise." She lowered a look at me.

"I know. But what ... what causes a shapeshifter to .. hey, that's a thought. Change shapes and see if it persists."

"I did. It does."

"Are you sure?"

"What, that I shapeshifted or that I still have the thing?" She was moderately irritated.

"Good point. Let me ask it this way. In the magical lore of the ancient Deft brindases, what does a tickley-pinch represent?"

"It doesn't. We don't have a spell for that type of communication."

"Maybe it's a voodoo doll and someone's sticking pins in it?" I sounded as excited as I was. It made real sense.

"That makes no sense, Uncle. There is no voodoo and there are no functional dolls with pins."

"But you said it was a form of communication."

"I did? Well, all spells are, in a certain light."

"No they are not," I protested. "When you lit those Cleinoids up at the park, was that an expression of communication? Maybe, *hey, I'd like to see you dead?*"

"All right, some spells are—" She stopped a second. "Uncle, are you listening any longer?"

"I wasn't. I knew the diagnosis. My dear," I said smugly, "can you name an individual who would send Mirraya/Slapgren the message, and I quote: *pain in the ass?*"

"You mean who thinks *I'm* a PIA?"

"No, no assignment of ownership. Let me put it this way. I'll say a sentence. You say the first thing that comes into your head."

"Okay."

"Biggest pain in the ass *ever*."

"EJ."

I opened my arms. "EJ is speaking to you. Up close and personal, it turns out."

Mirri craned her neck around to look at her behind in light of the new insight. Not sure she was pleased.

CHAPTER THIRTY-FIVE

"I've allowed you here against all rules and tradition. You are no scholar and you are most certainly no monk of the Cloistered Tower. Worse yet, you've come up with nothing. You must leave now." Seven Ways was actually trying to be tactful. Bless her huge heart, it just wasn't a skill set she possessed.

"What if I told you our entire universe was at stake? What if I said that if I didn't find a way to stop an unstoppable enemy we—you, me, and that whatever it is over there—will all be dead, gone, and forgotten?"

"You have told me that many times. Far too many, in fact. I hate weak excuses as much as I hate you. Up until now I have asked nicely. If you do not depart, I will ask not nicely."

"Losing those eyes and the hand are nice attempts?" EJ responded with incredulity.

"In my book they were cordial. *Overly* so, it would seem."

"Well until I—"

"Ah, excuse me," I said sheepishly. Whoever EJ was arguing with was most imposing and intimidating. Plus, she wore sacred robes. When I was a kid my mom taught me to never hit a girl or a preacher. This large cat was both. "I'm not interrupting anything important, am I?"

The Liolipod spun on me with hunger in her eyes. Oh, boy. Then she did an almost comical double take between me and EJ and back. "Are you twins? I shall say a prayer for your mother."

"No, more like good friends, except we don't like each other much," I responded cheerily.

"You are clones. I can see and hear it," she growled.

Mirraya stepped in front of me. She was still in her Deft-humanoid form. "Sister of the Cloistered Tower, I am Mirraya, a Deft brindas. I would ask your indulgence and welcome." She then bowed deeply.

Seven Ways' shoulders relaxed a bit. "Surely there are no brindas of Locinar left in the galaxy."

Mirri smiled as she transformed into a somewhat smaller version of the Liolipod, minus any clothes, of course. Arg. There we went with the nakedness again.

"It is true," marveled the monk. "You, sister of Locinar, are eternally welcome here." The Liolipod returned the deep bow. "I am Sister Seven Ways, a humble monk of this order, and I am at your service."

"Thank you, kindred spirit. We will not derail you long from your important work. We have come only to retrieve our ... our associate here." Mirri gestured to EJ.

"Then I am twice blessed this day. I have met a brindas *and* this mongrel will depart," she turned to address EJ, "*never* to return."

"I am honored to be of such utility," responded Mirraya.

"Gee gosh golly, I love being the butt of everyone's insults and abuse," wheezed EJ.

"You say you're leaving now?" pressed Seven Ways.

Back on *Stingray*, we all crowded around the mess table. Daleria, Toño, Sapale, Slapgren, Mirraya, EJ, and me. Ragtag was a word that kept flashing in my head.

"I see you got my message," EJ remarked to Mirri.

"Yes, and please never send it again. Your instant, painful, and irreversible death will ensue."

"Not a problem," he replied. "I'll never focus magical attention on your butt again."

Slapgren began to rise. He was someone no one wanted mad at them. Mirri forced him back down with a hand on his shoulder.

"Okay," I said quickly, so as to avoid a duel, "we came. Why did you call us? And it better be good, by the way. We can probably only transfer to and from that universe twice more."

"It's better than good. It's the solution we were looking for," EJ replied smugly.

"The solution to what, Jon?" asked Toño. He was the only one who still saw EJ as a friend. No wonder, I guess. He created the both of us.

"To how to eliminate the Cleinoid threat once, for all, and forever."

"That would be nice," said Sapale.

"Yeah, it would be, wouldn't it?" he responded glibly. He was *such* a tool.

"You gonna tell us, or do I have to beat it out of you, please?" I asked quite seriously.

"I found the ... I found someone in the know," he replied. "The source of the Cleinoids' power is Clein. End the Clein and you end the Cleinoids." He stared at Daleria as he spoke.

"What about that, Dal?" I asked. "Is that so?" *And why didn't you tell us if it is?*

"The *Clein?*" she puzzled. "Are you serious? The Clein is a legend, an old-man's tale told around a campfire. It isn't real."

"Oh, it's real, baby," EJ responded.

"It ... it can't be. No one has ever actually seen it, I mean. Where is it?"

"I got no clue," said EJ. "Hey, I can't do *all* the heavy lifting on our team. One or more of you'll have to help a little, too."

"Oh, so now it's *our* team, you included," snarked Sapale.

"It's always been that way, sweets. I was just working from home."

"We'll see—" she began to respond.

Mirraya cut Sapale off. "What *do* you know about the Clein, Daleria?"

"Oh, it's a very, very old story. It's said the Cleinoid gods were once mortals like anyone else. Then the Clein came to be and it imbued them with power; ultimate power. Something along those lines."

"Why did it come to be?" posed Mirri.

Daleria shrugged. "No idea. It's an origin myth. Those are always vague or require suspension of disbelief."

Mirri nodded. "I guess they do. What is it physically?"

"I have no idea on that either. I never paid much mind to the stories. No one discussed it and certainly nobody tried to research the topic. Not the almighty Cleinoids. We're too busy enjoying ourselves to be reflective."

"Hmm," responded Toño. "Creation myths can be hard to pin down, but in my experience, many are based on some real aspect of history."

"Could be," said Daleria. "I just can't tell you much more about this one."

"Is it said where the Clein is?" I asked.

"Not specifically."

"How unhelpfully nebulous," I replied.

"Well, it's said to be linked to our destruction. Not too surprising, I guess. No power, no us. Anyway, it's supposed to be located, and I'm paraphrasing I'm sure, here, *at the end of the Cleinoid path, when three miracles that are one work as two."*

"Yeah, we heard that cockamamie story before," I scoffed.

"No, Jon," corrected Toño. "We heard the last part, the one about the miracles. The first clue is new to us. My dear," he addressed Daleria, "is anything said about the path's location? Where it starts and where it finishes?"

"I don't think so." She blushed. "Sorry."

"Don't be sorry. You've been very helpful," reassured Toño. "If you do recall anything more be certain to tell us, all right?"

"Of course."

"So we go to their universe, find the stupid Clein, and we kill all the birdies with one stone," summarized EJ.

"The going back there is easy. The rest is kind of improbable," responded Sapale.

"Well, the journey of a thousand miles and all," I remarked as I stood. "Let's head back and take a stab at this new angle." I didn't add that I thought we had no chance of finding a Clein. Only certain failure and even more certain death. Oh well, no party lasts forever. Sooner or later the fat people gotta start singing.

CHAPTER THIRTY-SIX

Vorc sat behind his desk and he seethed. He seethed intensely. Everything that could go anywhere went the wrong way. Even his deep-cover agents had failed him. Bellicity was closing in on the next candidates for statues at Beal's Point. But she killed them before he could question them, find out who all was involved. And she somehow involved the drunken idiot Tefnuf in the stupidity. To top it off, Bellicity tried to blame some people who disappeared as if by magic instead of taking the responsibility for summoning Tefnuf. When one of his operatives screwed up, he only wished they'd own up to it before he cut them into little pieces.

Bellicity certainly hadn't. There she lay, small chunks oozing blood in that large barrel. Yet *she* never admitted her failure. *She* couldn't even find it in her soul to beg for mercy Vorc would never have shown her. Everything was going so badly for Vorc. If he thought he could abdicate without being executed, he'd do it in a hot second. He was such a good center seat, the best ever actually. Yet everyone around him foundered in the slick mud of incompetence and betrayal.

He shook his head. She said the person who actually cremated the two traitors was a dragon. A *dragon*. There were no dragons anymore. The only one there had been left with the first and only wave of egress. A stupid lie was a terrible lie. And Bellicity claimed the dragon worked for a humanoid mastermind who'd tried unsuccessfully to fool her into believing he was a would-be assassin. Such utter and absolute nonsense. She went on to describe with her dying breath a male who fit only one description. *Ryanmax*. He laughed in disbelief. She no doubt saw him at the vortex the day Rage departed. But she apparently didn't know Ryanmax had been killed and eaten by Gáwar. That sort of placed conspicuous holes in her fabric of lies. Why had he thought her loyal and clever? Bellicity was as bad as Tefnuf.

Well, unfortunately the bitch of the Lower Chambers still lived, unlike Bellicity. She tried to say Jon Ryan, the human whom she hallucinated long ago, had trapped her in a stasis bubble and released her at the massacre at the park. Was it possible for any brain to be that drunk? Apparently so. Vorc was so ...

Jon Ryan? Ryanmax? Jon *Ryanmax*? Could there be some connection?

Vorc slapped his face very hard. No, there could not be. Ryanmax had long since been crapped out by that hideous monster. If there was a connection, they were connected in excrement alone.

That's when the street-facing wall of Vorc's office exploded inward. He vaulted for the door. How many assassins were after him? He froze when he heard a hideous laugh. Only one blight on the universe had that laugh. Gáwar. Vorc turned to face the breach, but continued to slowly back toward the exit.

"Is that you, *Gáwar*?" he shouted with an unsteady voice.

"Of course, rodent droppings. Who else were you expecting?"

"I was not expecting you."

"Then," Gáwar bubbled as he entered through the large hole, "I'm a pleasant surprise."

Vorc started to respond, but wisely aborted any negativity.

"Why are you here?" Vorc demanded.

"To make you soil yourself. Thank you for your cooperation."

"I have not soiled myself. That is—"

"Oh you will before I depart."

"I very much—"

"Do you know who I tasted in the wind?"

"Tasted? You mean *smelled*?"

"No, moron. I taste the wind. The wind is my friend, my only friend. It tells me of things. Wondrous things and impossible things."

"Gáwar, I have no time for riddles and I have no time for games. What do you smell?"

"Ryanmax."

Vorc relaxed by leaning against the nearest wall. What a relief. No news was the only good news he'd receive that day. "Of course you *smelled* him. You *ate* him. So his lingering scent follows you around. Why is that—"

"Ryanmax lives, fool. When I tasted him in the air, I tasted his essence, his machinery, his foul breath. I tasted him, but it was in the wind, not my gut."

"Breath? You said he was a robot. Robots don't—"

"Stop saying words before I eat you whole, vermin," Gáwar thundered. "I say he lives. I tasted him."

"Tasted? That's the past tense. I'm confused. You're saying you tasted him before you smashed him, right?"

"Not exactly."

"Why is it I don't like the sound of that?"

"That would be hard for me to conjecture upon."

"I ... if ... how long has he been back? I mean, he can't be, but if he is, how long have you tasted him?"

"A few weeks."

"A few *weeks*? And you thought to tell me only now? What an outrage."

"Please calm yourself."

"What? Calm myself? My archenemy has defied the impossibility of it and returned from the dead weeks ago, and you only tell me now? Justify your action immediately."

"Ah, there is a twist ... no, a clarification I should make. He's gone again."

"Again? I like that less than the past tense thing earlier. Are you trying to say you killed him, he returned from the dead, but he's departed now?"

"Yes. Sort of, you know, in a way."

"You just said nothing."

"Yes, I did."

"Did what?"

"I said nothing. Actually, in my defense, I said *little*. Nothing is too harsh an assessment."

"Why didn't you tell me when you first realized the beast was back?"

"Well ... er ... there was the matter of ... well, you and I, we had an arrangement. Yes, that's it. We had—"

"You *reprehensible* slime," howled Vorc. "If I dealt you my soul and those of people I care for to kill him and you didn't, then our arrangement would be off. You dare try and dupe *me*? To swindle *me*?"

"Dupe, swindle, trick, those are such ... such *judgmental* terms. No. I was awaiting proper confirmation and a full review before *rashly* endangering your understanding and my stake. That's all. I was trying to be fair to *you*, friend Vorc."

"Lies. If I hear speech I hear *lies*."

"If that's how you feel, I suppose I won't be changing your mind on the subject. But know this. I will find Ryanmax and I will find him soon. Then I will kill him so completely and so many times that our deal will be fulfilled."

"Deal? What deal are you speaking of? You and I have not presently entered into any deal I know of?"

"You know very well we made a—"

"If we had or didn't have a deal, it was voided upon your failure to deliver. Arrangements such as that don't transfer forward unless so agreed upon."

"You'll pay for this betrayal, Vorc."

"Pay? Whatever are you talking about? Why would I pay someone anything unless we had a contract?" Vorc made a show of scanning the room. "I see no contract. Do you?"

CHAPTER THIRTY-SEVEN

Our ever-growing band materialized in one of our past hideout caves. With the screwy time in the ancient god universe, we were actually not gone very long. We had tried to hatch a plan to find the location of the Clein, whatever it was. Unfortunately, Daleria confirmed that there were no libraries, universities, or even museums to perform research in. The Cleinoids were totally not into knowledge, history, or culture. They were simple, free-spirited murderers. Nice. Every universe needs some of those.

I was so desperate, the first thing I wanted the second we were back in the Cleinoid universe was for Casper to appear. Yeah, I wanted to see that most annoying ghost. My best chance to quickly obtain information on the Clein was from him. That said too much about how weak our position was. But, any port in a storm was better than none.

"*Casper*," I shouted as soon as we materialized. "Casper, Mr. Ghost, are you here?"

Of course, he was right behind me when he replied rather loudly, "I've never been apart from you."

I basically jumped out of my polyalloy skin. Once recollected in one piece, I turned. I was instinctively going to chide or at least dis him, but I recalled I was totally reliant on him. Instead I somewhat pandered, "Hi, guy. Great to see you. How've you been?"

"Since I never left our side?"

"Sure," I replied uncertainly. Then his use of words hit me. "Our side? You mean my side?"

"Sure," he responded. I think he was playing me again.

If I didn't need him ... ah well. "Any side you want, buddy."

As was always the case, I noticed he'd morphed again. He looked like a human male. Incredible. Casper had gone from an amorphous blob to see-through homo sapiens in a handful of months. If my life got weirder, I was definitely asking Toño to reboot me.

"Say, you look different, kind of, you know, human."

"You are human, correct?" he responded.

"Last time I ... yes. I am."

"You are not transparent. I am. How is it I appear human to you?"

"I meant your form is human, your outline."

"And what is the significance of an individual having the form of a human in spite of not being one?"

"I ... have ... not ... one ... frakking ... clue." I surely did not. "Hey, since you're here, I had a question."

He was silent—yeah, I had to characterize it—as the grave.

"So I'll just ask it, okay? Have you ever heard of the Clein?"

"Clein."

"Yes."

"No."

"No?" My heart sank like the *Titanic*.

"No, it's called *Clein*, not *the* Clein."

"Ah. Then you have?"

"Have what?"

"Heard of th ... of Clein?"

"Yes."

"Thank the Sweet Lord in Heaven and all the little saints and angels."

"You want me to *what*?" Casper asked, confused.

"No, I was expressing relief and joy. It was not a command."

"Ah."

Silence.

"So what *is* Clein?" I asked, since he appeared not to be telling.

"It is the source of the Cleinoids' power. Surely she told you that much?" Casper gestured a human-looking hand at Daleria.

"Yes, we know that. I was ... checking to make certain. That's what I was doing."

"Why?"

"In retrospect, for no good reason."

"Ah."

You got it. Silence.

"Where is Clein?"

"I told him I didn't know because I don't," Daleria clarified before he could ask.

"Clein is everywhere."

Crap, we couldn't very well destroy it if it was everywhere.

"You told me yourself the Cleinoid gods are pulverizing your universe. They do so because Clein is there. It is everywhere."

"I guess that means we can't very well end it," remarked Toño. "It sounds like the Force of *Star Wars* fame."

"Apparently," I replied.

"No, it's not like that at all." Casper was sounding kind of huffy. Dude was odd as well as a ghost.

"How are they different?" pressed Toño.

"And excuse me for asking, but how do you know about *Star Wars?*" I challenged. "They don't rerun it in this universe, I know that for damn sure."

"I can't recall. I just know I know what you refer to," Casper responded.

"That's not very *helpful,*" I replied in an annoyed tone.

"I try," he said.

"I suppose you do. I suppose ... ah, how are the Force and Clein different?"

"The Force is fictional. Clein is real. It's everywhere."

"You know, talking to you is like riding a roller coaster," I declared.

"Shall I take that as a positive?"

"I hate roller coasters."

"Ah."

As the next insane silence progressed, I felt a strong desire to strangle his human neck.

"Any *other* way the two differ?" asked Toño.

"Yes. The Force was supposed to be generated by all living things and then be everywhere. Clein resides in a deep pit and spreads out to everywhere."

"But I asked you where it was and you ... you said where it was but not where I meant to ask where it was located—" I just stopped babbling. Casper could make me say such goofy things.

"I beg your pardon?" he responded.

"Never mind."

"But if I misled you in any way, I'd like the chance to apologize." He sounded sincere, probably too sincere.

"No, I asked a question and you answered it correctly. My bad."

"Ah."

Maybe *ah* was a word in Casper's native tongue meaning *I'm going to initiate an uncomfortable silent period now.*

"Do you know where this deep pit is?" asked Sapale.

"Possibly. I've never been there."

"Why?" asked Daleria.

"Why? Mostly because it's guarded by twelve thousand curses, not to mention hundreds of banshees, and that doesn't even count the dozen or so denizens."

"I ... I can imagine," Daleria responded weakly.

"All that stuff," I asked, "does it add up to *bad*?"

"No," replied Daleria absently.

"Excellent," I said, encouraged for the first time in a long time.

"It's soul-numbingly invulnerable," she added with no emotion.

"What? How bad can it be? Twelve thousand curses? Hey," I pointed at Mirraya, "we got a brindas. Hundreds of banshees? Duh. Slapgren over there is a minor god when it comes to war. And, what, only a dozen denizens? I can handle them with one arm tied behind my back."

"No, Jon, we could not," snapped Sapale. ""Even if I tied the arm behind you and left the ones with hands free. Do you even know what banshees are? Denizens?"

"Technically, no. But I have a vivid imagination and I've read a lot of science fiction and fantasy. Those genres basically list the options as to size, ferocity, and intelligence of potential foes."

"You say you *won* the war with those technologically advanced dogs?" asked Daleria with real judgment in her tone. "And he," you know who she rifled a finger at, "was on *your* side?"

"More in spite of him than because of him," grunted Sapale.

"Okay, Daleria, I'll bite. What's a banshee?" I said with justified indignation.

"Fairy spirits."

"*Fairies*," I scoffed. "How tough can those be? What, they kill you with flower petals and pleasant thoughts?" I harrumphed.

"I don't know about the fairies from where you come from," she responded, "but these are seriously bad. They are dead spirits. They feed on the souls of the living to keep from fading away. They are smart, relentless, and they are ravenous. Once they target you they will never stop—never—until they have your soul."

"Ah, so, no problema here," I said uncertainly. "I'm not entirely sure I have a soul for them to chomp on."

"Are you willing to bet your soul in the case that you're wrong?" she asked ominously.

"Maybe," I squeaked. "Okay, so we add them to Mirri's column more than Slapgren's."

"Oh, I inactivate twelve thousand curses *and* I combat soul-suckers?" challenged Mirraya. "You sure give me a lot of credit."

"Deservedly so," I defended. "A curse can't be *that* hard to unlock or whatever."

"Oh, they can't, can they?" she shot back angrily. "A well-crafted curse can take a master weeks to unravel. I've seen *some* that are unbreakable, Professor Clueless."

"Just for completeness, Daleria," asked Sapale, "what are these denizens Jon's going to kill seven of with one blow?"

"They are the stuff of nightmares. Of course, I've never seen one, but every description I've heard is consistent. Denizens are gigantic clouds of swirling spiked rocks. They move like an avalanche falling down a great mountain, and they do so with lightning speed."

"Clouds of rock?" I scorned. "That's ridiculous. You can be a cloud or you can be a rock, but you can't be a cloud made of rock."

"Before you slay the last one, maybe you can ask it how that works," replied Sapale snidely.

"The cloud is bound by unquenchable flames, by the way. Anything they touch flashes to ash instantly."

"Woah. How do we know the flame's unquenchable? Sounds like gratuitous assignment of powers to me."

"So if you *could* snuff out the fire you could handle twelve of them?" pressed Slapgren.

I shrugged. "Maybe. I've beaten some pretty tough cookies in my time."

"*General* Ryan," began Toño. I knew I was in for it because he used my rank. "I've known you a very long time. We have been involved in some amazingly lame and far-fetched discussions. This, however, is orders of magnitude worse than all others." He glowered a moment. Doc was way good at glowering. "We do not know, and I list these in no specific order, *where* Clein is, *how* to break the curses, *defeat* the banshees, *kill* the denizens, or *destroy* Clein if we ever got close enough to attempt to. Notice I have said nothing of our safe retreat, evasion of the unwanted attention you attacking Clein would absolutely spawn, or how stupid what you just said sounds."

"You know what I hear?" I responded hotly. "Blah blah blah—too lazy to work out a plan. Blah blah blah—too scared to try the plan I was too lazy to come up with that Jon Ryan force-fed to me."

"Uncle, don't you feel that's over-the-top harsh and insensitive?" exclaimed Mirri.

"Desperate times require desperate measures, Mirri. I need to see to it we remove the Cleinoids from the *living column* on the ledger of life."

"How about this? You solve *one*," Toño rotated a single digit in front of my nose, "just one of those problems to my satisfaction, and I will listen to the rest of your plan."

"You have yourself a deal, buddy. Shake on it." I held out my hand.

We shook. The whole while he had the smuggest smile on I'd ever seen.

"Oh, I forgot to mention that Vorc, Gáwar, and any number of lesser foes will be actively seeking you out the entire time." Toño released my hand.

"Doc, sounds to me like you *want* me to lose."

"No, very much to the contrary. I do, however, have some familiarity with statistical odds and the capabilities of powerful adversaries."

So, my course was clear. All I had to do was the impossible thrice. No, wait, four ... no, five times. I really did need to count avoiding the wrath of Vorc and Gáwar separately. Aw, hell. After three impossible chores were on any to-do list, one didn't need to mind any others.

CHAPTER THIRTY-EIGHT

Trethnaur was a sidle worm on Calveras. It had spent as long as it could remember screening the mud and sandy bottom of the great ocean it did not know it lived under. Trethnaur was a simple beast. Self-aware? Yes, it was. Weighed down by a complex thought process? No, it was not. It had noted recently, though, that food was more plentiful. Much more plentiful. That was nice. It sieved out ever increasing particles of protein and a rich slurry of other nutrients. If Trethnaur was capable of joy, it would have experienced it. It would seem the Darwinian forces on Calveras directed toward sidle worms were indifferent to happiness.

A true boon was that Trethnaur was able to asexually breed with proclivity. It was ejecting upwards of ten thousand eggs per day. And twice in its memory it exchanged sperm sacks with other sidle worms. Again, it experienced a feeling short of pleasure. But Trethnaur definitely looked forward to sperm-sack swaps again, if the food supply held up. Life was good.

The main predator of sidle worms and related species was the rapacious Guild fish. It swam with dart-like speed and had a long needle-nosed set of three jaws to dig juicy prey out of the ooze.

Trethnaur noted that their scent in the water was considerably reduced of late. It was also encountering more and more worms, burrowing crabs, and shellfish. The muck was getting very crowded, what with the increased eating and the decreased being eaten. Life was good.

Why was nutrition up and predation down? Trethnaur never gave that question a passing thought. It was not concerned with existential matters like how, what, when, where, or why. Its focus was on open mouth, take in a gulp, squirt it through its filter-mesh. As noted, it was a simple creature. Taste for other sidle worms and Guild fish. End of intellectualization.

Twenty-thousand leagues above the barely sentient Trethnaur, two ancient gods lay supine on a beach. Berral and Mugwan could hardly move they were so stuffed. Like the goose destined to aid in the production of *foie gras,* they'd force-fed to the point of intestinal distress. Were it not for the enormous smiles on their faces, a passing observer might have thought them to be suffering. They were not. They were taking a necessary break in their rampage across the face of Calveras. Even a god had to pace himself or herself when the pickings were so good.

When the pair of demons first arrived, a not insignificant resistance was put up by the two main races of inhabitants. Though they called themselves the Dopla and the Bastic, Berral and Mugwan dubbed them the Grindier and the Squishier, based on their mouth feel. Neither was as delicious as species they'd obliterated earlier in the jaunt. But, to their soon-ending credit, what they lacked in taste the locals more than made up for with their spunk and pluck.

"Do you suppose," asked Berral, once he was able to speak, "it would be worthwhile plundering the sea life on this blighted planet?"

"Now?" replied Mugwan with a nauseous tone.

"No, no. *Breathing* is a struggle presently. No, I meant eventually, as in before we move on."

"I don't know. Your affection for aquatic life is, as you know, well beyond me."

Berral, being a lithe monster with pinfeathers and light fur on his hide, was a natural water baby. He was only ten feet long and shaped very much like a python. Mugwan, on the other hand, was an ox reminiscent of Paul Bunyan's Babe the Blue Ox. Well, Babe the Blue Ox, with electric bolts for horns. He also sported three smaller heads protruding forward from his chest with razor-blade teeth coated in the most deadly poison known to exist. In water, without magic, he sank faster than a comparably sized boulder.

"Waste not, want not. That's what my father always used to say," reminded Berral.

"Yes, you say that to excess. Recall please you so hated your father that you falsely accused him of treason, just so he'd be immortalized on Beal's Point and not in your daily life."

"I knew he'd make such a better statue than a father figure, I simply had to pull the trigger on that plan."

They both tried to chuckle but the pressure generated made the pair queasy, so they settled for a shared grunt.

"I say we agree to disagree on the need to sweep the planet's oceans free of life. We have, at *someone's* insistence, picked off the larger animals that chance to come near the surface. I say let the rest rot in place."

"But what if there's a creature of unsurpassed delicacy and delectability down there somewhere? To leave it uneaten would be a sin."

"I'm comfortable with sin. Have been all my life," replied Mugwan.

"It *is* easy once you get the hang of it, isn't it?"

They grunted again.

"Look, you and I have been together for a very long time. We've never done one nice, considerate, or merciful thing in our lives."

"Perish the thought," responded Berral with a heartfelt shudder.

"So I vote to leave the bottom dwellers to their own devices and call it a mitzvah. That way if we're ever held to an accounting, we have one good deed to our credit."

"And you stay warm and dry."

"And I stay warm and dry."

"So be it." Berral sat halfway up, for that was all he could tolerate, and looked out to sea. "So long, tasty morsels left alive by the grace of Berral and Mugwan, gods of some measurable merit."

"Now shut up so I can sleep off my last meal," grumbled Mugwan.

"Not yet. As a god of detectable virtue, I must bless the sea creatures I have just pardoned."

"Can't you do that quietly?"

"Nonsense. Noble acts require loud acclamation." He felt to his right for a bone he seemed to recall he'd picked clean but not consumed. Yes, there it was. He held it aloft. "With this bone I thee bless." He tossed the tribute into the calm waters far offshore. Then he collapsed to the sand, asleep before his head hit the ground.

Half a meter under the seabed, Trethnaur took in another gulp and forced it out his sieve. It was rich and fulfilling. It quickly sucked in an even larger mouthful. But as it tried to extrude, a long thin object emerged from the goo and lodged against a cheek. It twisted and turned violently, but the bone would not dislodge. Trethnaur drew in more substrate, hoping to move the bone. It not only didn't budge, but Trethnaur found it was unable to expel the load because the affected cheek wouldn't contract. Unable to breathe, Trethnaur slowly died in tortured anguish, writhing in the mud and sandy bottom of the great ocean it did not know it died under.

Trethnaur's last act of intellectual insufficiency was to *not* appreciate the irony. Berral, a foul and hateful monster, blessed Trethnaur with death. The inclination to sin was both inescapable and eternal for the ancient god.

CHAPTER THIRTY-NINE

A semi-didn't-suck idea came to me. The morons who did the fabrication of the neutral matter might be of some help. They were *sort* of scientists. Scientists were into knowing stuff. Maybe they knew something about Clein. They certainly were dumb and gullible. Easy to manipulate was always a plus in my book. Of course, after the *Mission Impossible* stunt we pulled, all the technonerds might be dead. Vorc was not a fellow who possessed mercy one would want to test by failing as completely as they had failed him.

Having no other options at least made checking out the fabrication drones a permissible waste of time. I took Mirraya and Daleria along. My entire posse was too large and would draw unwanted attention. If nothing else, I'd learned that Godville was a paranoid place. Everyone suspected everyone else of plotting and conniving. That was good, because the whole damn lot of them probably were. The day was, as all were, pleasant. A long walk was nice. Unfortunately, it was also rather short.

From behind something hit me like an ICBM. I tumbled forward multiple times, coming to a stop on my back. I was looking up at

Gáwar. He was frothing and drooling and he panted like a worn-out dog.

Daleria screamed bloody murder, which I do believe she anticipated seeing any second.

Mirraya transformed into an armor-plated bull with nastified horns and heaved into a charge.

"Nice to *see* you again, undead robot," snarled Gáwar. Dude was seriously enjoying himself.

"Ca ... can't say the ... same," I wheezed. It was hard to speak with his enormous hands around my neck.

"That's okay, toy human. You won't be around long enough to hate me much." He bent his head back and roared convincingly.

"Cur ... curious, you asshole?" I managed to state clearly.

Gáwar began pounding the back of my head against the street, hard.

Mirraya slammed into the side of his head with everything she had. It turned out that wasn't enough. Gáwar batted her away like she was a stuffed animal.

"Oops, that's gotta hurt," he sprayed in my face. "I hope your little bitch is well enough to try again. She's fun."

"Say ... again. Curious?"

"About what, pathetic speck?"

"Me."

"Oh," he shouted. He stopped banging my head and returned to throttling me. "No, not really."

"Get off and I'll tell you how."

He pretended to consider my proposal. "Nah, I'm good. I'll kill you again, eat you again, then I'll get off."

"If ... you eat me how ... can you get off ... me?"

He angled his head. "Hmm. I'll deal with that incongruity when the time comes."

I managed to free my left hand. "Do you ... like surprises?"

He puzzled his lips a second. "No, I'd have to say I don't." He started with the head pounding again.

I slammed my right thumb onto his forehead hard. I drew a

wiggly cross on his skin as I shouted the words, "I bless you in the name of the Father, the Son, and the Holy Spirit." Then I set my hand on his chest and pushed him away.

The look on his face was absolutely, positively priceless. First, he was confused. Second, he slapped his head and glared at his hand. Third, he cried out in agony. Fourth, his skin began to simmer. Fifth, and my personal favorite of all, the cross burst into white-hot flames.

"What have you done?" he howled. Gáwar shoved his big claw-hand toward me and screamed, "One drop of blood ... ahhhhhh." He rolled off me in pain and began slamming *his* head against the pavement. All he accomplished was to make a bloody, flaming mess of his ugly face.

"What ... have ... you ... done, *infidel*," he cried out in terror and torment. The terror part, that's what I really loved to hear exiting the monster.

I stood and towered above him. "Something you should thank me for. I *blessed* you, pig fart."

"What is this ... ahhhhh. What blood *is* this?" He held out his now flaming hand.

"The blood of Christ. You know of Him?"

"I ... oooooh, this hurts." He slammed his claws against his mangled forehead. "Make it stop. Make it ... ahhhh."

"Not on your life. You are now the *sanctified* god of demons." I toed him with a boot tip. "Get it? Yeah, funny, isn't it. A sainted dark lord. You gotta love it."

I doubt he did, but he didn't answer. Gáwar just kept slamming his head on the street in between slapping himself. He proved to be a slow learner, there at the end. Einstein once said that the definition of insanity was doing the same thing over and over again and expecting a different result. Silly demon god. He proved the great physicist's admonition.

Within five minutes Gáwar lay still. His forehead was down to smoldering. Maybe he was dead or maybe he was just unconscious.

Either way he was my bitch. I had half a mind to try and eat him, but my wrath and my stomach couldn't go there.

Mirraya, naked and back in her Deft form, stepped up to my side. "Uncle, what did you do to him?"

"You heard me. I blessed him with the blood of Christ."

She looked at me in disbelief. "Where did ... Ah *ha*. The Pillars of Creation."

"Yup. I really gotta shop there more often."

"So you're telling me that—what'd you say his name was—Pravil?"

I nodded.

"You thought to ask and Pravil agreed to make you a drop of the blood of your culture's deity?"

"What part seems challenging to believe?"

"All of it, you goon. And I don't wish to seem to be Captain Obvious here—"

"But why did I *hallucinate* that the human deity was actually deific enough to polish off Gáwar?"

"Thank you," Mirri popped back.

"He's the most holy person I could think of. Look, Jesus was an actual historic figure. Even if he wasn't God, he's been worshiped so much and so long that had to add power to the application of his name." I pointed to the flaccid Gáwar. "Worked like a charm any way you cut it."

"You are the luckiest uncle, Uncle."

"Yeah, guess I am."

"So what's in your other thumb?"

I held it up and inspected it. "Nothing. Why?"

"You passed on a chance to have, I don't know, a double dose?"

"If the first one didn't work the second wasn't going to either." I kept studying my thumb. "What should I have packed it with?"

"Let's focus on the smoking demon god at our feet. What do we do with him?"

I looked at him. "If he's dead I suppose leave him." I nodded my head toward him. "Why don't you check?"

She set her palm on her chest. "Me? Why not *you?* I'm not touching *that*." She tossed the back of a hand at the body.

"Big baby brindas," I taunted.

She dropped to her knees instantly and felt for a pulse or whatever. "I do not want to hear you say that ever again." Soon she held her hand over his chest. "I'm pretty sure he's alive."

"Bind him up like EJ did that Cleinoid and let's take him back to the ship."

"Say *what*? Take evil incarnate to our safehold?"

"You will have bound him. Hey, he could be useful down the line. Plus, remember, because he may be sensitive on the point. I sanctified him. No more evil incarnate quips, please. I anticipate you will be sensitive to his life choices."

"You are so impossible." She stood and began casting her spell. "I should bind you to him. It'd serve you right."

When I opened the membrane aboard *Stingray* and revealed Gáwar, boy did I get an impressive reaction. Not a very positive one, but if intensity was the measure of success, I did good.

"Are you insane?" shouted EJ.

"You are insane," screamed Toño.

"Insane, that's what you are," declared Sapale.

"Cool," exclaimed Slapgren. He was the only one other than JJ who always got me. Good kid.

"He may be useful," I defended.

"He may eat us in our sleep," responded EJ.

"Simple solution. Then don't sleep." I stuck my tongue out at him.

"Well, I'm keeping him," I said with finality.

"How does holding him prisoner advance our position, Jon?" asked Toño.

"He knows where all the bodies are buried."

"Yeah, he *buried* them," exclaimed EJ.

"Why would he cooperate?" posed Daleria.

"Maybe he won't. If not, I'll let you kill him."

She backed away. "No. I'm not that brave. *You* kill him."

"We'll have a raffle when the time comes. For now, someone'll stand watch over him twenty-four/seven."

"Okay," responded EJ. "You take the first watch because it looks like our guest is waking up."

I turned and checked. Gáwar was moving a little and groaned softly. I sure hope he had a bad headache.

"Can I question him?" asked an energetic Slapgren.

"We'll see. I'll take the first turn at bat but you're on deck, okay?"

"Which means *no,*" he said with a pout.

I walked over to Gáwar's exposed face. "Hey, cupcake, you back?" I slapped what passed for his cheek. "Can I get you an aspirin?"

He groaned louder. Might have been a moan.

"Take your time, big guy. I'm immortal. No rush to consciousness required on your part."

Within a couple minutes he was sort of awake. Man did he look at me with studied rage.

"Just because I blessed you, bound you, and took you prisoner, please don't let it stand in the way of our budding friendship. Deal?"

"Ever the funny wind-up toy. When I'm free you will know the worst death—"

"Ah ah." I wagged a finger. "Remember you're one of the good guys now. No threats, no murders. Only happy thoughts."

"I am *not,* and I *will* see you dead."

"Stubborn little shit, aren't you?"

He deferred a response.

"Here's the deal." I was pretty sure something brilliant was about to exit my mouth. "You seem, I don't know—unhappy." I addressed Mirri. "You think he looks down and moody?"

"Yes, Uncle. I believe you're right."

"I *knew* it. Are you not pleased with your blessed state of being, pal?"

"I am not. That is all I will say to you until I hold your broken body in my claws."

"You're not warming much to the good guy role. FYI. Work on it, 'kay?"

He was silent.

"Here's my offer. I will extend it to you once, now, and never again." I held my left thumb in front of his face. "This one contains a drop of the water Pontius Pilate used to wash his hands after sentencing Jesus to death." I rotated it to myself and whistled. "Yeah, purely evil stuff." I then made a show of appearing surprised by a new thought. "You know what? It's evil, kind of like the old Gáwar."

His eyes opened wider.

"If you help me, I'll reverse the blessing with this." I placed it right in front of his eyes. "What'll it be? Eternal angel, or back to the old god of demons gig?"

"You know I don't trust you. Even if that is what you say it is, I know you'll betray me."

"You're right to be suspicious, I'll grant you that. Two points to keep in mind. One, if you do nothing, you stay blessed." I rolled my eyes. "I would pay good money to be a fly on the wall of the next meeting of the demon society when you show up in a frilly dress with flowers for all your buddies."

"I hate you."

"Thanks. Two, I'm desperate. I really need help. I need it so badly I will make a deal with the likes of you *and* I will keep it."

He grumbled a bit. "What do you want to know?" he growled.

"Where Clein is. How to get past the protection. Mostly how to destroy it."

He did an extended version of a classic demon laugh. Asswipe. "That's *all*?" he mocked. "Betray my kind and guarantee my own death?"

"Maybe. Or it's the dress and the flowers forever. Your call. What'll it be?"

He howled with blind rage.

"Ah, *indoor* voice, please," I taunted.

"I will help *if* you take me with you," Gáwar finally spat at me.

"Now doesn't that strike you as a silly wish to grant? If you're here you can't stab me in the back a million different ways."

"Then no deal."

"Okay, big guy. I'll bring you, but you stay bound."

"No deal." He turned his head away as best he could.

"Slapgren, you're up. But no cattle prods for at least two minutes. You got that?"

"How about anal probing, Uncle? Is that fair game from the get-go?"

"Of course. Anal probing is *always* a nice opening play. Ah, I'll be in the other room." I pointed to somewhere else.

"You can't be serious," yelped Gáwar.

I looked at Slapgren, then to Gáwar. "He looks serious to me. Have a nice probing." I left quickly.

"*Ryan*," he bellowed. "Come back. I'll take your deal."

"My deal expired. Now I'm not saying Slapgren won't offer you the same one, but I am saying it's unlikely to come for, oh, I don't know, six or seven visitations. Take my word on this, please. Dude's got serious issues with probing, the sicko."

"Ryan, return. If that fiend touches me there'll be no deal."

I think he was ready for the fork test. He was done.

"Okay, here's the plan," I said very sternly. "You direct us to where Clein is located and I lug you along in a membrane. If you get us all the way in, I free you. If you betray me then I'll do something unspeakably worse to you than I already have. Got it?"

"What's worse than this?" he asked, trying to move his claws.

"It wouldn't be *unspeakable* if I said it, now would it?"

"I hate you so much even I am amazed," he seethed.

"Back atcha, boobie." I flicked the still smoldering cross on his forehead.

He winced satisfyingly.

"Now let's do this, people. We have countless innocents to save and the hopes of millions of evil gods to transform into unfulfilled expectations."

. . .

To be continued ... What a stinker am I, right?

GLOSSARY:

Als (1): The original ship's AI on Jon's first flight long ago was Alvin. Jon shortened that to Al. When Al was joined to Jon's vortex in the Galaxy on Fire Series, Al and Blessing fell in love and got "married." Since then Jon refers to them combined as the Als.

Antigods (1): A group of reclusive, über-powerful gods. They have been the bane of the Cleinoids' existence since time began.

Apractolith (3): The proper name of the antigods.

Beal's Point (1): An area of monuments to disgraced Cleinoid gods. All living gods must visit to be made ill so they stay loyal.

Bellicity (3): A conspirator allegedly with Festock against Vorc.

Bethniak (1): Child appearing, vengeful, powerful, and really really mean god.

Blessing (1): See *Stingray*.

Brindas (3): High master of Deft traditional magic and psychic ability.

Brood-mate/brood's-mate (1): Male and female members of a Kaljaxian marriage.

Calfada-Joric (2): The Deft master brindas, or witch/magician, on Rameeka Blue Green. Went by Cala. After the war with the Adamant was over she was given Evil Jon to rehabilitate.

Calrf (1): A Kaljaxian stew that Jon particularly dislikes.

Carol (2): An antigod. Generally takes the form of a rock being with rattling pebbles.

Casper (2): The name Jon gave to the mysterious ghost who helped him fight the ancient gods.

Central Seat (1): The official leader of the Ancient Gods' conclave.

Cleinoid gods (1): Ancient and malevolent mix of gods. They have destroyed many universes before and are eyeing ours now. The five ranks or groupings for their invasion were to be Rage, Torment, Wrath, Fury, and Horror.

Command Prerogatives (1): The thin fibers Jon extends from his left four fingers. They are probes that also control a vortex.

Cragforel (1): Friendly Deavoriath Jon met after he first escaped the Adamant in the far future.

Cube (1): Jon's alternate name for the vortex he captains.

Daleria (2): Demigod and innkeeper whom Jon and Sapale

befriended. She worked with them against the ancient gods as she'd grown to hate them.

Dalfury (1): Vorc's right hand, or chief assistant. A demigod of cloudy memories, hence, he has the form of a cloud.

Davdiad (1): Kaljaxian divine spirit.

Deavoriath (1): Three arms and legs, the most advanced tech in the galaxy, and helpful to Jon.

Deca (1): One of the witch gods skilled at prophecy. Sister of Fest.

Dominion Splitter (2): The name of the transfolding vortex the ancient gods use to transport to our galaxy. He has a lot of issues and is very conflicted. Actually he's just a total asshole, period. Aka DS.

Evil Jon Ryan/ EJ (1): Alternate time line version of the original human to android download. Over time, he turned to the darker side of his nature. He studied "magic" under a Deft master.

Felladonna (2): Vorc's second assistant or so called *right hand.* A demigod of lists and communication.

Felnastop (2): A delicious vegetable that runs like the wind.

Fest (1): One of the witch gods skilled at prophecy. Sister of Deca.

Festock (3): Old friend of Daleria who was part of a conspiracy against Vorc.

Fire of Justice (2): A metallic rod given to the center seat as a sign of power. A powerful incinerator also.

Form One/Form Two (1): A Form is the title of a vortex pilot. If more than one is aboard they get numerical designations based on seniority.

Gáwar (2): Seriously badass god. The god of demons. Ten-foot-long lobster claw front hands. Multiple tentacles serving in place of antenna. Block-shaped bull head. Gáwar's torso was a snake with human legs. Yeah, badness on the doorstep, I couldn't take one more step.

Genter-ban-tol (1): Prime Minister of the Joint Galactic Parliament. A Bezathy, basically the Galaxy's largest snail species.

Gorpedder (1): Ill-tempered boulder Cleinoid god.

Hemnoplop (1): Demigod of Fool's Island. On pilgrimage to Beal's Point with Jon.

Hollon (3): The complete joining of two Deft shapeshifters.

Kalvarg (1): The planet Jon took the orphan Kaljaxian population to as the Adamant were destroying their home world. An island solar system long ago ejected from the Milky Way Galaxy.

Lorpamoor (1): Cleinoid vampire god. Nasty nasty fellow.

Joint Council for Interplanetary Defense and Cooperation (1): Group of allied free world who fought the Adamant. Remained as a central quasi-UN for the surviving planets. JCIDC to its friends.

JJ (3): Sapale's first son. Raised by Jon as his own son, whom he loved very much. JJ is short for Jon Junior.

Marropex (1): A reaver. The Cleinoid god of atrocities.

Mirraya-Slapgren (3): A pair of Deft shapeshifters joined as one in hollon. Jon rescued Mirraya from certain death as a child and found Slapgren shortly after that. They are joined in the form of a large golden dragon. Very impressive, really. They are a powerful magician. Referred to as *Mirraya* generally because she is the one who speaks for the pair.

Nassel (2): Leader of the Rage faction of Cleinoids. She had served as such for the last three transheavals. A god of conquest.

Probe Fibers (1): Aka command prerogatives, they allow piloting of the Vortex spaceship and can analyze whatever they touch.

Quantum Decoupler (1): A most excellent weapon that pulls the quarks apart in a proton. The energy released as they rejoin is amazing.

Racdal fat (2): A food animal from Kaljax's abundant fat stores.

Sapale (1): Jon's Kaljaxian wife from his original flight to find humankind a new home. At first just her brain was copied, then, eventually, she was downloaded to an android host. Traveled with the corrupted Jon Ryan from an alternate time line.

Space-time congruity manipulator (1): Hugely helpful force field. Aka a membrane.

Stingray (1): Jon's Deavoriath spaceship. Her name in the Deavoriath language is pronounced "crash." Hence, silly Jon renamed her after one of his favorite cars. It makes Jon-sense.

Stone Witches (2): Another name for the antigods. See also Apractolith.

Tefnuf (1): The first ancient god Jon encountered. She was saddled with an uncanny ugliness and a profoundly bad temper.

Toño DeJesus (1 of TFL): The creator of the android Jon became and his lifelong friend.

Transfolding (1): The mechanical process of moving from the land of the ancient gods to somewhere else.

Transheaval (1): The term the Cleinoids use to describe their migration from one universe to another. Accomplished via a mean vortex-cloud know as Dominion Splitter.

Visant (3): The proper name for a pair of Deft joined in hollon.

Verazz (2): The first antigod introduced. Also one of the most powerful.

Vorc (1): Current central seat of the conclave.

Vortex (1): Super-advanced Deavoriath sentient spaceship. Moves by folding space. If you get a chance to own one, do it.

Vortex (alternate definition) (1): See Dominion Splitter.

Walpracta (2): Ancient god of consumption. Positively revolting.

Wul (1): God of business and enterprise. Humanoid. Befriended Jon.

Zastrál (2): A three-meter long, one-meter tall fuzzy siamese-twinned python with paddles for legs. Used to extract knowledge. Very unpleasant chap.

AND NOW A WORD FROM YOUR AUTHOR

WHO DOESN'T LOVE SHAMELESS SELF-PROMOTION?

Thank you for continuing your journey through the Ryanverse! Along with this series, please check out *The Forever Series*. Beginning with The Forever Life, Book 1, learn Jon's backstory and share his many incredible adventures.

The second series in the Ryanverse, *Galaxy on Fire*, begins with Embers. Learn what happened to Jon and his companions long after humankind safely left Earth.

Audiobooks, you ask? Why yes, there is The Forever on Audible, and it's superb.

Along with joining by reading, hop aboard the bandwagon. There's plenty of room. Follow me at Craig Robertson's Author's Page on Facebook. Partake of the conversation and fun. Best of all, sign up for my Mailing List by emailing me [contact@craigarobertson.com] That way you can stay abreast of news and new releases. You'll be so glad you did. Finally, I love emails. No, I'm not that needy. I just love emails. contact@craigarobertson.com.

A final favor. Please post a review for this book, especially on Amazon. They are more precious to us authors than gold.

Well, I hate to say goodbye, so I ...
Craig

www.ingramcontent.com/pod-product-compliance
Lightning Source LLC
Chambersburg PA
CBHW070104030726
47506CB00002B/588